Emancipation Job

A Righteous Wrong Heist Novel

Walden Gray

waldengray.com

For my family, who give me the strength every day . . .

and

For those trapped in darkness, searching for light—
may you find your path to redemption,
knowing there are people fighting for you,
even if you can't see them yet.

Once you have set yourself a goal and believe in it, have the audacity to believe that you can achieve it . . . Do not go at tasks with a return to the past.

Ralphy Waldo Emerson

Author's Note

Dear Reader,

Before you embark on this thrilling journey with the *Righteous Wrong* crew, I wanted to take a moment to address the sensitive subject that forms the backdrop of this story. *The Emancipation Job* deals with themes related to the adult entertainment industry, including pornography and trafficking. I want to make it clear that I have written this as a work of fiction and I strongly condemn the exploitation and abuse that frequently takes place within these industries.

It is important to me that readers understand that the purpose of this novel is not to glorify or sensationalize these issues, but rather to shed light on the real-life struggles and challenges faced by those who find themselves trapped in these situations. Through the experiences of the characters, I aim to explore themes of redemption, justice, and the power of friendship in overcoming adversity.

While the subject may be sensitive, I have attempted to approach it with care and respect. You will find that the story does not contain explicit sexual content, drug or alcohol use, or excessive profanity. My goal was to tell an interesting story that entertains and engages readers while also prompting reflection and discussion about important social issues.

If you or someone you know has been affected by the topics addressed in this book, please know that there are resources and support services available. You are not alone, and help is always within reach.

Thank you for trusting me to take you on this journey. I hope that *The Emancipation Job* not only captivates you with its thrilling plot and dynamic characters but also leaves you with a sense of hope and the belief that even in the darkest of times, there is always a chance for redemption and a better tomorrow.

With gratitude,

Walden Gray

Contents

Prologue		1
1.	Outside Hitter	8
2.	The Broker	13
3.	Broken Angels	18
4.	Merry Men	24
5.	Breaking Character	30
6.	James Bond	35
7.	Prodigy	43
8.	Witch City	52
9.	Interview: Josh	67
10.	Nirvana	69
11.	Interview: Tony	81
12.	Patience and Fortitude	84
13.	Three Years	97
14.	Interview: Tommy	100
15.	M's	103
16.	Walls	114
17.	Interview: William	121
18.	Instant Ramen	124
19.	Interview: Zack	133
20.	Breathe	135

21. Interview: Big Mike ... 144

22. Good Gray Poet ... 146

23. Chez Tortoni ... 153

24. Arnie the Mason ... 157

25. Running Hills ... 165

26. Interview: Justine ... 172

27. Breadcrumbs ... 174

28. Mercedes Sprinter ... 181

29. Tick Tock ... 186

30. Interview: Chloe Jane ... 192

31. Interview: Lilly ... 196

32. Crisscross Applesauce ... 203

33. Interview: Darby ... 214

34. Conversation Pit ... 218

35. Daddy-O ... 222

36. Interview: Charles ... 229

37. Ready to Ride? ... 232

38. Interview: Chase ... 236

39. Interview: Lolita ... 240

40. Floor-to-Ceiling Windows ... 245

41. Interview: Ella ... 253

42. What Lies Within Us ... 258

43. Interview: Sydney ... 268

44. Existential Resilience ... 271

Epilogue ... 275

Afterword ... 278

Acknowledgements ... 280

About the Author ... 281

Prologue

The moonlight caught the razor wire, making it shimmer like a crown of thorns atop the high fence. Justine pressed her forehead against the cold glass of her third-story window, watching the guards make their rounds below. Their shadows stretched long across the manicured grounds of the compound, dark figures moving with mechanical precision through pools of artificial light.

Her breath fogged the window, and she absently traced patterns in the condensation with her finger. The luxury of her room—all chrome and marble, more five-star hotel than prison cell—felt like another form of mockery. Even the vast shower with its rainfall head and the kitchen with its high-end appliances couldn't disguise what this place really was: a gilded cage where dreams came to die.

Heavy footsteps in the hallway made her freeze. Through the solid steel door, reinforced with a deadbolt that would laugh at anything short of explosives, came Lilly's sharp voice: "Lights out in five minutes!"

Justine bit back the urge to respond. She'd learned early on that drawing Lilly's attention meant risking a "special session" with Lolita, and those sessions left scars that no amount of time could heal.

Three years. She could hardly believe it had been that long since she'd walked through these gates willingly, head full of dreams and promises of stardom. The invitation felt genuine; the opportunity, perfect. After years of bouncing between companies, never quite finding her place, Lilly had made this feel like home.

What a fool she'd been.

But tonight felt different. As the crew rushed to prepare for tomorrow's big event, she'd noticed small cracks in the compound's usually ironclad security. Gaps in the patrol routes. Distracted guards. A chance, however slim, to finally break free.

Justine stepped back from the window, her heart beating faster as possibilities raced through her mind. She needed something subtle—no dramatic escapes through sewer tunnels or desperate rappelling attempts. She'd been watching, waiting, learning the compound's rhythms. It was time to use that knowledge.

A plan began to take shape in her mind, fragile as a spider's web but growing stronger with each passing moment. They thought they'd broken her, turned her into another empty-eyed performer going through the motions. But deep in her chest, an ember of defiance still burned. And tonight, she would fan that ember into a flame.

She knew her captors saw her as just another pawn in their twisted game, a disposable asset to be used and discarded. But they had underestimated her—and that would be their undoing.

Her fingertips drummed against the windowsill as she surveyed her prison. "Too high to jump, door's reinforced steel . . . what options does that leave?"

The ventilation shaft caught her eye—a rusted grate secured by four large bolts in the corner of her room. Narrow, maybe too narrow, but she'd lost enough weight in this place that she might just fit. The real question was where it led.

"Only one way to find out," she whispered, already moving toward the grate. "Good thing I kept up those contortionist skills from my circus days."

Working quickly but quietly, she pried the grate free, her hands trembling with a mixture of fear and anticipation. The dark tunnel gaped before her like a throat. Inch by inch, she pulled herself into the shaft, biting back a gasp as cold metal pressed against her skin. The stakes were too high to let discomfort stop her now.

"Keep moving, stay quiet, don't get caught," she repeated, the words becoming a mantra as she navigated through the compound's steel arteries.

She paused at a particularly tight bend, twisting her body into an impossible angle. "Five-star accommodations," she said, brushing aside a cobweb. "Though the housekeeping could use some work."

The shaft opened into a small security room, dimly lit and mercifully empty. She dropped down silently, pressing her back against the cold cinder block wall. Outside, two guards were engaged in conversation, their voices reaching through the door.

"Did you see that new movie?" one asked, practically giddy. *"Double Trouble Delights?"*

"Quality stuff," his colleague agreed.

She rolled her eyes. Perfect timing—their discussion of porn would cover any small sounds as she disabled the surveillance system. Her fingers flew across the keyboard, muscle memory from her time working the company's security protocols making the task almost too easy.

The guards' conversation continued as she slipped past their station, her heart thundering so loud she was sure they must hear it. But they remained oblivious, lost in their crude analysis of the latest release.

She eased the door open,

Easy now. Just a few more steps . . .

She emerged into the corridor, keeping her footsteps light as she made her way toward the side exit. Freedom was close—so close she could taste it. But she knew better than to celebrate too early.

After all, she hadn't just come here to escape. She had come to expose this place, to bring justice to all the others trapped within these walls.

The Great Porn Compound Escape. Chapter one down, rest of the story to go.

The night air hit her like a wall as she slipped outside, thick with humidity and the metallic tang of approaching rain. Moving through shadows between the floodlights, she kept her footsteps silent and her bright red hair tucked beneath a makeshift cap torn from her shirt. Her heart hammered against her ribs, but her movements remained steady, deliberate.

She pressed against the rough concrete wall of the building, peering around the corner. No guards were visible, no cameras pointed her way. A stack of shipping crates beckoned from the storage yard—temporary cover, if she could reach them.

She was halfway there when voices drifted from behind the crates. Panic surged through her veins, but she channeled it into focus, sliding into the deepest shadows as two more guards emerged, deep in conversation.

"Can't believe that Hail Mary in the last five seconds," one said, gesturing animatedly. "What kind of idiot makes that call?"

"The kind that just cost me fifty bucks," his partner said, an unhappy growl in his voice.

She held her breath until their footsteps faded, sardonic amusement flickering through her fear. How fitting that while she fought for her freedom, they argued about football.

The compound sprawled before her like a maze, all sharp angles and stark lighting. She moved between buildings and trees, each step calculated, each shadow offering a brief sanctuary. The surge of adrenaline made everything sharper, clearer than it had been in years of captivity.

Finally, the perimeter fence rose before her, razor wire glinting like teeth in the moonlight. Freedom waited on the other side—if she could scale it without being spotted. Without being shredded.

"One last Hail Mary," she whispered, appreciating the irony as she studied the barrier. It was daunting, but she had come too far to balk now. Every muscle tensed, ready to sprint.

A final glance confirmed the yard was clear. She took a deep breath and ran.

The cold metal of the fence bit into her fingers as she scaled it. She gritted her teeth, ignoring the pain and focusing on the freedom that lay just beyond it. As she reached the top, a jagged edge tore through her skin, eliciting a sharp gasp.

"Ugh," she said under her breath, gripping the fence tighter to keep from losing her balance. "Razor wire, of course."

As blood trickled down her arm, she fought against the urge to cry out in pain. No one ever said escaping was gonna be easy.

Despite the throbbing in her arm, she managed to swing her leg over the fence and began her descent. Her heart pounded in her ears, drowning out the sounds of the compound behind her.

Almost there.

Her muscles screamed with every movement. She dropped to the ground, wincing at the impact but not allowing herself to dwell on it.

Okay, time to run like hell.

She forced her legs into motion. The scrubland before her seemed to stretch on forever, the sandy floor of the land beckoning her forward. Terror and desperation fueled her as she sprinted through the trees and bushes, branches whipping at her face and snagging her clothes.

"Seriously?" she huffed, swiping away a particularly aggressive branch. "Could this get any worse?"

Her thoughts raced alongside her pounding footsteps, each one bringing her closer to freedom—or capture. As much as she tried to focus on her escape, the pain in her arm demanded attention. It throbbed with every heartbeat, a constant reminder of the danger she'd left behind and the risks she still faced.

"Keep going," she urged herself, her breath coming in ragged gasps. "If you stop now, they'll catch you for sure."

She couldn't afford to slow down. Not when she'd come this far, not when her life—and her sanity—were on the line. The darkness of the land without streetlights enveloped her, offering both concealment and a disorienting maze that threatened to swallow her whole.

God, I hope there's some kind of path out of here. Or at least a friendly woodland creature who can show me the way.

But as the trees and brush closed in around her and her breaths became more labored, she knew there would be no magical solution to her predicament. It was up to her alone to find a way out—or die trying. She pushed herself harder, running through the pain and the fear, determined to put as much distance between herself and the compound as possible.

The unforgiving underbrush tore at her exposed skin, leaving fresh scratches and welts in its wake. But she barely noticed the pain; her focus was solely on the faint glimmer of light that signaled the edge of the expanse—and the road beyond.

"Almost there," she said, the words both a reassurance and a prayer.

Her strength was nearly gone, but she clung to her determination like a lifeline, willing herself to keep moving. And then, finally, she emerged from the treacherous forest, collapsing onto the hard asphalt of the road with a gasp of relief.

"Never thought I'd be so happy to see pavement," she said, her vision beginning to blur. "At least now I have a chance."

As she lay there, the cold ground leaching away what little warmth she had left, she couldn't help but wonder if it would be enough. But for now, she was alive—and that would have to do.

A sudden gust of wind whipped across the pavement, chilling her to the bone. She shivered, each tremor sending jolts of pain through her battered body. But as much as she wanted to curl up and hide from the world, she knew that wasn't an option.

Come on, girl. You didn't come this far to die by the roadside.

Forcing herself to sit up, she scanned the deserted highway for any sign of life. The darkness seemed to stretch on forever, but she refused to give into despair. Instead, she slapped her cheeks lightly, trying to keep her fading consciousness at bay.

"Any minute now, some charming prince will come whisk me away in his shiny car," she said, a bitter smile tugging at her lips. "Or, more likely, some trucker looking for a little action. But beggars can't be choosers, right?"

As if on cue, a pair of headlights appeared in the distance, cutting through the inky blackness like a beacon of hope. Her heart leaped with a mixture of relief and trepidation, knowing that whoever stopped could either save her or seal her fate.

"Alright, time to turn on the charm," she said, doing her best to strike a pose that was equal parts desperate and alluring. She winced as the effort sent fresh waves of pain shooting through her injuries, but she gritted her teeth and held her ground. "Here goes nothing."

The car slowed to a stop beside her, and the driver's side window rolled down smoothly. A middle-aged man with salt-and-pepper hair and a kind, weathered face peered out at her, his eyes wide with concern.

"Good God, what happened to you?" taking in her battered appearance with shock. "Do you need help?"

"Only if you're offering a ride to the nearest hospital and a fresh set of clothes," she said, doing her best to keep up the façade of nonchalance despite the agony that tore through her with every breath. "Otherwise, I'll just wait for the next guy."

"Get in," shaking his head at her bravado. "I'm no prince charming, but I think I can manage both requests."

She climbed gingerly into the car, wincing as her injuries protested the movement.

As the car pulled away from the side of the road, she allowed herself a moment of relief, feeling the weight of her captivity lift ever so slightly. She wasn't out of the woods yet—both literally and figuratively—but for the first time in longer than she could remember, she had something resembling hope.

She had escaped the clutches of her captors, armed with the evidence to dismantle their empire and ensure they would hurt no one again.

But her journey was far from over. She would need allies, support, and a plan to expose the truth. With renewed determination, she stared out the front windshield, ready to face the challenges ahead and fight for the justice she and so many others deserved.

"By the way," she said, turning to her rescuer with a coy smile as the last vestiges of fear fell away, "you can call me Justine."

Outside Hitter

Darby's long legs carried her across the crowded office like a gazelle, striding through a field of predators. She had once ruled the volleyball court, an unstoppable force that left opponents shaking in their sneakers. Now she worked for different kinds of sharks, collecting debts and gathering intel for an underground gambling syndicate.

"Ms. Darby, I presume?" Cam Johnson asked, rising from behind his desk as she entered.

"Guilty as charged." Darby's face wore a practiced smirk, her sky-blue eyes locking onto his with predatory ease. Darby was known for treating her hair like a constantly evolving art project, never afraid to experiment with new styles and colors. Today she wore it her blonde hair in a blunt collarbone cut, and her tailored blue pantsuit projected authority while highlighting her athletic frame.

"Please, have a seat," he said, nervously adjusting his cufflinks. "I assume Charles sent you to discuss the . . . ah, payment plan?"

"He did." Darby settled into the chair, crossing her legs. "You're behind on your markers, Mr. Johnson. Charles is concerned."

Johnson wiped sweat from his brow. "I just need more time. The market's been volatile, but I have some deals in the pipeline—"

"Charles doesn't care about your excuses," she cut him off smoothly. "He cares about his money. But I'm authorized to offer you an . . . alternative arrangement."

While Johnson rambled about his venture capital firm and promised future payments, Darby subtly surveyed his office. She spotted his computer, noting the USB ports clearly visible on the desktop tower. Perfect.

"I'll need to use your restroom," she said, rising gracefully. "Then we can discuss terms."

Once Johnson stepped out to point her to the executive washroom, Darby moved swiftly. She inserted the USB drive into his computer, the custom malware immediately beginning its work. Within seconds, she'd have access to all his financial records—and more importantly, evidence of his illegal gambling operation that could prove useful leverage.

"Let's skip the excuses, Mr. Johnson," Darby said when she returned, noting how he'd loosened his tie in her absence. "Charles is willing to write off forty percent of your debt in exchange for something more valuable than money."

"What does he want?" Johnson asked, his fingers drumming nervously on his mahogany desk.

"Information." Darby leaned forward, her voice dropping. "We understand your venture capital firm isn't only putting money into tech startups. You've got other interests. Interests that align with certain establishments in Vegas and Atlantic City."

The color drained from Johnson's face. "I'm not sure what you're—"

"Please," she cut him off with a wave. "The USB drive in your computer right now is copying everything. Bank records, shell companies, offshore accounts. Charles doesn't care about your gambling habits, Mr. Johnson. He cares about your connections."

"You bitch," Johnson snarled, half-rising from his chair.

Darby's smile turned razor-sharp. "Careful now. Remember, I'm the one offering you a way out. Charles gets access to your network of high rollers, and you get to keep your kneecaps. Seems fair to me."

She stood, smoothing her pantsuit. "You have twenty-four hours to consider the offer. Though based on what my little device is finding right now, I don't think you'll need that long."

Darby strode out of Johnson's office, her heels clicking authoritatively on the polished marble. She could feel the weight of curious gazes from the cubicles she passed, but she wore their scrutiny like armor. This wasn't the volleyball court anymore, but she was still playing to win.

The receptionist gave her an envious look as she passed.

"Thanks, hon. Keep those dreams alive," Darby offered with a wink before boarding the elevator.

"Ground floor, please," she told the older operator, who couldn't keep his eyes off her impossibly long legs. As the doors closed, she allowed herself a moment to exhale, letting her mind wander to the upcoming workout session that awaited her.

"Here we are, Miss," the operator announced. "Enjoy your day."

"Oh, I will." Darby flashed him a dazzling smile and sauntered out of the building. The sun beat down as she hailed a cab, already anticipating the familiar burn of exertion that would soon course through her veins.

"Iron Paradise Gym," she instructed the driver, settling into the leather seat. "And step on it. I've got muscles to sculpt."

As they sped through the city streets, Darby thought about Johnson and the information she'd just stolen. He was just another mark in a long line of wealthy men who thought they were untouchable. She'd learned long ago that the real money wasn't in breaking kneecaps for bookies—it was in gathering leverage on the power players, the ones who thought they could gamble with other people's lives without consequences.

"A different kind of game," she mused, watching the city blur past. The thrill of the con, the intricate dance of power and manipulation—that's what she lived for now. The gym was her refuge, where she kept her body as sharp as her mind, always ready for the next move in this dangerous chess match she played.

She settled back to review the intel from Johnson's computer on her phone. A list of high-stakes players scrolled past—venture capitalists, tech moguls, and there, near the bottom, a name that made her pause.

Unlike the others, his file was thin. Former addict turned professor turned author, now living in Omaha. But what caught her eye was the amount—he'd recently lost big at an underground poker game in Los Angeles. The kind of loss that would have Charles salivating for fresh blood.

At the gym, Darby pounded the heavy bag, her mind churning over the file. Something about him was different. Most of their marks swaggered through life, convinced of their own superiority. But not this one . . . his losses seemed almost calculated. Like he was trying to work his way into the circuit.

"Hey, Darby!" Big Mike called out, using her old volleyball nickname. "Someone left this for you at the front desk."

The envelope was unmarked, but she recognized Charles's handwriting inside: "Los Angeles. Next Friday. Details on the teacher." A plane ticket was paper-clipped to the note, along with a grainy photo of the subject at a poker table, his expression unreadable.

Darby's instincts, honed by years of reading people, tingled. This wasn't just another mark to be squeezed. He was hunting for something—or someone—in the gambling world. And now Charles was sending her to find out why.

She smiled, already plotting her approach. This could be interesting. Very interesting indeed.

· · · ● · ● · · ·

She changed into black spandex volleyball shorts and a tight, dri-fit sleeveless light blue top. She pulled her hair into a high bun as she exited the locker room.

A hulking figure covered the door to the free weight room. It was Big Mike again; Mike was a trainer and occasional lifting partner who frequented Iron Paradise.

"Hey! Ready to get your ass handed to you today?" she said playfully, earning a hearty guffaw from the mountain of a man.

"Bring it on, volleyball queen."

Iron Paradise was an old school gym. Its original focus was on free weights. But as times changed, machines (first Nautilus, then Universal, then the popular functional equipment used today) were added, cardio was added, aerobic studios with specialized classes like Zumba and Yoga were added, eventually they added a boxing area with a roped-off ring. The goal of the never-ending *progress* over the years—blasphemy to many—was to compete with the other fitness facilities like Jazzercise and CrossFit. Despite the changes, Iron Paradise struggled financially.

She knew of the challenges, but as she and Mike entered the gym together, Darby couldn't help but feel a sense of purpose wash over her. This was where she belonged, pushing herself to the limit in pursuit of her goals. With each bead of sweat that fell, she moved closer to the justice she craved, inching ever nearer to the redemption she so desperately needed. And nothing or no one would stand in her way.

The Broker

Once a prominent residential district in the late 19th and early 20th centuries, the Bunker Hill district of Los Angeles went through significant changes over the years. Today, a blend of commercial buildings, cultural institutions, and modern high-rises occupy the area. Its steep streets, staircases, and terraced landscaping define the area which offers panoramic views of the cityscape. Angels Flight, the iconic, funicular railway, with its colorful railway cars, connects the top and bottom of the hill, providing a charming nod to the area's history.

Cultural institutions thrive in Bunker Hill, attracting visitors from near and far. The Museum of Contemporary Art (MOCA), The Broad contemporary art museum, and the Music Center, which houses renowned venues like the Dorothy Chandler Pavilion, are among the cultural gems that enrich the area's artistic landscape.

Bunker Hill has an ambiance. The area is dynamic, reflecting the essence of Los Angeles. It is a place where history and modernity converge while creativity and progress thrive.

• • • ● • ● • • •

Josh stood in front of the large glass window of an office in the 2Cal building in this thriving section of Los Angeles, nibbling on garlic-flavored pretzels. The office was medium size with the obligatory framed degrees (USC undergrad, Stanford Business School) and modern artwork. He had a small office, but he was proud of it and the work it took to get there.

He was born here, went to school here, and had been working as a banker for the past two years, and yet every time he looked out at the sprawling city, it still felt like a foreign land.

In his late 20s now, his sharp mind had earned him an excellent reputation among his colleagues, but few knew about the haunted past that lurked just beneath the surface.

When Josh looks back at his college days at USC, his time working at one of the Big Four accounting firms seems innocent enough. But that internship led him down a darker path—from basic auditing to forensic accounting for clients who needed their books *cleaned up*. By his senior year, he was secretly cooking books for mob-connected businesses, making dirty money look legitimate. The money was incredible for a college student, but the guilt ate at him as he saw how his work enabled exploitation and crime.

"Hey Josh, you daydreaming again?" teased one of his coworkers, a boisterous man named Rick.

"Something like that," Josh said with a wry smile, not wanting to reveal the true nature of his thoughts.

"Come on, snap out of it! We're heading to The Yard for lunch, you in?"

"Sure, why not?" He was eager to escape the confines of his office and the memories that seemed to reach out and grab him whenever he lingered too long in the silence.

As they walked through the newly renovated outdoor area, Josh recalls coming here with his father as a child. The plaza used to be centered around a large water area—they called it a water court. It was changed a few years ago to protect the parking lot it covered. The new space was nice, it was greener, and it allowed visitors to get closer to the staged performances that crowded the summer calendar. But if he was being honest, he missed the water.

"You seem a little off today," Rick said around bites of his turkey sandwich, his brow furrowed with concern.

"Ah, just some old ghosts coming back to haunt me," Josh responded with an attempt at nonchalance, hoping to deflect the conversation away from his troubled past.

"Dude, I'm with you. I used to have this job selling knives door-to-door. Let me tell you, there are some things you can't unsee," Rick said, completely oblivious to the weight of Josh's confession.

"Knives, huh? Yeah, that sounds rough."

Josh laughed at the absurdity of the comparison. But deep down, he wished his demons were as simple as an ill-advised sales job.

Rick's eyes lit up with excitement. "Hey, I've got an idea. I heard about a new bar . . . let's go tonight. It's supposed to be amazing. What do you say?"

"Sure, why not?" He hoped a night out would ease his guilt.

"Great! I'll round up the troops. Trust me, it's gonna be epic," Rick promised, giving Josh a friendly slap on the back before bounding off to spread the word.

As the sun dipped below the horizon and the shadows grew longer, Josh couldn't help but feel a sense of trepidation creeping in. He knew that no amount of alcohol or laughter could ever erase the ghosts of his past, but perhaps, just maybe, he'd find some temporary relief in the company of friends and the dimly lit corners of a seedy Los Angeles bar.

• • • • • • • • • • •

Darby's laughter rang through the air like a bell, resonating in the dim lighting of Iron Paradise as she easily held her own during their sparring session. Josh couldn't help but grin back at her, admiring her athleticism and clever wit; it was no wonder she could charm and disarm her clients with such finesse.

"Alright, let's switch it up," Darby said, wiping the sweat from her brow and throwing back her long hair before tossing him a pair of gloves. "Time for some boxing."

"Are you sure about that? I wouldn't want to hurt your moneymaker," he said, referring to her face.

"Please, just try not to break a nail while we're at it," she shot back playfully, slipping on her own gloves with a smirk.

Josh had met Darby just over a year ago at this very gym and they'd quickly become close friends, bonding over their shared experiences in the seedy world that inhabits certain corners of their city. Although they came from different backgrounds, they found solace in each other's company, driven by their desire to make amends for their past and achieve their goals.

"Alright, come on big guy, show me what you got," Darby dared as they began their boxing workout.

Trading jabs and crosses, they pushed each other to their physical limits. Each punch thrown and received served as catharsis, allowing them to cope with their past experiences in an environment free from judgment.

As the workout progressed, the intensity increased, and Darby's movements became fluid and graceful, her muscles rippling with every punch. Josh found himself mesmerized by her form, her lithe body moving with a grace he'd never seen before.

As they landed their final blows, sweat pouring down their faces, Josh knew that no matter what haunted him from his past, he had a genuine friend by his side.

"Thanks for the workout, Darby," he said, panting slightly as they removed their gloves.

"Anytime, Josh. You know I'm always up for some sparring."

As they made their way towards the exit, Josh felt a sense of peace wash over him. Progress in his journey to redemption gave him a feeling he hadn't had in a long time. He was making progress.

But as they stepped out into the dark, bustling streets of LA, he couldn't shake the feeling that his past was still lurking in the shadows, waiting to tackle him.

"Hey, remember when you had to collect from that guy who tried to pay his gambling debt in rare coins?" Josh asked as they walked down the street.

"Ugh, don't remind me," Darby said, rolling her eyes as they both laughed. "At least they were worth something. What about that time you had to hide all those shell companies for that *entrepreneur* who was really running an underground fight ring?"

"God, that was a nightmare," he said, laughing at the absurdity of it all. "I'll never look at incorporation paperwork the same way again."

Darby stopped.

"Hey, I'm finally ready," Darby said, her voice full of determination. "I'm quitting this life. I can do more than chase down gambling debts and ruin lives."

"You absolutely can," Josh said, his own experience of leaving the criminal accounting world behind making him the perfect person to understand her decision. "Best thing I ever did was walk away. The straight life suits me better than cooking books ever did."

Darby received a text that made her pause. It was from a business associate she had recently started working with. She stopped where she was to read it again.

"Darby, can we meet? I have a job that requires a special set of skills that I believe you possess."

The words suggested to Darby that this job wasn't her typical assignment. She was intrigued.

"Broken Halo, next Tuesday, midnight."

She and Josh kept trading playful banter, and a sense of anticipation for what lay ahead in their friendship and individual lives charged the surrounding air.

Broken Angels

The neon lights flickered, casting an eerie glow upon the grimy streets of the Los Angeles underbelly. Nestled in a forgotten corner, a seedy bar emerged from the darkness like a den of vices and secrets. Its weathered façade displayed a faded sign that read "The Broken Halo," barely clinging to the promise of redemption long abandoned.

The dimly lit room revealed a motley crew of characters huddled together, seeking solace or escape from the harsh realities of their lives. The walls, adorned with peeling wallpaper and graffiti, whispered tales of shattered dreams and shattered lives.

A worn wooden structure with nicks and scratches etched into its surface, the bar itself stood as a testament to countless nights of reckless abandon. The bartenders, weary souls with hardened expressions, moved with a practiced efficiency, serving drinks that danced with the devil's elixir.

The patrons, a collection of lost souls, clung to their barstools like anchors in a storm, drowning their sorrows in glasses half-empty or half-full, depending on their perspective. Smoke hung lazily in the air, intertwining with the haunting melodies pouring from an old jukebox, each note echoing the melancholy that permeated the room.

In the corner, a pool table stood as a battleground for those seeking to prove their worth or forget their troubles. The clatter of billiard balls mingled with bursts of raucous laughter and the occasional muttered curse, creating a discordant symphony of broken dreams and fleeting moments of joy.

The flickering lights reflected in the eyes of its patrons, revealing glimpses of pain, longing, and a yearning for something more—a glimmer of hope buried beneath layers of regret and despair.

Time halted, the outside world irrelevant. It was a haven for the lost, the forgotten, and the broken, where shadows danced and stories unfolded in whispers, creating a tapestry of human experiences woven from threads of darkness and shattered illusions.

The Broken Halo was a far cry from their usual workout spots. Swapping punching bags for dim lighting and sweaty gym rats for the smell of stale beer, Josh found himself quickly submerged in an atmosphere that seemed to cling to him like the grime on the walls.

The sticky floors seemed to hold on to the secrets of countless nights gone awry. Shady characters lurked in the shadows, eyes darting, waiting—and looking—for trouble. Raucous laughter rang out, punctuating the cacophony of drunken conversations and off-key karaoke performances.

"Josh! Over here!" Darby called out, waving at him from a booth near the back. He made his way through the crowd, avoiding the occasional elbow or spilled drink, and slid into the seat across from her.

Darby—wearing a black shift dress with cap sleeves and a point collar with split neckline—had her long blonde hair parted in the center, a classic look that framed her face and drew attention to her facial features.

"Wow, this place is . . . something else," he said. Josh sat in his tailored navy blazer, looking oddly pristine against the grimy backdrop of the bar, taking in the surroundings with an amused grin and quickly diving into the beer nuts on the table.

"Right? It's like we stumbled into the set of *Kiss Kiss Bang Bang*. But I figured we could use a change of scenery."

"Definitely," Josh said, nodding as he signaled for the bartender to bring them some drinks. "I just hope we don't end up end up in someone's trunk being dumped in Big Bear Lake."

"Hey, if we do, at least we'll have a good story to tell." She made a face after taking a sip of her seltzer water. "Ugh, this tastes like they haven't cleaned the soda lines in months."

"Let me try," Josh said, swapping his glass with hers. He took a sip and grimaced. "You're right. That's awful. Tastes like carbonated metal. Cheers to surviving this place, I guess."

They clinked glasses again as they both forced down another sip.

"You know, most people would question two friends meeting in a dive bar to drink nothing but soda," Darby said with a wry smile. "But I guess we've both learned the hard way that keeping a clear head is the better choice."

"Definitely," Josh agreed, eyeing his questionable seltzer. "Though with drinks this bad, maybe we're just smarter than everyone else here."

As they drank and chatted, the pair couldn't help but find humor in their surroundings. From the man at the bar who seemed to attempt an impromptu stand-up comedy routine, to the woman in the corner who was passionately singing a love ballad to her pet iguana . . . the bar offered no shortage of entertainment.

"Y'know, there's something kind of liberating about being in a place like this," Darby said as she watched a couple stumble onto the makeshift dance floor. "It's like everyone here has just embraced the chaos."

"True," Josh conceded, rubbing his chin thoughtfully. "Maybe that's what we need sometimes. Life doesn't always need to be serious. Maybe we need to embrace more chaos."

"Exactly," she said, nodding vigorously.

• • • ● • ● • ● • •

"Hey, watch this," Darby said, grabbing a handful of bar napkins. With practiced precision, she began folding one into an intricate shape. "Back in my volleyball days, we'd have origami competitions during tournaments to stay calm between matches."

"No way," Josh said, reaching for his own napkin. "I used to do this too—though usually to impress dates at fancy restaurants." He grinned sheepishly. "Care for a little folding challenge?"

"You're on," Darby said, her competitive spirit ignited. "Best paper crane in under two minutes. Loser buys the next round."

"Deal," Josh replied, already working on his first fold. "Though I should warn you—I once made a whole paper zoo during a particularly boring budget meeting."

They hunched over their napkins, faces screwed up in concentration as their fingers flew. When time was up, Darby's crane was elegant but slightly lopsided, while Josh's looked more like a rumpled seagull.

"I think we can both agree who won this round," Darby smirked, gesturing to her creation.

"Hey now, mine has . . . character," Josh protested, but he was already flagging down the bartender with a good-natured laugh.

"Now, about that story you were going to tell me . . ."

"Ah, yes," Darby said, rolling her eyes. "I call it *The Tale of the Perpetually Sweaty Gambler.*"

"Sounds . . . delightful," he winced, taking a sip of his beer.

"Trust me, it's not as bad as it sounds. This guy—let's call him Mr. Drippy—would get so anxious about his gambling debts that he'd be drenched in sweat during our 'collection meetings.' I mean, we're talking Niagara Falls levels of perspiration here."

"Ugh," Josh grimaced. "I've had my fair share of anxious clients, but that might just take the cake."

"Wait, it gets better," she said, pausing for dramatic effect. "One time, he tried to pay his debt in vintage baseball cards—showed up wearing a full-on raincoat and galoshes, carrying a climate-controlled briefcase. Had an entire presentation about why his Mickey Mantle rookie card was worth double what he owed."

"Stop!" He laughed so hard he nearly choked on his drink. "I can't handle any more!"

"Okay, okay," she said, laughing as well. "Your turn. Top that."

"Alright," he said, wiping tears from his eyes. "This one happened back when I was handling accounts for this tech entrepreneur. There was this guy—we'll call him Mr.

Crypto—who was convinced he'd invented a revolutionary new cryptocurrency. He needed me to set up all these elaborate offshore accounts for his 'imminent billions."

"Go on."

"Turns out, his revolutionary crypto was just pictures of his cat wearing different hats, and he'd literally mortgaged his house to buy servers to mine *KittyCoin*. Had a whole whitepaper and everything. Would only meet me in different cat cafes around the city."

"Okay, my turn," Darby said, taking a gulp of her beer. "I know we were moving past those days, but this is too good. I had this high-roller who insisted on meeting me at the Bellagio fountains to pay his debt. Full tuxedo, champagne, the works. He even had *Viva Las Vegas* playing from a portable speaker."

"Seriously?"

"Swear to God," she said, stifling a laugh. "I felt like I was in some twisted *Ocean's Eleven* fantasy."

"Did you at least get your money?"

"Let's just say he made it worth the theatrics," Darby said, rolling her eyes.

• • • ● • ● • ● • •

Darby saw him walk into the bar and take a seat at a corner booth. She continued chatting with Josh, but knew she needed to talk to him; Darby didn't know the job, and she knew she would likely turn it down. She was serious when she told Josh she was done with sex for money. But something in the way he moved and something that he texted caused her to agree to the meeting tonight.

"It's been a long night, Josh. I'm going to hit the Ladies' Room and head home. Why don't you take off without me? We can catch up later this week. Maybe for another epic boxing match!"

"You're on! I've got an early morning as it is. 'Til we box again!"

．．．●．●．●．．．

"Hello, Chuckles, it's good to see you again."

Merry Men

A crystal chandelier cascaded fragmented light over the room as Darby sipped a vodka tonic—ok, all tonic, but she needed to blend in—her eyes scanning the sea of well-dressed guests. The party was a cacophony of laughter, clinking glasses, and techno music. But she felt oddly detached from it all. Wearing a black strappy pleated bust corset detail crop top with khaki cargo pocket detail baggy boyfriend jeans, she navigated the sea of bodies, her senses assaulted by the overpowering scent of cologne and sweat. The bass from the speakers reverberated through her chest as she squeezed past a group of tipsy dancers. A kaleidoscope of colors reflected off the chandelier, casting an ever-changing pattern across the room. A woman with fire-red hair caught her eye.

A new client hired Darby to be at this party tonight. She didn't know his name and only saw her boss, Charles, as he gave her an envelope and details. Besides a rather sizeable sum of money, she was told to find a red head and to listen to her story. That's it. Just listen.

Darby was just fine with this.

"Hey babe," the woman said, sidling up beside Darby with a mischievous grin. "You look like you could use a little excitement."

"Excitement, huh?" Darby raised an eyebrow, her lips curling into a smirk as she took another sip of her drink. "I'm listening."

The woman introduced herself as Justine and ordered a dirty martini from a passing server. As they exchanged pleasantries, Darby observed her more closely—there was a magnetic air about her, something that made it impossible to look away. Her sky-blue satin halter neck plunge skater dress perfectly highlighted her body.

"So what brings you to this shindig?" Justine asked, swirling her drink in one hand while absently twirling a strand of red hair with the other.

"A former client is hosting and invited me. Getting invited to events like this is always fun. It beats being forced to work." Darby kept her tone light, masking the seething anger beneath her words. "And you? What's a girl like you doing in a place like this?"

"Retirement, believe it or not. I used to be a porn star, if you can imagine that," Justine admitted, her voice tinged with a hint of nostalgia.

"Really?" Despite herself, this intrigued Darby. "Now that's a conversation starter."

"Isn't it, though? But I'm through with that. My life was nothing but working seemingly nonstop."

Darby drifted back to her own checkered past. "Tell me about it."

"Anyway, I got out of the business, but the shadows never leave you. It's like a looming presence, threatening to engulf you again." Justine's eyes darkened with unease, and for a moment, a sense of vulnerability replaced that magnetic air.

"Sounds rough," Darby sympathized, her mind racing with questions she dared not ask just yet. "But hey, we've all got our demons, right?"

"True enough," Justine conceded, raising her glass in a mock toast. "So here's to exorcising those demons."

"Cheers to that."

The party swirled around them as they continued to talk. Justine's stories of her past life in the porn industry were fascinating, and Darby found herself drawn in. But as the night wore on, the music became louder, and the guests became more intoxicated. Darby realized she was no longer interested in the party or the surrounding people. The alluring red head intrigued her and she wanted to learn more.

"God, parties like these bring back memories," said Justine, her gaze flicking around the bustling room. "Once, I was at this gig in Vegas, and you wouldn't believe the people who showed up. The things they expected of us . . ."

"Sounds . . . interesting?" Darby ventured cautiously; her curiosity piqued.

"Interesting doesn't begin to cover it. You wouldn't believe what they did to break us down," Justine said, her voice trembling slightly. "One time, a producer gathered several of us in his suite, showing us off to his business partners like we were property. Made us serve drinks, act as entertainment. We were just there for his amusement." She shuddered, taking a sip of her drink. "He loved humiliating us in front of his friends. Called it 'breaking our spirits.'"

"Jesus, that's disgusting."

"Tell me about it," Justine said, her eyes clouded by the memory. "That's just the beginning. Another time, they forced me to work with this director who had a reputation for being cruel . . . emotionally abusive to everyone on set. And they knew it, but they didn't care. Made me sign an NDA—which I'm obviously breaking now—saying I wouldn't tell anyone about the psychological abuse or sue them if things went wrong. They trapped us in these situations where we felt completely powerless."

"Did you ever consider walking away?"

"More times than I can count," Justine admitted, her voice cracking. "Each time I tried to leave, they would reel me back in. 'Just one more job,' they'd say. 'We'll make it worth your while.' And like an idiot, I'd fall for it every time."

"Money talks," Darby said, her empathy shining through. "But it's never too late to break the cycle, right?"

"Maybe," Justine conceded, her optimism wavering. "But the industry's like a black hole. Once you're in, it's nearly impossible to claw your way out again."

"Hey," Darby said, leaning forward. "You've made it this far, right? That's gotta count for something."

"Thanks. I appreciate that. But I feel like I'll never completely escape it, you know?"

"Trust me, I get it," Darby said, her thoughts drifting to her own struggles. "The past has a way of sticking around, no matter how hard we try to shake it off."

"Isn't that the truth? But there was more to it."

She took a big gulp and continued.

"The last studio I was at loved me so much that they . . ."

Justine began to tear up.

Darby put her hand on Justine's forearm, noticing the healing scar for the first time.

"Darby, the last place . . . they wouldn't let me leave. Not just I can't break my contract. I couldn't leave the compound. Leaving my room was limited to shooting, eating, or exercising. I was a prisoner. I lost my life there. Or at least I almost did."

She stared straight ahead as Darby looked on with a degree of compassion she didn't know she possessed.

"I got out—through a ventilation duct, over a razor wire fence, through a thorn-riddled forest—just two weeks ago."

The music pulsed around them and they both sat there, letting Justine's story sink in. They were both survivors, bound by their determination to escape the darkness that threatened to swallow them whole.

Darby broke the silence with a wicked glint in her eye. "Have you ever thought of doing more than just walking away?"

"What do you mean?

"What if we could hit the bastards where it hurts most while also making a serious payday?"

Justine cocked an eyebrow. "How could we possibly hurt them?"

"I'd love to rob the bastards blind and bring them down to Earth." Darby leaned back in her chair, savoring the weight of the idea. "It seems like you have no qualms about breaking a few laws. I've got connections, and I know my way around the darker corners of society. We combine your inside knowledge with my skills, and we walk away with the studios in shambles."

"Damn," Justine said, a slow smile spreading across her face. "You're not joking, are you?"

"Never been more serious," Darby said, matching her grin. "We'd be like modern-day Robin Hoods, taking from the corrupt and giving back to ourselves."

"Okay, let's say I'm on board with this insanity," Justine said, her eyes sparkling with mischief. "How do we pull off something of that magnitude? Because I doubt they keep all their dirty money in a single vault somewhere."

"True," Darby admitted, tapping her chin thoughtfully. "But I bet there are key financial pipelines we can tap into. You know, choke points where a lot of transactions flow through."

"Like what?" Justine pressed, caught up in the plan's audaciousness.

"Think about it," Darby began, her voice low and conspiratorial. "All those payments from subscriptions, onetime purchases, ad revenue—they must use a centralized platform to handle all that cash."

"Sure, but even if we find it, how do we access it without getting caught?" Justine asked, her practicality reasserting itself.

"Leave that to me," Darby said with a confident smirk. "I'm motivated by your sincerity and your story. Plus, I've got some friends in high and low places who owe me favors. We'll need a team, of course. A hacker, finance expert, maybe even some muscle if things get physical. Maybe more than that, but it's a place to start."

"Sounds like a bad heist movie," Justine said, shaking her head. "But you're right. If we can assemble the right crew and come up with the right plan, we might just get somewhere."

Darby leaned in closer, her eyes alight with excitement. "We'll be doing more than just stealing money. We'll be making a statement. Showing the world that they can't keep exploiting people like us without consequences."

Justine laughed at the irrationality of it all. "Okay, okay! I'm in. Let's bring down the house of smut and walk away rich. How's that for sweet revenge?"

"Sweet as sin. Here's to our grand heist and an epic middle finger to the industry that tried to break you."

As the music roared around them, they drank deeply, thoroughly intoxicated by the promise of retribution and redemption.

Breaking Character

Thirteen-year-old Justine sat cross-legged on her bed, surrounded by movie posters and playbills, her eyes glued to the latest issue of Backstage magazine. The soft glow of her bedside lamp cast dramatic shadows across the glossy pages as she devoured articles about audition techniques and method acting.

"Lights out in ten minutes, sweetheart," her dad called from the doorway, a gentle smile playing on his lips as he took in the familiar scene.

"Just five more minutes, Dad? I'm reading about how Brandon Thaylen went from community theater to Hollywood." Her eyes sparkled with enthusiasm. "Did you know he started acting when he was even younger than me?"

He leaned against the doorframe, his expression softening. Ever since losing her mother, Justine had thrown herself into acting with an intensity that both impressed and worried him. "You remind me so much of your mother sometimes," he said softly. "She had that same fire in her eyes when she talked about her passions."

Justine beamed at the comparison. Her memories of her mother were hazy, more feelings than concrete images, but she cherished every story her dad shared. "Tell me about her theater days again?"

"Tomorrow. School night, remember?"

But instead of protesting, Justine was already lost in another article, her fingers tracing the path of her dreams across the pages.

· · • · • · ● · • · • · ·

The years flew by in a whirlwind of school plays and community theater productions. By sixteen, Justine had transformed from a starry-eyed dreamer into a serious student of her craft. Her bedroom walls were now covered with acting awards and show photos, each one a stepping stone on her path to stardom.

"You were born for this," her drama teacher said after watching her bring the audience to tears as Juliet. "You have a gift, Justine. A way of making people feel every emotion as if it were their own."

Her dad watched from the wings, pride warring with concern in his heart. He saw how the stage lit her up from within, how she came alive in ways that nothing else could match. But he also saw the darker side of the entertainment industry, the broken dreams and shattered lives that littered the path to fame.

Then came the Brandon Thaylen scandal. Justine's childhood idol, the actor whose career she had followed religiously, exposed as a predator who'd exploited young actresses and embezzled millions. She spent hours in her room that night, tearing down posters and ripping up magazines, her sobs echoing through the house.

Her dad found her surrounded by the wreckage of her innocence, her face streaked with tears. "I'll be different," she promised him fiercely. "I'll never let the industry change who I am."

"I know you won't, sweetheart," he said, pulling her into a tight embrace. "But maybe this is a sign to consider other options? You could study theater in college, get a degree to fall back on . . ."

But Justine was already shaking her head. "The scandal just proves we need more good people in the industry, Dad. People who'll stand up against the corruption, who'll use their platform to make real change."

By her senior year of high school, Justine had accumulated an impressive portfolio of leading roles and glowing reviews. College acceptance letters poured in, including several prestigious theater programs. Her dad dared to hope she might choose a more traditional path.

"Stanford has an excellent drama department," he suggested over dinner one night. "You could double major, maybe combine theater with business or communications?"

Justine pushed her food around her plate. "I've been thinking," she said slowly. "What if I took a gap year instead? Really focused on auditioning, building my professional resume?"

The words hung heavy in the air between them. Her dad set down his fork, choosing his next words carefully. "Justine, you know I support your dreams. But the world of professional acting . . . it's not just about talent. It can be cruel, exploitative. I've seen too many young people get chewed up and spit out by that machine."

"I'm not naïve, Dad," Justine said, her chin lifting with determination. "I know it won't be easy. But I have to try. I feel it in my bones—this is what I was meant to do."

In the end, they compromised. Justine would attend college locally, majoring in theater while pursuing professional auditions on the side. For a while, it seemed to work. She excelled in her classes, landed a few small commercial roles, began building a name for herself in the local acting community.

But the fire in her burned too bright to be contained by lecture halls and student productions. Los Angeles called to her like a siren song, promising bright lights and bigger stages. The tension between father and daughter grew with each passing semester.

"You're throwing away your future," he argued during one particularly heated discussion. "At least finish your degree first!"

"My future is out there, Dad, not stuck in some classroom! I'm suffocating here!" Justine shot back, her red hair seeming to crackle with electricity. "I've already booked some promising auditions in LA. I just need a chance to prove myself!"

The night she left, her dad stood in her doorway one last time, watching her pack her dreams into a single suitcase. "Just . . . be careful out there," he said, his voice rough with emotion. "The world isn't always kind to dreamers."

"I know, Dad," Justine said softly, pausing to hug him tightly. "But I have to do this. I have to know if I can make it."

• • • ● • ● • • •

Los Angeles greeted her with indifference, a city too busy chasing its own dreams to notice one more hopeful arrival. Justine threw herself into the audition circuit, her determination undimmed by countless rejections. Minor roles trickled in—a line or two in a TV pilot, background work in commercials, student films that never saw distribution.

But the bills piled up faster than the callbacks. Her savings dwindled. Then vanished. Soon she was juggling three part-time jobs, snatching sleep between auditions and shifts, her dreams fraying at the edges.

That's when Marcus Bentley found her, his designer suit and calculated charm a stark contrast to her growing desperation. Over coffee in a sleek downtown cafe, he painted pictures of fast fame and faster fortune.

"I've seen your work, Justine," he said, his voice smooth as aged whiskey. "You have a rare talent. But the reality is, it's a tough industry. Thousands of talented women vying for a handful of roles."

She nodded, trying to ignore the gnawing emptiness in her stomach. Another missed meal to make rent.

"Have you ever considered the adult entertainment industry?" Marcus asked, the words sliding out like silk. "It's evolved, become more legitimate. With your talent and beauty, you could be a star. Making six figures within a year, living the life you've always dreamed of."

Justine's fingers tightened around her coffee cup. "I . . . I'm not sure that's the right path for me."

"Of course, I understand your hesitation," Marcus said, his tone gentle, understanding. "But think about it—financial security, creative freedom, a chance to build your brand. Many successful actresses started in adult films. It could be a stepping stone to bigger things."

The promises swirled around her like smoke, seductive and suffocating. She thought of her mounting debts, her fading dreams, the look of disappointment in her dad's eyes if he knew she was even considering this.

But desperation has a way of reshaping moral boundaries, of making the unthinkable seem almost reasonable. Before she knew it, Justine found herself in a sleek office building, signing a contract with Cum As You Are while the studio's CEO, Tony, smiled his predator's smile.

"Welcome to the family," he said, his eyes glinting with something darker than mere satisfaction.

Beside him stood his assistant, Lolita, her spiky blonde hair and chiseled abs giving her an otherworldly appearance. Her cold, calculating gaze seemed to strip Justine bare, dissecting her deepest insecurities with surgical precision.

As she was led to her new *living quarters*, Justine couldn't shake the feeling that she had just made a terrible mistake. But it was too late—the cage door had already swung shut behind her, and the key was in Tony and Lolita's hands.

She stared at her reflection in the small bathroom mirror, hardly recognizing the woman who stared back. "What have I done?" she whispered, her voice breaking. The bright-eyed dreamer who had stepped off the bus in Los Angeles seemed like a stranger now, a ghost of possibilities lost.

But even as fear and regret threatened to overwhelm her, something fierce and unbreakable stirred in Justine's core. She might be trapped, but she wasn't broken. Not yet. And somehow, someway, she would find a path back to freedom—or burn everything down trying.

James Bond

Darby and Justine sat on a sun-drenched outdoor patio at a chic coffee shop in the heart of Los Angeles. The aroma of freshly brewed coffee and the murmur of idle gossip filled the air. A young couple nearby engaged in a passionate debate about which Marvel superhero would win in a fight, while a well-dressed woman in her forties tapped away furiously at her laptop, undoubtedly working on the next great American novel.

"Alright," Darby said, taking a sip of her iced latte as she flipped through her mental Rolodex of likely accomplices, her hair perched atop her head in a messy bun. "If we're going to do this, we'll need someone who understands how shady money works."

"Like a banker." Justine said, twirling a strand of her red hair around her finger. "This *banker* needs to understand the process from online payments to where the money goes to how the companies spend the money, They don't use checks anymore, it's all ones and zeroes now."

"Exactly. Moving to the tech side. We need someone who can hack into security systems, disable alarms, and get us inside information."

"Like a modern-day Q from James Bond?" Justine asked with a grin.

"Sure, if Q had a penchant for internet memes and a serious caffeine addiction," Darby said as she laughed. "But seriously, we'll need someone who knows their way around the digital world like it's their own backyard."

"Doesn't everyone these days?" Justine said, raising an eyebrow. "I disabled some cameras and grabbed a couple passwords, but I don't think I can do that."

"True, we need someone who's fantastic. I'm talking next-level hacking skills."

"Got anyone in mind?" Justine asked, sipping her Americano.

"Actually, no. But I think I know someone who might . . . an old friend," Darby said, a mischievous glint in her eye. "I've got a banker in mind. A friend of mine—Josh—works in a bank nearby. He's a wizard with money and has his own motivation."

"Think he'd be up for our little escapade?"

"There's only one way to know. I'll set up a meeting with him tomorrow morning."

· · · · ● · ● · ● · · ·

The following day, Josh nibbled on a blueberry scone as Darby and Justine walked into the pastry shop to meet him. It was rainy, so they met indoors. Darby introduced Justine as they both laid out their audacious plan. He listened, wide-eyed, as they detailed their desire to bring down Cum As You Are—CAYA—and make off with a fortune in the process.

Justine shared her personal connection to the studio and the desire to do this. And Darby added she loved a good challenge. She then turned to Josh, her eyes sparkling with hope and enthusiasm. "We need your help, Josh. While we've got the inside scoop on the company, we don't have the financial know-how to pull off a major heist. You have a lot of friends in this world. You could be our financial eye in the sky and lead us to the weak points in the system."

Josh sat there listening, his fingers drumming away on the wooden table as he contemplated the idea. He might be getting ahead of himself—he'd only met Justine this morning—but it made sense. "Like you, I love a moral challenge," he said after a moment. "And I know many people in finance. I could make some calls, get some leads."

"That would be amazing," Darby said, placing her hand on his forearm.

When they finished, Josh was quiet for a time, contemplating the sheer magnitude of what they wanted to do. "This is a lot to take in," he said eventually, running a hand through his hair. "And like I said, my contribution is in the information. If you would like help with the plan, I'll put you in touch with the right people. We can meet here tomorrow and talk strategy. Justine, hit me up on Discord, if you don't mind. I need to get a handle on what they have. Let me go over the security of the studios and see where we're most vulnerable. I might have some ideas on how to hack into their accounts."

"So are you in?" Darby asked, her voice laced with equal parts hope and urgency.

"I'll have to think about it. I get the goals, I do, but . . ."

"Take your time, big guy," Justine said as she tried to assure him, her own nerves betraying her calm exterior. "It's a big decision."

As Josh returned to work on the 33rd floor of 2Cal later that day, he couldn't shake the thoughts of Darby and Justine's proposal from his mind. He found himself constantly distracted, his fingers hovering over his keyboard as he stared blankly at his computer screen. When his boss inquired about his lack of productivity, he mumbled something about feeling under the weather.

Lunchtime rolled around and Josh retreated to an isolated corner of the break room and began doing research on his phone. His heart raced as he discovered that his bank indeed held the primary account for CAYA—the very same company that had once exploited and tormented Justine.

Wow.

He suddenly felt the weight of the decision before him. He thought about the countless lives that the porn industry had ruined and, with his own past participation with sketchy finances, he wondered if he could really turn a blind eye any longer.

• • ● ● • ● ● • • •

Josh stared at the blinking cursor on his computer screen, the dissonant hum of the office around him fading into the background as he wrestled with his conscience. It was a match made in hell: on one side, his loyalty to Darby and now Justine, one used by countless men, the other who had seen the worst of what the porn industry could do; on the other, his career, which was now tangled up in that same web of exploitation.

He felt his fingers tremble above the keyboard. "What the hell am I supposed to do now?"

As evening approached, the tension inside Josh's chest continued to grow. He knew that staying silent would only allow the cycle of abuse to continue, but the prospect of betraying his employer to bring down CAYA filled him with dread. Trapped between a rock and a hard place with no escape, he grabbed his phone and made a call.

The familiar FaceTime tone.

Darby.

"Hey, Josh," her voice interrupted his thoughts. "Anything I can help with?"

Josh hesitated for a moment, then released a heavy sigh. "Yeah, actually. I've been thinking about your plan all day, and I've got some thoughts."

Darby raised an eyebrow, a smile playing on her lips. "Oh? Do tell."

"Fine," he said, mustering up a grin. "But only because you asked so nicely. I'll let you know what I've learned. I've also decided I'm in."

"Really?" Darby's face broke into a smile, her eyes shining with relief. "That's fantastic, Josh. Thank you."

"Alright, alright," Josh said, waving off her gratitude. "Now, what's the plan, boss?"

Darby leaned in, lowering her voice conspiratorially. "Here's what we're going to do: we'll need to access the bank's mainframe and reroute the funds from CAYA's account to several offshore accounts. Once that's done, we'll leak evidence of their corruption and illicit activities to the media, effectively bringing them down. And, of course, we'll be keeping a little something for ourselves as compensation."

"Sounds risky," Josh noted with a wry smile. "But what's life without a little danger . . . right?"

"Exactly," Darby said, her eyes twinkling mischievously. "Now, are you ready to help us take down this industry and make some money in the process?"

"You know I am," Josh said, his chest swelling with newfound determination. "Let's show these jerks what they're up against."

"Welcome aboard, partner," Darby said, clapping him on the shoulder. "Now let's get to work."

• • • ● • ● • • •

Darby—her hair in a textured lob—stood by a wall-sized whiteboard, tapping the marker against her chin as she contemplated the intricate web of plans and contingencies laid out before them. The room was dimly lit, casting dramatic shadows across the serious faces of the assembled team members. Justine stood nearby, arms crossed, and eyes narrowed in focus, while Josh leaned back in his chair, grabbing a handful of popcorn.

"Alright, folks," Darby began, her voice low and determined, "this is what we've got. Insider intel is our priority. Justine with the company, Josh, with the money."

"Of course. Who else would you trust with the delicate task of corporate espionage?"

"Your humility is truly inspiring," Justine said, rolling her eyes.

"Thank you," Josh said with a mock bow. "I try."

"Moving on," Darby said, ignoring their banter. "I need to reach out to an old friend for help with the computer systems."

Justine asked, "You mentioned this *old friend* before. Who is this person?"

"William."

"Just William? No story?"

"I met William—no idea if that's his real name—several years ago. We were introduced professionally and struck up a bit of a friendship. He wrote a book a few years ago about his experiences in the world of gambling."

"Ah, good old William," Josh said. "Never thought his encyclopedic knowledge of card counting and odds would come in handy for anything other than lonely Saturday nights."

"Everyone has their strengths," Darby said, suppressing a smile. "He just seems to know everyone, so he almost certainly has a hacker extraordinaire, to break into their systems.

We'll use them to siphon off the funds to multiple offshore accounts, leaving just enough breadcrumbs for the authorities to follow."

"Like Hansel and Gretel, only with more money and less cannibalism," Justine said, a wicked grin playing at the corners of her mouth.

"Exactly," Darby said, nodding. "Now, we'll also need someone on the inside, someone who knows the ins and outs of the company. That's where you come in, Justine."

"I'll get you what you need. Speaking of which, we may need some muscle. CAYA has a huge security force in their complex."

"Security . . ." said Darby. "We need someone keeping watch and providing backup if things get hairy. Security plus a hacker—we talked about that early on, Justine. Two areas we don't have covered. I think William can help us here. Once we have everything in place, however, we'll release the incriminating evidence to the media, ensuring that CAYA meets a very public and very messy demise. With any luck, other companies will take notice and think twice before exploiting their employees."

"Sounds like one hell of a plan," Josh said, his expression growing serious. "But are we really ready for this? I mean, we're not exactly professional criminals here."

"Speak for yourself," Justine said.

"Look," Darby said, meeting each of their gazes, "I know this is risky. But if we pull this off, we can make a real difference. Not just for us, but for everyone who's been hurt by this disgusting industry. So are you with me?"

There was a moment of silence as they considered her words, the weight of their decision heavy in the air. Then, one by one, they nodded.

"Let's do it," Josh said, his voice steady and resolute.

"Damn right," Justine said, her eyes gleaming with anticipation.

"Alright then," Darby said, a fierce grin spreading across her face. "Let's bring this sleeze down."

With that, they set to work.

• • • • ⬤ • ⬤ • ⬤ • • •

As the sun dipped below the horizon, casting a fiery orange glow across the city, Darby leaned against the railing of her rooftop patio, a glass of wine in hand. She took a deep breath, inhaling the cool evening air as she surveyed the sprawling metropolis below.

"Remember, you can't spell 'heist' without 'h,' 'e,' and 't'," Justine called out from the doorway, a mischievous grin on her face. "And those are the first letters of 'hell,' 'eat,' and 'tacos.'"

Darby couldn't help but laugh at the absurdity of Justine's remark. "You're right. We should definitely have some victory tacos after we pull this off."

"True," Justine said, sauntering over to join Darby at the railing. "Are we sure Josh is up for this? I mean, he's got a lot at stake here—his job, his reputation . . ."

"Josh is tougher than he looks," Darby reassured her, her gaze fixed on the distant horizon. "Besides, I think he's secretly enjoying the idea of sticking it to the man. Or, well, the men who've been exploiting women like you. Speaking of which, how, exactly, did you end up in this world?"

Justine sighed, her eyes clouding with a mixture of pain and resignation. "Long story short, I was an out of work actress, I needed money, and it was simple work. At least, that's what they told me. But once you're in, it's not so easy to get out."

"Kind of like trying to escape quicksand," Darby observed.

"Exactly," Justine nodded. "Except with more silicone and less dignity."

There was a brief silence between them, punctuated by the distant hum of traffic and the faint sounds of laughter from a nearby party. Darby glanced at Justine, her thoughts racing as she considered the immense challenge they were about to undertake.

"Listen," she began hesitantly, "if we pull this off—*when* we pull this off—what do you want to do with your life afterward?"

Justine mulled over the question for a moment before answering. "You know, I've always loved animals. Maybe I could open up a sanctuary or something."

"From porn star to animal savior . . . I like it."

"Hey, stranger things have happened," Justine said, grinning back at her. "What about you? Once we've toppled the empire, what's next for Darby?"

"World domination, obviously," Darby deadpanned. "But first, maybe a nice long vacation somewhere tropical, where the soda comes decorated with tiny umbrellas."

Just then, Josh appeared in the doorway, his expression a mix of determination and anxiety.

"Alright," Darby said, "Tomorrow we start!"

Prodigy

The gymnasium echoed with the sound of sneakers squeaking on polished wood as Darby, a precocious middle school volleyball phenom from Phoenix, leaped into the air to deliver a powerful spike. The ball whizzed past her opponents and slammed onto the court floor, sending up a puff of chalky dust that hung in the air like an exclamation mark.

"Another point for the unstoppable Darby!" the announcer said as teammates exchanged high fives and the opposing team, looking on, mouths gaped in disbelief. Darby's hair was pulled into a high ponytail as her charming smile lit up the room, her eyes sparkling with mischief. She knew she had a rare talent, and it was impossible not to love her for it.

"Great job, Darby!" shouted Coach Jennings, their overly enthusiastic coach, clapping his hands together with a little too much gusto. "You're going places, kiddo!" He patted her spandex covered butt.

Did he just do that?

Ugh . . . here we go. Just last week, Coach Jennings invited Darby to *friend him* on social media. She politely declined, but he got into a habit of texting her.

"Thanks, Coach J." Darby flashed a forced grin before turning back to her teammates and rolling her eyes, pretending not to notice his inappropriate behavior. She knew she had to focus on her game and not let anyone distract her, especially not a coach with ulterior motives. They were a tight-knit group, bound by their shared passion for the sport and their love for their star player.

As the weeks went by, it became increasingly apparent that Darby's talent and charm attracted more than just the admiration of her coach and her peers. A handful of teachers paid her special attention, offering extra help and encouragement that sometimes strayed into inappropriate territory.

"Darby, darling, you really should join the drama club," Mrs. Carmichael said one day during lunch, her fingers lingering on Darby's shoulder for a moment too long. "With your charisma, you'd be a natural on stage."

This was more than simple encouragement from a teacher. It was abuse. What started as a soft caress of her shoulder transitioned to Mrs. Carmichael running her fingers through Darby's hair.

"You have such beautiful hair, Darby."

Why do these adults think they can treat me this way?

"Uh, thanks Mrs. Carmichael, but I'm kind of busy with volleyball right now," Darby said, shifting uncomfortably in her seat as she tried to extricate herself from the woman's touch and away from her hideous perfume.

A stench I will never forget.

"Of course, of course," Mrs. Carmichael said with a disappointed sigh. "But if you ever change your mind, you know where to find me."

There was also her math teacher, Mr. Thompson.

"Darby, I noticed you were having some trouble with that last algebra problem," Mr. Thompson said as he sidled up to her desk after class one day, his voice dripping with faux concern. "I'd be more than happy to give you some one-on-one tutoring, if you're interested."

"Thanks, Mr. Thompson," Darby said, trying not to cringe at his too-close proximity and the way his eyes lingered on her legs. "I think I'll just ask my dad for help, though. He's pretty good with numbers."

"Suit yourself," Mr. Thompson said with a shrug, walking away with the air of someone who had just been denied a tasty treat.

Despite her attempts to deflect their advances, the lecherous attention from her teachers began to wear on Darby. She felt like a fly trapped in a web of unwanted desire, her every move scrutinized by predatory eyes. Yet, she refused to let their inappropriate behavior diminish her love for the game or her determination to succeed.

"Hey, Darby, you okay?" asked Sara, Darby's best friend, as they walked off the court after another victorious match. "You seem kind of . . . distracted."

"Nothing I can't handle," Darby said, forcing a smile onto her face. "Just focusing on the game, you know?"

"Alright," Sara said, giving her a concerned look. "But remember, we're here for you. If anything's bothering you . . ."

"Thanks, Sara," Darby said, touched by her friend's support. But deep inside, she knew that to truly escape the web of exploitation that threatened to ensnare her, she would need more than just the love and loyalty of her friends. She would need to fight back.

* * * * * * * * * * *

The volleyballs whistled through the air, their trajectories as varied as the countries represented on the gymnasium floor. With each country's flag proudly hanging from the rafters above, Darby and her U16 teammates fought for victory in an international tournament that brought together some of the world's best young volleyball players.

"Darby! Heads up!" shouted Sara, drawing her attention back to the game. Darby leaped into action, her powerful serve slicing through the air like a hot knife through butter. The opposing team scrambled, unable to return the ball, and Darby's teammates erupted in cheers.

"Nice one!" Sara high-fived her as they rotated positions on the court.

"Thanks," Darby grinned, her hair in her now common high ponytail. Her eyes scanned the crowd. She spotted a group of coaches watching intently, a mix of admiration and something darker in their gazes. Shivering involuntarily, she focused back on the game, refusing to let their presence rattle her.

As the season progressed, Darby traveled across the globe, competing in matches in Canada, Mexico, England, France, and Spain. While the thrill of playing the sport she loved while representing her country was exhilarating, it also exposed her to a whole new array of potential predators.

"Have you ever considered playing at UCLA?" asked a handsome older man with a French accent at a post-match celebration. He introduced himself as a coach and scout for the renowned university, his eyes lingering on Darby a little too long.

She began receiving letters from colleges and universities in middle school. Penn State, Minnesota, Nebraska, Stanford, UCLA. And many others. She loved the tradition of Penn State and Nebraska, and Stanford's academics, but maybe loved the beaches of southern California more.

"UCLA? Well, yes, I've thought about it. But I haven't decided yet."

"Let me know if you change your mind," he said, slipping her his business card. "We'd love to have someone with your . . . talents on our team."

Darby pocketed the card, unease settling in her stomach. But as she considered her options, the lure of the beaches and, of course, playing for one of the top volleyball schools proved too tempting to resist. She accepted a scholarship to play at UCLA and found herself immersed in a world that seemed both familiar and utterly foreign.

"Darby, meet Professor Langston," introduced her coach as they walked through the athletic department. "He's one of our most esteemed faculty members."

"Ah, Darby," Professor Langston said, his eyes sweeping over her appreciatively. "I've heard so much about you. I think we're going to get along just fine."

"Nice to meet you," Darby managed, fighting the urge to roll her eyes. Even at UCLA, her charm and talent were still acting as magnets for inappropriate attention.

Despite the unwanted advances, Darby continued to excel on the court, her fierce determination driving her forward. She refused to let the lecherous gazes of others define her or her love for the game. With every hit, every block, and every victory, she would prove to herself and the world that she was more than just an object of desire—she was a force to be reckoned with.

"Another win, Darby!" Alexa said, wrapping her arm around her friend's shoulders. "You're unstoppable!"

"Thanks," Darby grinned.

· · · ● · ● · ● · ● · ·

During a raucous post-game celebration, Darby met Craig, a charming and seemingly genuine student, with an irresistible smile. She couldn't help but feel drawn to him as they swapped stories over drinks, their laughter filling the dimly lit bar.

The two began dating and were soon inseparable. She didn't feel the love Craig gave her, but it was nice to be wanted. It was nice to have someone.

During one night at dinner, Craig appeared distracted.

"Darby, you're amazing," he said, his breath warming her neck. "But you know what would be even more amazing? If you could help my buddy Steve out. He's on the lacrosse team, and he's failing three classes. He'll lose his scholarship if he doesn't pass."

"Help him how?"

"Steve just needs a little academic assistance. You're so smart, especially in statistics. You could probably write his papers, take his online tests. Make him look like a million bucks."

"Wait, are you asking me to cheat for him?" Darby began, but Craig cut her off with a laugh.

"It's not cheating—it's helping a friend in need. Come on, you've seen how the system is rigged against athletes. This just levels the playing field."

"Fine," Darby said, knowing that she wouldn't be able to shake off Craig's request. "I'll help him pass."

"Great! And hey, maybe if things go well, you could help some of the other guys too. The whole team struggles with academics."

"Sure," Darby said, feeling the weight of Craig's manipulation settling onto her shoulders like a leaden yoke. This was a dangerous game she was playing—one that threatened to pull her further into resignation and despair.

. . . ●.●.● . .

"Darby, you're a godsend," Craig said as they approached Steve in the library. Steve looked up from his textbook with a calculating gleam in his eye. "Steve, meet Darby. She'll make sure you don't lose that scholarship."

"Nice to meet you," Darby managed, plastering on a fake smile and rolling her eyes internally at the all-too-familiar introduction. Her hair was down tonight with a slight wave to it.

"Likewise," Steve said, sliding over a stack of assignments. "Let's talk about my upcoming midterms."

As the weeks went by, Darby sank deeper into the morass of Craig's scheming. He began accepting money from professors and students alike for her *academic services*—a chilling reminder of the corrupt and exploitative nature of college athletics. She wrote papers, took online exams, even hacked into the university system to change grades. Each task pulled her further into a web of academic fraud that could destroy her own future if discovered.

"Five hundred," Craig said one night, handing her a thick envelope. "That's what Professor Jenkins gave me for changing his son's transcripts."

"Transcript fraud? Is that what we're calling it now?"

"Come on, babe," Craig said, wrapping an arm around her waist. "You know how this works. Just keep the grades flowing, and we'll both come out ahead. Think of all the good we're doing—helping kids keep their scholarships, stay in school."

"Fine."

She pocketed the cash with a feeling of self-loathing that gnawed at her soul. She knew she was trapped, ensnared by the very intelligence and computer skills that had once seemed like her greatest assets. What had started as *helping* one student had evolved into a full-scale cheating operation that served wealthy students, athletes, and even faculty members' children.

Craig kissed her cheek, his breath hot and sour.

"Remember, Darby, you're doing this for us."

"Us," Darby echoed hollowly, already plotting her revenge against those who sought to exploit her. No matter how deep she sank, she vowed she would rise again—and when she did, there would be hell to pay.

. . . ● . ● . ● . .

Darby stared at her reflection in the mirror, her hair down in a textured shag as she smudged her lipstick with a practiced swipe of her thumb. She took in her own eyes and felt a surge of disgust. This wasn't who she wanted to be. Craig had pushed her too far.

"Enough. I'm done."

"Done with what, babe?" Craig's voice slithered into the room like an unwelcome guest, his slimy presence behind her in the mirror.

"Us," Darby said, her voice resolute. "I'm done with you."

"Come on, don't be like that," he said, feigning hurt. "We're good together, you know that."

"Good? You call running this cheating ring, exploiting students and athletes good?" Darby said, not bothering to hide her disdain.

"Hey, I thought we were doing this for us, remember?" Craig said, his tone suddenly sharp.

"Maybe that's what you thought. But I won't let you control me anymore."

With that, she slammed the door behind her, leaving Craig gaping after her in disbelief.

• • • • ● • ● • • •

Somehow, despite cutting ties with Craig, Darby found herself unable to escape the web of influence she'd woven. The power that came with knowing everyone's secrets, the thrill of outsmarting the system—it had become intoxicating. She continued to operate her academic services, but now on her own terms, building a network of contacts that stretched beyond the university.

"Darby," Professor Collins said one evening after class, her hand brushing against Darby's arm in a gesture that was anything but accidental. "I have someone I'd like you to meet. Someone who appreciates . . . talent like yours."

"Really?" Darby's voice dripped with sarcasm. "And what kind of talent would that be?"

"The kind that knows how to keep secrets," Collins replied with a knowing smile. "The kind that understands how the real world works."

As if on cue, a knock echoed through the office. A man in an impeccably tailored suit entered, his presence commanding immediate attention.

"Charles," Collins nodded. "This is the student I was telling you about."

Charles studied Darby with calculating eyes. She met his gaze unflinchingly, her volleyball player's height and natural confidence evident even seated.

"I hear you're quite the problem solver," he said.

"Depends on the problem," Darby shot back. "And who's asking."

A smile tugged at the corner of his mouth. "Direct. I like that." He settled into a chair, his movements deliberately casual. "Your reputation precedes you. Managing a complex operation, keeping multiple parties happy, ensuring everyone pays what they owe . . . That takes a certain finesse."

"You seem well-informed," Darby said, leaning back with easy confidence. "But I'm guessing you're not here to discuss my academic consulting business."

Charles's smile widened. "I run what you might call an alternative gaming enterprise. High-stakes poker, private games for discerning clients. But I'm looking to expand into sports betting. The market's about to explode."

"And you need someone to handle collections," Darby said. It wasn't a question.

"Someone to manage relationships," Charles corrected. "My organization doesn't rely on crude intimidation. We prefer a more . . . sophisticated approach."

"And what makes you think I'd be interested?"

"Because you understand people, Darby. You know how to apply the right pressure without leaving marks. How to make someone want to pay up, just to stay in your good graces." He leaned forward. "That's a rare talent."

"Flattery will get you everywhere," Darby said, but her mind was racing with possibilities. "Tell me more about these *relationships* you need managed."

Charles's eyes glinted with approval. "Let's discuss the details over dinner. I have a feeling you'll fit right in with our organization."

As she followed him out, Darby felt a familiar thrill course through her veins. This was different from running campus schemes—bigger, more dangerous, but also more aligned with her talents. Here was a chance to step into a world where her ability to read people and control situations could really shine.

Maybe someday she'd find a way to turn it all around, to use her position to right some wrongs. But for now, the game called to her. After years of playing by others' rules—Craig's manipulation, the university's hypocrisy—the chance to operate on this level was too tempting to resist.

The only question was how far she'd go.

Witch City

The crisp autumn air carried a chill through the streets of Salem as Darby, Justine, and Josh arrived in search of William, Darby's old friend, and hopefully a new co-conspirator. The trio made an eye-catching group as they strode with purpose, each reflecting a distinct facet of their colorful pasts.

Darby's blonde hair fell in a straight cascade down her back, contrasting with her all-black outfit that hugged her tall, lean silhouette. Her steely blue eyes scanned the surroundings, a testament to her resourcefulness and determination. Justine wore casual jeans and a leather jacket; neither of those stood a chance of taming her comely curves. Her green eyes sparkled with cunning, hinting at the depths she'd plumbed to survive the treacherous world she'd left behind. And then there was Josh, the brooding banker with a dark past, his fit frame clad in a tailored suit pants and jacket with blue shirt—no tie today—that whispered of his power. His dark hair was flecked with gray, a striking reminder of the wisdom—and pain—he'd accumulated over the years.

"Remind me again why we're in Witch Central?" Justine said, casting a sarcastic grin at her companions.

"Because, my dear friend William might be our ticket to revenge," Darby said, her voice dripping with sarcasm. "And I swear, if he's dressed as a witch when we find him, I'll—"

"Laugh?" Josh interjected, a sly smile playing on his lips. "I know you, Darby. You've got a twisted sense of humor."

"Alright, enough," Darby admonished with a bit of a grin. "Let's focus on finding William."

William had once been one of Darby's clients in her days navigating a nationwide gambling ring, but their relationship had grown into a genuine friendship over the years. He'd since moved to the touristy town of Salem, seeking solace in its history and charm. A gambling addict in recovery, he'd penned several well-received books; the most recent detailed his journey to recovery. He still wrote and occasionally taught at local universities as an adjunct, but he was mostly retired. It was his gambling expertise and extensive network that were invaluable for their mission.

• • • ● • ● • • •

Salem Common was a large, wide open grassy green park with an iron fence encircling it. This former swamp had evolved into a training ground for the militia to its current use as a gathering place and spot for recreation and relaxation. Several paved paths crisscrossed the green while a primary dirt path wound around the outskirts, just inside its iron fence. The park was surrounded by the Salem Witch Museum and Conant statue on one side, the Hawthorne Hotel on another, and old homes on the last two.

Today, the golden hues of early October bathed the Common with sunlight, with leaves just beginning to change color. A crisp breeze carried the faint scent of burning wood from nearby fireplaces, and children's laughter filled the air as they chased each other around the park. Near the beautiful Washington Arch—with its elaborate gold carvings, including an image of George Washington on the front and a proud golden eagle on top—the trio sat on a bench, taking in the picturesque scene before them.

"Nice place for a clandestine meeting, huh?" Justine said, adjusting her leather jacket against the chill.

Josh's eyes scanned the area as he took a bite of his muffin. "Very cloak and dagger."

"More like running shoes and a heart rate monitor," Darby said as she recalled a meeting she had years ago.

• • • ● • ● • • •

During this scheduled appointment, Darby slid into the dimly lit hotel room, the scent of stale cigarettes and cheap cologne assaulting her senses. Her client stood by the window, gazing out at the neon-lit streets of LA below.

She cleared her throat. "I'm here to collect."

Her client turned, eyes red-rimmed behind wire-framed glasses. "I shouldn't have asked for more time. I don't know what I was thinking."

Darby sighed, kicking off her stilettos and padding over to the minibar. "At least let me have a drink on your dime before I do what I came here to do."

"Go ahead. I'm sorry to waste your time." He scrubbed a hand over his face.

Darby popped the cap off a tiny bottle of water and knocked it back in one go. She sauntered over to him, her stance intimidating despite her smaller frame. "Now, now. No need to be sorry. I'm happy to provide . . . motivation . . . if that's what you need."

He grasped her wrist, surprising her. His touch sent a jolt through her body, but not from fear—something else entirely. "I don't think you understand. I'm an addict and can't pay anymore. Gambling's ruining my life."

"Oh." Darby blinked. This was new. In all her years of collecting debts, she'd never had a mark break down quite like this. "Well. That's . . . unfortunate."

The client laughed bitterly. "Unfortunate. Yes, that's one way to put it."

The first hints of sympathy flickered in Darby's chest. She sat on the edge of the bed, patting the spot next to her. After a moment, he joined her.

"Talk to me," she said. "And not about the money. Talk to me about the addiction."

And so he did. About the emptiness, the shame, the endless chase for a high that remained out of reach. About the way each win only fueled the need for a bigger one. The thrill of betting it all, the crushing despair of losing everything, then crawling back to do it all again. She listened, struck by the raw pain in his voice, a pain she understood all too well from the countless lives she'd seen destroyed by gambling debts.

When he finished, he sagged against her, tears dampening her shoulder. Darby wrapped an arm around him, her throat tight. Usually, she was here to break spirits, not mend them.

Maybe, just this once, she'd do something different.

Darby held him as he wept, her mind wandering to her own past sorrows. How many times had she been the one causing this kind of pain? How many lives had she helped destroy in the name of collecting debts?

Too many.

When the client's tears subsided, he lifted his head, eyes glassy but clear. "I'm sorry. I shouldn't have—"

"Hush." Darby squeezed his shoulder. "No apologies needed."

A wry smile twisted his lips. "Now there's a first. A debt collector showing mercy."

Darby arched a brow. "I may not be in the forgiveness business, but even I can spot a man in need of mercy when I see one."

Her client's smile softened into something almost fond. "You're full of surprises, aren't you?"

"So I've been told." Darby stood and wandered to the minibar, cracking it open. "Drink?"

"Please."

She poured two glasses of seltzer and passed one to him. They clinked glasses, the crystal chiming in the quiet room.

The liquid burned pleasantly down Darby's throat. She eyed him over the rim of her glass, this strange, sad man who'd walked into her life and refused to play his assigned role of desperate debtor.

Perhaps it was foolish, but part of her didn't want to be just another enforcer tonight.

"Tell me about yourself," the client said. "The real you, not whatever persona you put on to frighten people into paying."

Darby blinked. When was the last time someone had asked her that?

"Only if you do the same."

He nodded. "Fair enough."

And so they talked through the night, trading stories and secrets, sorrows and scars. She told him about volleyball, about her fall from grace, about how she'd ended up working as muscle for a gambling syndicate. He shared tales of his academic career, his spiral into addiction, the shame of losing everything he'd worked for.

By the time dawn peeked over the horizon, Darby knew his soul as well as her own.

A soul that, much like hers, had wandered long in the dark. But perhaps, together, they could find their way to the light.

He swiped a hand over his eyes, scrubbing away tears that threatened to fall. His voice cracked. "The gambling has ruined so much of my life."

Darby's heart squeezed with sympathy. She knew that pain, having seen countless lives shattered by addiction and debt, though she was usually the one doing the shattering.

"How so?" she asked gently.

He slumped onto the edge of the bed. "This addiction—my addiction—cost me everything. My friends. My career." He sighed. "Even after losing everything to the sharks and bookies, I still couldn't stop. I'd tell myself every day was the day I'd quit betting, but . . ." He shook his head. "Here I am, waiting for an enforcer to break my kneecaps."

"Here you are," Darby echoed. She settled beside him, close enough to offer comfort but not crowd him. "Gambling addiction is a disease. It's not your fault."

"Isn't it?" The client's laugh held no humor. "I had tenure. A great life. And I threw it all away for the rush of a poker game, the thrill of a winning bet."

His self-loathing radiated from him in waves. Darby recognized that feeling all too well.

"The past is done. You can't change it. But you can choose to do better going forward."

He slanted her a sideways glance. "And you're one to talk? A syndicate enforcer giving advice on morality?"

The barb struck deep, but Darby didn't flinch. "I never said I was perfect. But I know what rock bottom looks like—I've pushed enough people there. And I know the only way out is up."

She nudged his shoulder with her own. "The fact that you're here, realizing you have a problem, that's the first step. You can beat this . . . if you want to."

"And if I don't? If I'm too weak?"

"Then I'll help you." Darby threaded her fingers through his, squeezing tight. "You're not alone anymore. Together, we're strong enough to face any demon."

Her client stared at their joined hands, eyes suspiciously bright. When he looked up at her again, something close to wonder lit his face.

"Well, aren't you full of surprises?"

"So I've been told."

He cleared his throat, blinking hard against the sting in his eyes. "I don't know why I'm telling you all this. You're supposed to be here to collect a debt, for God's sake."

"Sometimes it's easier to open up to someone who's seen the worst of it," Darby said. "No judgment. No history."

"And you won't go reporting back to Charles about my deep, dark secrets?" He tried for a joke, but it fell flat. He scrubbed a hand over his face with a sigh. "Christ, listen to me. Like my sad, insignificant life matters to someone who breaks legs for a living."

"Don't do that. Don't diminish what you're going through. Your struggles are real, and they matter."

Her client huffed out a breath, raking both hands through his hair. When he dropped them on his lap, he looked lost. Defeated. "I don't know if I can beat this. The gambling. It's had its hooks in me for so long . . ."

His voice trailed off, but Darby heard the unspoken fear behind his words. She reached out again, curling her fingers around his.

"One day at a time. Every day you stay away from the tables is a victory. Focus on the battles you can win right now instead of the war."

He peered down at their joined hands, his thumb idly stroking the side of hers. The touch was startlingly intimate, but Darby didn't pull away. She sensed he needed the contact. The reassurance that he wasn't alone.

"How do you know all this?" he wondered out loud. "You're what, 25? How did you get so wise about addiction?"

Darby's smile turned wry. "I've watched enough people lose everything to know the pattern. I'm a fast learner. And an even faster enforcer."

"Somehow, I doubt that's all there is to you." The client gave her hand a gentle squeeze. "You're smarter than you let on, aren't you?"

"Maybe." Darby tilted her head, studying him through lowered lashes. "But in my line of work, it's better to be underestimated."

"A gift, that," he said. His gaze drifted to the window, pensive. "The future's unwritten. That's what you said. So I guess . . . there's still hope."

"There's always hope. As long as you don't give up the fight. And as long as you stay away from Charles's poker games."

Her client's eyes found hers again, soft with gratitude. "Thank you. For listening. For . . . not breaking my kneecaps."

Darby felt her throat tighten at the raw emotion in his voice. She gave his hand another squeeze, hoping the simple gesture conveyed what she couldn't say aloud.

After a long moment, he cleared his throat and pulled away. Darby let her hand drop, missing his warmth.

"I should let you get going." He fished a wad of bills from his pocket and held them out.

Darby eyed the money but didn't move to take it. "Keep your cash. Use it to get help instead."

The client's brow furrowed. "But Charles—"

"I'll handle Charles. Just promise me you'll get clean. Every day, remember how far you've come. How much further you have to go?"

"I will. Thank you, Darby. For everything."

Darby nodded, a lump forming in her own throat. She walked to the door on wooden legs, acutely aware of his gaze following her every step.

At the threshold, she paused. Glanced over her shoulder to find him still watching her, eyes dark and unreadable. She offered a faint smile.

"Goodbye, William."

And then she was gone, the door clicking shut behind her. William was alone again—but for the first time in longer than he could remember, the solitude didn't seem so bleak.

• • • • • • • • • •

William's strides were long and purposeful as he ran past historic landmarks. He spared a glance at the House of the Seven Gables, its dark façade casting an eerie shadow despite the sunny day. He headed up the short hill, past a statue of the author that made that house famous—Nathaniel Hawthorne—and then the proud, almost regal hotel named in his honor, The Hawthorne Hotel. Everywhere he looked, he recognized a testament to the town's storied past. Last, he passed the Salem Witch Museum, where tourists snapped photos of the ominous black building. As William neared the end of his run on the common's crushed gravel path, he noticed Darby, Justine, and Josh waiting for him near the gate, which caused him to momentarily stumble in surprise.

• • • • • • • • • •

"Can't miss him," Darby remarked as they spotted William from a distance. He was thin. The lean muscles and sculpted calves told of someone who pushed his body to the limits. His shaved head looked like it'd been sanded down, and his arms and shoulders were wiry . . . sinewy, ready to break at the slightest touch. His athletic shorts and sweat-stained shirt spoke of a man who'd traded one addiction for another—this time, a healthier pursuit.

"William!" Darby called out, waving her arm to catch his attention.

"Dammit, Darby! You could've warned me," he grumbled in a low, husky voice, like a man reborn. His heavy breathing was like a train, loud and noisy as his chest heaved from the exertion.

"Where's the fun in that?" Darby smirked, offering him a water bottle.

"Fun? I almost face-planted in front of a group of those witchy tourists," he said, accepting the water and downing half of it in one swig.

"Think of it this way, runner dude: you'd have made their trip even more memorable," Justine said, raising an eyebrow playfully.

"Thrilling," William deadpanned, wiping the sweat from his brow. "Not that I'm sad to see you, but what are you doing here, Darby?" His breath wasn't labored in the slightest, but harsh demeanor aside, his eyes warm with genuine affection.

"Well, you're a creature of habit. I know you end every long Saturday run on the common. I wanted to see an old friend to introduce him to some new ones, so I knew this would be the place and I knew you'd end up here right around now."

William just shook his head with half a smile. Any smile is a big deal for Darby's gruff friend.

"William, this is Josh, and this is Justine. They're friends from Los Angeles. During our trip to this corner of New England, I recalled you lived here and thought it would be nice for all of us to get together."

"Have you been running away from your past or just tourists?" Josh said, earning an eye roll from Darby and another sly smile from William.

"Both, actually," William said, wiping the sweat from his brow. "So what really brings you all the way to Salem? I don't believe you just happened to be here and just randomly wanted to meet."

"True enough. It's a long story that involves kidnapping, revenge, and a bit more," Darby began, her voice firm and resolute, "is there somewhere we can talk? Preferably without witches?"

"And without so many eavesdropping squirrels?" said Josh.

"*Not until we are lost do we begin to understand ourselves,*" William said, quoting Henry David Thoreau as he leaned back on the park bench, crossing his arms. "Alright, you've got my interest. But before we dive into this, let's grab some lunch. We can catch up more and discuss the details there."

"Sounds good to me," Justine said, her stomach rumbling audibly.

"My house is just over there. Let me grab a quick shower, change my clothes and we can meet at Red's. They've got the best Reubens in town. And Darby, whatever it is," William said, his expression turning serious, "you know I've got your back."

· · · ● · ● · ● · ● · ·

As the group approached Red's, they took in the charming, red painted clapboard exterior of the restaurant. The black sign with gold lettering declaring this 'Red's Sandwich Shop' provided a colorful contrast to the otherwise traditional façade. What a place. It still has an old time red and white newspaper box for "The Salem News." Yes, the newspaper's logo has a witch on it.

Upon entering, the warm, inviting atmosphere of the bustling diner greeted the group. The comforting aroma of fried food, an open grill with eggs, and savory meats filled the air, while the sound of laughter and clinking silverware indicated a lively lunch crowd. Vintage posters showcasing classic Americana and retro advertisements hung over green, flowery wallpaper. A diner-style eating counter surrounded the grill on three sides by. The large, laminated menu boasted an impressive array of breakfast staples on one side, sandwiches and sides on the other.

As they settled into a booth near the grill, William leaned back and crossed his arms. "So let's hear it," he said, his voice laced with sarcasm. "What's this big plan you've cooked up that requires you to disrupt my retirement?"

Darby slid a menu across the table to him before answering. "We're going after a high-profile target. Someone who's made a career out of exploiting people."

"Sounds noble," William said. "But why me? I'm retired, remember? I don't do this kind of thing anymore."

"Come on, William." Darby gave him a pointed look. "Your connections are invaluable. I also recall you sharing a couple jobs you pulled before you retired. Plus, you're my friend. And most importantly, I trust you."

"Flattery will get you everywhere," William said, his gruff exterior momentarily cracking to reveal a hint of affection. "Alright, tell me more. But remember, I'm not promising anything."

Josh chimed in, describing the plan. "We need to infiltrate a heavily guarded complex that serves as the base for Cum As You Are, the huge, famous porn production conglomerate. By exposing their exploitation and abuse, we intend to bring them down. To destroy them."

"And that's where your knowledge comes in," Justine added. "You understand the ins and outs of this world better than anyone. And yes, I have heard stories of some of your capers. Combine that with my experience acting for them . . ."

William frowned, unsure how he felt about others knowing about his former exploits.

He considered their proposal. "I won't lie," he admitted, rubbing his shaved head in thought. "The idea of taking down someone like that is appealing. But it's risky. And I've got a quiet life here in Salem. What if things go south?"

"Look, we know there's risk involved," Darby acknowledged. "But we also know you're great at what you do. We wouldn't be asking if we didn't think we could pull this off."

"Besides," Josh interjected, "think of all the people you'd be helping by bringing this guy down. You'd be a hero."

"Hero, huh?" William smirked, a glint of mischief in his eyes. "That's not something I ever thought I'd be called." He took a deep breath, weighing his options.

"It's not just a guy though Josh," said Justine. "Sure, Tony has issues. Lolita is his *hench-woman*. She has most of the power. And she's evil."

"Interesting," offered Josh and William at the same time.

"Alright, I'm in. But only on one condition: we do this as a team. No unnecessary risks, no flashy moves. We get in, we get out, and we don't leave a trace."

"Deal," Darby said, extending her hand for William to shake.

"To heroes and villains," William offered, raising his water glass in a toast, clinking glasses with the group.

They finished their sandwiches—Red's Reuben for William, Cuban for Justine, Monte Cristo for Josh, and Turkey for Darby—and ventured outside to join the teaming masses prepping for Halloween.

• • • ● • ● • ● • •

At 10am the next morning, Darby, Justine, and Josh stepped inside the grand entry of William's house on Winter Street. His is one of the few brick homes on this street, and one of the few brick Greek Revival houses in Salem. Most houses on Winter Street are painted yellow or green or purple.

"The sea captain, John Bertram, had this home built in the mid-1800s. Not to be confused with the John Bertram House Assisted Living Facility on the square. Winter Street has even more history; it's an ancient road dating back to 1668," William was in teacher mode now. "And Red's Sandwich Shop yesterday? That's been here since sometime after WWII. But the building was formerly the London Coffee House, dating back to just before 1700. I love the warmth of Los Angeles and I loved the people in the Midwest when I lived there, but the history here is tough to top."

William lowered his voice as if sharing a secret, "Alright, let's shift gears. If we're going to do this, we'll need some extra help. I count at least two others, maybe more: a computer expert and muscle."

"I agree. Any leads on who these two could be?" asked Josh.

"Well, there are two people I know who could be invaluable to our mission."

Darby leaned in, her curiosity piqued. "Who are they?"

"First, there's Tommy."

He took a sip of his coffee thoughtfully before continuing. "Tommy's a tough guy with military experience. Street smart. He was born in Cuba but came to the US when he was very young. His family settled in West New York, New Jersey. Unfortunately, he had a bit of a . . . mishap while serving in Afghanistan and got dishonorably discharged."

Josh raised an eyebrow. "A *mishap*?"

"Let's just say it involved a theft that would make you question his sanity. But don't let that fool you—he's fiercely loyal to those he trusts and knows how to handle himself in high-pressure situations. Plus, he's built like a tank: six-foot-four and all muscle. Tommy's the kind of guy you want watching your back."

"Sounds like a handful, but useful," Justine conceded.

"I know Tommy," Josh said. "we crossed paths a couple of years back when he was doing security consulting for the bank. We hit it off and kept in touch."

"Good, good . . . next up, we've got Ella," William said. "I lived in Omaha for much of my life; a teenager down the street used to fix my electronics and computers (I'm no good at that). We actually partnered on a few different adventures . . . we were a pretty good team back then. She disappeared for a few years, but I know she's back now.

"She's a prodigy computer hacker. Only nineteen years old and already making a name for herself in the digital underworld. She's had a rough life, forced to grow up too quickly because of her past. But she's got nerves of steel. I lost track of her over the years. But her dad tells me she's determined to use her skills for good—or at least, what counts as good in our line of work."

"Smart and courageous? Sounds like a keeper," Justine remarked.

"Remember, though," William warned, "she might be a bit of a wildcard. She and I used to be close, but that's before some bad things happened to her. Her dad, Jim, tells me that her emotions can sometimes get the better of her, and she's been known to go rogue if she feels it's necessary. But if we can keep her focused, she'll be an invaluable asset.

"Ella can help us hack CAYA's system."

"Alright," Darby said, considering the new information. "So, how can they help us?"

"Well," William said. "Tommy's military background and *oneness with the street* give us an edge in planning and executing the physical aspects of the heist. He knows how to navigate dangerous territory and deal with unexpected obstacles. The security at CAYA is, I would imagine, extensive and elaborate. As for Ella, she'll be our eyes and ears in the digital world. She can hack into security systems, monitor communications, and pinpoint vulnerabilities in CAYA's firewalls and other defenses. Like the security, I would be shocked if their IT people slacked off during the planning process."

"And with their help, we stand a much better chance of pulling this off," Justine said, nodding in understanding.

"Exactly," William confirmed. "We'll need every advantage we can get, and Tommy and Ella, I believe, are the missing pieces of the puzzle."

"If you're sure, then let's not waste any time," Darby said, determination etched on her face. "We've got a heist to plan and two more allies to recruit. And we'll need to strategize carefully if we want to bring Tommy and Ella on board without tipping our hand."

"Agreed," William said, his eyes shifting between the trio. "First, we should split up. Darby and Josh, you two head to Manhattan and locate Tommy. Josh already knows Tommy, so that will help. Get a feel for him before making any moves. Meanwhile, Justine and I will fly out to Omaha and do the same with Ella. I have a connection, but besides me mending some fences, I think Ella might need some additional convincing. Justine can help there."

The out-of-town trio looked at him with concern before Justine asked, her brow furrowed in concern, "Will that be enough to convince them?"

"Only one way to find out," Darby said with a wry smile. "But we'll need to be persuasive. We're asking them to risk everything for a shot at revenge."

"Revenge is a powerful motivator," Josh remarked, staring into the remnants of his coffee cup as he took a bite of an apple. "And we've all got our reasons for wanting it."

"Absolutely," Darby said, her eyes flashing with determination. "So let's make sure they understand what's at stake and why we need their help. If we can appeal to their sense of justice or personal vendettas, they might just be willing to join us."

"Sounds like a plan," William nodded. "But remember, neither Tommy nor Ella will jump into anything without carefully weighing the risks."

"Understood," Josh confirmed. "We'll tread lightly until we've earned their trust."

"Good," William said, satisfied. "Now let's get moving."

The group stood up. "Let's take a walk around the Common," suggested Justine, "this place is growing on me." Leaving behind half-eaten muffin, bagels, and lukewarm coffee, they made their way toward the door.

"I just love your home, runner dude," Justine remarked, as she held the door open for the others. "Feels like we're in some sort of time warp."

"It has character for days," Josh said, smirking at her. "If we pull this off, we'll be able to buy houses built by other sea captains and merchants. We could be neighbors with William!"

"Great," Justine deadpanned, sarcasm dripping from her words. "Just what I always wanted."

As the cool autumn air greeted them outside, Darby felt a surge of anticipation mixed with anxiety. They were taking a leap of faith on two strangers, but their mission demanded it. If they could recruit Tommy and Ella, the odds of success would increase significantly. But first, they had to find them.

"Alright, team," Darby announced, her voice filled with resolve. "Let's go make ourselves some new friends."

Interview: Josh

Inspector: *Good afternoon, Josh. Let's get right to it. Can you deny any involvement in the heist targeting Cum As You Are?*

Josh: *Inspector, I've already told the others asking questions. I don't know anything about a heist or what happened at CAYA . . . just what I read in the papers. I'm just a banker trying to make an honest living.*

Inspector: *Josh, I've seen your type before, playing innocent to protect your own interests. But here's the thing: we have evidence linking you to this operation. Now, I suggest you start being honest with me.*

Josh: *I swear, Inspector, I simply don't know what you're talking about. I'm not involved in any heist, and I can't help you with your investigation.*

Inspector: *Oh, I think you can help, Josh. Did you hack into the company's computers?*

Josh: *No.*

Inspector: *Did you steal billions of dollars from their accounts?*

Josh: *What? Billions with a 'B'? No way.*

Inspector: *Come on Josh, you're a banker. You know how money works. You have valuable information, and it's in your best interest to cooperate.*

Josh: *I'm sorry, Inspector, but I really can't help you. I don't have any information, and I'm not involved.*

Inspector: *Did you work with anyone else who helped you hack into the bank's network?*

Josh: *Absolutely not. I could lose my job if I did that.*

Inspector: *Precisely. So your answer remains 'no?'*

Josh: *Correct.*

Inspector: *Did you work with others on this?*

Josh: *Again, I had nothing to do with this.*

Inspector: *Josh, let me be clear. I'm giving you an opportunity here. Help us solve this case, and you might find yourself in a better position. Continue denying your involvement, and things will get much worse for you.*

Josh: *I understand what you're saying, but I truly don't know anything. I'm just as perplexed by all this as you are.*

Inspector: *Fine. For now, I'll let you maintain your innocence. But remember, the truth has a way of catching up with people. Don't let it catch up with you, Josh.*

Nirvana

Tony leaned against the smooth walnut counter of the reception desk in the lobby, tapping his fingers to an imaginary beat. The sprawling San Fernando office complex was a testament to his contribution to the adult film industry and its proliferation in modern society, and he couldn't help but feel a sense of pride as he awaited the arrival of a potential investor.

"Tony," Lolita's voice cut through the air like a knife, snapping him back to reality. Her pencil-thin figure towered over him as she approached, her short spiky blonde hair giving her an almost feral appearance. She wore designer black suit pants, black heels, a white crop top to display her well-toned abs, and a black blazer. "You know you need to be serious about this tour. Chase Harrison's money would help us a great deal. We could explore some things we dreamed of in the past."

"Of course, my dear Lolita," Tony said, straightening up and adjusting his designer suit. "I was just taking a moment to appreciate what we've built here."

Tony started CAYA in the mid-1990s; a common story for ecommerce, what started in a college dorm room had become the largest purveyor of porn in the US and third in the world. (The Russian porn producers get bigger and more proliferative by the day.) Online porn sites are generally divided into two primary types: some distribute porn produced by others with minimal product creation, and others focus on creating pornographic movies with only small online storefronts. CAYA is one of the few that excels at both. Its success in these areas has allowed it to branch out in several directions. Interactive cam shows, a platform for amateur and professional pornographic content creators—think Only Fans—old school pornographic magazines, phone sex—yes, still a thing—and they've dipped their toes in the dark web.

Last year, they had 40 billion visits to their sites and their annual revenues topped $100,000,000,000 for the first time. With the non-stop progression of service lines and products, they expect to reach over 50 billion site visits and revenues of $125 billion this year.

Lolita escorted Chase Harrison into the Frank Lloyd Wright-style conversation pit, where Tony was waiting to greet him.

This was Tony's favorite part of the compound. Styled after Wright's Taliesin West in Scottsdale, the conversation pit was in the building's living room. The room was large; it had windows on two sides broken up by structural stone columns. For a Frank Lloyd Wright-style building, the ceiling in this room was tall and included two cathedral-like peaks. While there was plenty of natural light and wood paneling, like Taliesin West, there were other notable differences. The living room's floor was concrete—not wood—and it was more of a large hallway that separated the front reception and lobby areas with Tony and Lolita's offices. A walkway surrounded the square pit of built-in seating. Stairs were available on all four sides, and there was a low table in the center of the pit.

Chase was a tall man in his mid-fifties, with salt-and-pepper hair and a stern expression that betrayed nothing of his thoughts.

"Welcome to our operation Mr. Harrison," Tony announced proudly, gesturing beyond the pit to the open-plan office space filled with chic furniture and groundbreaking technology. "Everything we do, from marketing and sales to website creation and strategic decisions, happens right here. I'm proud of the complex we've built beyond these four walls, but this building will always have special meaning to me. It was originally a private home owned by my parents. They died when I was in high school; I moved here during college, and I guess you could say I never left."

"Very impressive," the Chase remarked, his eyes darting between the office spaces, what lied beyond the windows, and the high-tech gadgets on display. Tony could see the wheels turning in his head, calculating the worth of this empire.

"Thank you," Tony said, his tone dripping with sarcasm. "We try our best to create a working environment that is both functional and stylish. You know, like something out of a James Bond movie."

In keeping with the design approach, the compound was a collection of mostly low-lying buildings linked by walkways, courtyards, and terraces built over several years. The main headquarter building was a large single-story building that oozed sophistication and style. Besides the conversation pit, the former home, which was decorated with a mid-century vibe, was a mixture of old Hollywood glamor and modern sensibilities. It was an honest place of beauty that welcomed natural light, with generous glazing that framed picturesque views and seamlessly connected the indoors with the lush outdoors. Polished concrete floors separated the exposed brick walls, which were adorned with vintage movie posters and neon signs, a subtle nod to the company's core business without being overtly vulgar. The building mimicked Frank Lloyd Wright's iconic Usonian-style—*Usonia* was Wright's alternate word for America and his vision for what the country's landscape could be.

"Speaking of movies," Lolita interjected, shooting Tony a warning glance, "we should show Mr. Harrison some of the film sets we have here on the grounds."

"Ah, yes. A unique part of our little empire. Follow me."

As they ventured deeper into the complex, Tony knew Lolita was right; impressing Chase Harrison was crucial to the continued growth of CAYA. If they could secure their investment, the possibilities would be endless.

This anticipation raced through Tony's head as he led the tour, expertly highlighting the best aspects of the company while downplaying any potential weaknesses. He knew that success in this business was a delicate balancing act, and that one wrong move could bring everything crashing down.

But for now, as he guided Chase through the impressive maze of film sets, Tony couldn't help but feel confident that he had everything under control. "Mr. Harrison, welcome to the heart of CAYA," Tony greeted the potential investor with a slick smile, extending his hand out for a firm handshake.

"Quite the operation you have here," Harrison remarked, taking in the vastness of the production building. His tone was neutral, but there was a glint of curiosity in his eyes as he scanned the room. This building was quite different in its build and esthetic. It was a four-story building; each floor had a different purpose.

"First, we have our more domestic sets," Tony said, leading them into a building filled with various home interiors. This first floor included traditional set rooms like two living rooms, three bedrooms, two showers, and four kitchens—who knew so many would like to watch sex in the kitchen!? They styled each set differently, and they could change each design at a moment's notice.

The *professional* zone was on the second floor. Here CAYA has several unique rooms and sets: doctor's offices, classrooms, massage rooms, fitness centers, a mall, and even a church. This was where they filmed many of the stories set in professional offices.

Floor three had only two rooms, both very large living rooms, and there were balconies on all four sides to allow filming of different balcony scenes.

The basement. This was an area Tony rarely ventured to. He was perfectly relaxed around sex and porn of every kind; however, the S&M rooms downstairs were a whole different story. Sure, they were just actors, and it was all a façade, but it still freaked him out a bit.

Outside, the sets continued; there was a street scene to one of the building's side while the back had an infinity pool that overlooked the Pacific Ocean with Point Dume in the background. The variety and diversity of sets provided an almost endless array of filming options.

"*Rule #34*, am I right?" said Chase, citing the often-invoked comic from the early 2000s that stated, *If it exists, there is porn of it. No exceptions.*

"Well, we do try to cover our bases. We have a department that does just that . . . think of new scenarios," agreed Tony, thinking of his development studio. Their task is simple: come up with any kind of pornographic concept—no matter how unusual or innocent—and create movies, chat rooms, or phone sex operators that match it.

"Your development and production value must be astronomical," Chase observed, running his fingers along the upholstery of a luxurious chaise lounge.

"High quality and wide variety are what we're known for, and those efforts keep us at the top of the industry," Tony bragged, puffing up his chest. Inside, he couldn't help but feel a spark of amusement at Chase's genuine fascination with the sets.

"Remarkable," Chase said, his lips curling into a faint smile. "The flawless execution of every element, down to the smallest detail, makes the attention to detail truly outstanding."

"Indeed," Tony said, beaming with pride. He turned to Lolita, who nodded in response. "Always attentive," he thought appreciatively.

"Here we have our first film set," Tony announced, spreading his arms wide as they entered a faux city street lined with brick buildings and cobblestone roads.

"Is that so?" Chase said, raising an eyebrow. Tony could sense his interest growing, and he knew they were close to sealing the deal.

"It is," Tony confirmed, shooting a glance at Lolita. Her sharp eyes never missed a beat, and she gave him a curt nod of approval. *She has my back,* he thought, feeling a surge of gratitude for her unwavering loyalty. "While we had an online presence during those early years, we didn't actually do any of the filming. This room was our first foray into film, and it just took off from there. Lolita and I liked the idea of keeping the room in its original form. Almost like a shrine to our beginnings."

They left the building and Chase turned to look at it once more.

"You showed me three floors, but it appears there's a fourth. What's up there?" asked Chase.

"Very observant," offered Lolita. "We're saving that floor for future expansion. We have some ideas of what sets we'd like to house there."

"Shall we continue?" Tony offered, wanting to change the subject before gesturing towards the next building with a flourish.

"By all means." Chase's voice was laced with intrigue as they moved on to explore the other film sets that CAYA offered.

As they walked through the grounds, Lolita's heels clicked authoritatively on the pavement while she maintained an air of stoicism, her gaze constantly scanning their surroundings. Nothing would get past her watchful eye.

"That building is for production, including editing and casting."

As they walked, Tony's thoughts raced. He knew he'd sold Chase Harrison on their plan, now to close the deal. He silently reassured himself, mentally preparing for the final pitch.

"Mr. Harrison, what we do here at CAYA is provide entertainment for adults who appreciate a certain type of . . . artistry," Tony explained, his voice dripping with sarcasm. "Have some have called it exploitative? Sure, but I disagree. Everything we produce is consensual, and we treat everyone involved fairly and with respect.

"Besides," he said, a wicked grin forming on his lips, "aren't there more pressing matters in the world than what people choose to watch in the privacy of their own homes?"

"Point taken," Chase conceded, nodding reluctantly. "Now, what's in that multi-story building over there?" he asked, pointing to a gray, nondescript structure that stood like a fortress amid the lavish sets.

"Ah, that would be our security headquarters," Tony said, his tone suddenly serious. "Lolita oversees the entire security operation, ensuring the safety and well-being of everyone on our grounds."

Lolita chimed in, her voice an icy whisper that sent a shiver down Harrison's spine. "We take security very seriously here at CAYA. And to maintain that protection, we cannot go in that building."

"Of course," Chase said, shifting his gaze between Tony and Lolita. *I wouldn't want to cross her*, he thought.

"Let's keep going," Tony said, sensing Harrison's unease. "There's still so much more for you to see."

"By all means," Chase managed, hoping his voice sounded steadier than he felt. As they moved on, he couldn't help but marvel at the intricate world Tony had built—equal parts fascinating and unnerving.

"And I'm about to become part of it," he said to himself, steeling himself for what lay ahead.

Tony led Chase away from the security building and towards a small utility shed situated inconspicuously among some trees. "Now, this next part of our tour," Tony began, his voice dripping with barely contained excitement, "is a hidden wonder."

Chase raised an eyebrow, unable to imagine what could be so special about a run-of-the-mill shed. *Probably just more props and equipment*, he thought wryly. *Though in this business, you never know what surprises await.*

"Behold," Tony announced, swinging open the shed door to reveal an ordinary-looking storage area filled with gardening tools and maintenance equipment. But as Chase stepped inside, Tony pressed a concealed button, and a section of the floor slid aside, exposing a staircase that led down into darkness.

"Welcome to the electronic, AI-monitored brains of CAYA," Tony said, descending the steps with Lolita close behind. Chase hesitated for a moment before following them, wondering if he was stepping into some kind of underground crypt.

As they reached the bottom of the stairs, the lights flickered on, revealing a warehouse-sized state-of-the-art computer data center, complete with rows of humming servers, high-tech workstations, conference rooms, and an enormous wall-mounted monitor displaying real-time analytics. Chase stared in awe, trying to reconcile the cutting-edge technology with the seedy business it seemed to support.

"Wow," he said, feeling slightly dizzy at the sight of it all. "This is . . . extraordinary."

"Isn't it?" Tony said. "From here, we manage every aspect of our empire: production, distribution, marketing, you name it. And, of course, there's the bonus of keeping our most sensitive information safe from prying eyes. No one would ever suspect that beneath this humble shed lies the nerve center of the world's largest pornography company."

Lolita said, her eyes narrowing as she surveyed the room. She didn't correct him; CAYA was the largest porn company in the USA, but ranked third in the world. "And anyone who tries to infiltrate our system will find themselves in a world of pain."

"Uh, noted," Chase said weakly, already regretting any thoughts he'd had about taking a souvenir. "What's that door lead to there?" pointing to a single black barn door against a cold, blank concrete wall.

Lolita and Tony glanced at each other and, rather than answer, Tony gestured for Chase to follow him back up the stairs. "Let's head back outside, shall we?"

Chase Harrison made a mental note that not all is as it seems.

As they emerged from the concealed entrance, Tony led Chase towards another area of the sprawling complex—a cluster of sleek, modern buildings that looked more like a luxury resort than anything else.

"The building over there is housing and next to it is medical," beamed Lolita.

"Wait, housing? What do you mean *housing*? And *medical*?" Chase shot back.

"We provide a comfortable place to stay for all our actors. On-campus stays are not required, but we encourage them." Lolita was clearly proud when she described this. She knew their competitors didn't have many of these things.

Tony explained, his voice taking on the tone of an enthusiastic real estate agent. "We want them to feel comfortable and at home, so we provide top-notch accommodations. Each actor has their own private suite, complete with a spacious bedroom, ensuite bathroom, and fully equipped kitchenette. In addition, they have access to a variety of amenities: a gym, pool, and even an onsite masseuse. Oh, and we provide all the food here at no cost to our staff."

"Sounds like heaven," Chase said, marveling at the opulence that surrounded him. "Who knew the porn industry was so . . . cushy?"

"The key to a successful business is keeping your employees happy, wouldn't you agree?"

"Absolutely." Chase was suddenly feeling as though he were part of some twisted sitcom. He couldn't deny, however, that Tony had built an impressive empire. And if everything went according to plan, he would soon be a vital part of it.

He followed Tony and Lolita, who led the way to another sleek building, this one with frosted glass windows and an air of sterility. As they entered, the faint scent of antiseptic greeted their nostrils.

"Welcome to our onsite medical clinic," Tony announced with a flourish. "We take the health and well-being of our actors seriously. Top-notch medical professionals who specialize in sexual health staff our facility."

"Very . . . responsible of you," Harrison said.

"Of course," Tony said. "We're not monsters, after all."

Lolita, who had been a mostly silent but ever-present figure throughout the tour, kept a watchful eye on their surroundings. Her gaze never wavered as she assessed the security measures and ensured the smooth operation of the tour.

"Is it just me, or does your assistant remind anyone else of a hawk?" Chase whispered to Tony, nodding towards Lolita.

"Ah, Lolita," Tony said. "She's certainly got keen eyes. And believe me, you don't want to be her prey."

"Good to know," Harrison thought, making a mental note to stay on her good side if such a thing existed.

The group continued through the clinic, where they observed several exam rooms stocked with more state-of-the-art equipment, a small pharmacy, and a recovery area for post-procedure care.

"Every actor undergoes regular health screenings—like STDs and HIV—and comprehensive testing," Tony said. "We also offer a range of services, from birth control consultations to treatments for work-related injuries."

"Work-related injuries?" Chase raised an eyebrow. "I thought this was supposed to be fun."

"Even the most pleasurable of activities can have its hazards, my friend," Tony responded, his tone a mix of amusement and seriousness. "But our actors are in excellent hands. We do our best to provide a safe and comfortable environment for everyone involved. After all, a happy performer is a productive performer."

With that, they concluded the tour of the medical clinic. Tony and Lolita exchanged satisfied glances, confident that they had left a lasting impression on their potential investor.

"Shall we head back to the main building to discuss the finer details of your investment?" Tony proposed, his voice oozing charm and confidence.

"By all means," Chase said, unable to deny the allure of the empire Tony and Lolita had built.

As they walked back, Chase couldn't help but think that he might just be in way over his head with this one. But then again, where would be the fun in playing it safe?

• • • ● • ● • • •

"Tony, this is a breathtaking view," Chase said as they stood on the rooftop of the main building, gazing out at the vast complex sprawled before them.

"Isn't it?" Tony said, his chest puffing up with pride. "From up here, you can really appreciate the scale of our operation."

Chase took in the panorama of immaculate lawns, perfectly aligned palm trees, and an array of film sets that could rival any Hollywood back lot. "You've certainly built an empire."

"More like a kingdom," Lolita chimed in, her voice dripping with sarcasm. "And every kingdom needs a king, doesn't it?"

"Of course," Tony said. "But a king is nothing without his loyal subjects, and I must say, we have some of the most talented and dedicated people in the industry working for us." He glanced at Lolita, who gave him a nod of approval.

"Speaking of which," Chase said, trying to steer the conversation toward more practical matters, "I noticed quite a few security personnel around the complex. Is that standard for this type of business?"

"It is," Lolita said, her eyes narrowing slightly. "There are always those who would seek to disrupt our operations or harm our employees. We take security very seriously."

"Clearly," Chase said under his breath, recalling the small army of uniformed guards he'd seen patrolling the grounds.

"Besides," Tony said, "it's not just about protecting our assets. It's about creating an atmosphere where our performers can feel safe and comfortable. That's essential for their, ahem, creativity."

"Ah yes, creativity," Chase said, thinking back on the various film sets they had toured earlier. "I must admit, I was rather impressed by the range of film set *rooms* displayed."

"Thank you," Tony beamed. "We pride ourselves on catering to a wide variety of tastes and fantasies. You never know what might strike a chord with our discerning clientele. And as you so perfectly mentioned, *Rule #34* is certainly a consideration."

"True," Chase conceded, "though I can't help but wonder about the morality of some of these productions."

"Morality? My friend, we're in the business of pleasure, not judgment. Besides, as long as everything is consensual and legal, who are we to impose our own values on others?"

"An interesting perspective," Chase admitted, his mind racing with thoughts of profits, but also on the veracity of what he's been pitched and the resulting moral quandaries.

"Isn't it just?" Lolita said, her icy gaze fixed on Chase's face, daring him to challenge their way of doing things.

"Anyway," Tony said, clapping his hands together, "I think we've seen enough for one day, don't you? I hope our tour has shown you we're serious about what we do and the level of quality we maintain."

"It certainly has," Chase said, his expression finally softening into a genuine smile. "Consider me impressed."

"Then I'm delighted to have you aboard as our newest investor," Tony said, extending his hand once more.

"It's a deal as far as I'm concerned," Chase assured Tony, while shaking his hand firmly. "But I represent an investment group. We want to diversify, so we are interested. I will run it by leadership and our board and get back to you. But I believe with what you've shown me, including the financials you sent last week . . . I think we can get this done." His curiosity piqued by the complex web of power, desire, and ambition that seemed to permeate every corner of CAYA.

"Well, I hope our next conversation includes a welcome to the family," Tony grinned, feeling a rush of triumph wash over him. Beside him, Lolita smiled ever so slightly, her gaze still fixed on the horizon, always vigilant.

As they walked down to Tony's balcony that overlooked the ocean, Chase couldn't shake the feeling that he was about to step into a world unlike any he'd ever experienced before. And yet, as the sun dipped low over the horizon, casting long shadows across the impeccably manicured grounds, he couldn't deny the allure of the empire that Tony and Lolita had built. Time would tell if he'd made the right choice, but for now, he couldn't resist the siren call of their kingdom.

Interview: Tony

Inspector: *Good day, Tony. Thank you for agreeing to meet with me. I would like to discuss recent events and your involvement in the incident that occurred at your studio. Can you confirm or deny any knowledge or participation?*

Tony: *Good day, Inspector. I appreciate the opportunity to speak with you, but I must strongly deny any involvement in any illegal practices or the events that transpired at our company. As the CEO, I am committed to upholding the highest standards of integrity and conducting business within the bounds of the law.*

Inspector: *I didn't ask if there were illegal things happening there. I asked about your knowledge of the theft that occurred.*

Tony: *Oh, well, yes. I mean no; I know nothing about that. Besides having our money taken and our computers decimated, I know nothing.*

Inspector: *Interesting. Let's stick with company operations. Our investigation has uncovered evidence linking you to various irregularities within the company, including financial discrepancies and potential exploitation of performers. Witnesses have come forward with accounts that suggest your knowledge and involvement. Can you explain these allegations?*

Tony: *I understand the seriousness of the situation, but I must reiterate that I deny any involvement in illegal activities. CAYA operates within legal frameworks, adhering to industry regulations and ensuring the well-being of our performers. Any accusations made against me are unfounded and based on false information.*

Inspector: *The evidence we have suggests otherwise—*

Tony: *We were the ones who were wronged. They stole our money. They hacked our system. They ruined us. Why don't you see that?!?*

Inspector: *I do see that. But back to this other question of illegal practices. Witnesses have provided detailed accounts of your role in orchestrating the company's operations, as well as your direct involvement in exploitative practices. We have testimonies that point to your direct participation in the events that unfolded. How do you respond to these claims?*

Tony: *These claims are baseless and without merit. As the CEO, I oversee the company's operations, but my focus has always been on creating a safe and consensual working environment for our performers. Any allegations of exploitative practices or illegal activities are simply untrue.*

Inspector: *Our investigation will continue, and we will uncover the truth behind these allegations. It is in your best interest to cooperate fully and provide any relevant information to assist us in our efforts.*

Tony: *Inspector, I am fully committed to cooperating with your investigation. However, I must reiterate that I am not involved in any illegal practices. If there are issues within the company, I would encourage you to scrutinize them, as I am confident that the truth will show we always acted appropriately.*

Inspector: *Tony, I want to go back to the missing money. Did you orchestrate all of this? Were you the mastermind behind it?*

Tony: *What? No. Absolutely not.*

Inspector: *You didn't do all of this for publicity?*

Tony: *This is surreal. No.*

Inspector: *So if we uncovered evidence to suggest you did, that would be?*

Tony: *Ridiculous. And false.*

Inspector: *No insurance fraud?*

Tony: *This is unbelievable. We were robbed. We are the victims.*

Inspector: *Thank you for your time, Tony. We will continue our investigation and ensure that justice is served.*

Tony: *But what about what they took from us? We're finished!*

Inspector: *We're done for now, Tony; we will be in contact.*

Patience and Fortitude

Tommy left the building after manning the early shift. Sure, he preferred working nights at Vivid—it was certainly more active then. But working early had its advantages as well. The club's clientele was a little classier during the day, and the strippers were not yet wasted. He also didn't need to bust as many lap dances that went past the constraints the club had set.

Vivid is a gentlemen's club on W. 37th Street in Manhattan that promotes itself as the best strip club in New York City. It boasts a dizzying array of colorful walls, bouncing lights, and spiral staircases. They placed a handful of outdoor umbrellas inside to cover some of the club's tables, providing a kind of intimacy. Like so many other clubs in the city, Vivid embraced the bottle service business model with bottle girls doting on tables to be sure their needs are met. This service allows patrons to enjoy their drinks in a dedicated space while receiving attentive service and avoiding the lines and crowds typically associated with busy bars and clubs. Customers pay a lot for these VIP packages and the women serving in this role ensure their return is high with such an outlay of money.

But bottle service is not as common around lunch—another reason Tommy likes this shift occasionally. Instead, the club has a lot of businessmen—not businesspeople; these were almost always males—entertaining current and potential clients from around the world.

Happy hour just ended and so did his shift.

The sun was setting in the heart of Manhattan's Garment District as golden rays cast a warm glow on the busy sidewalks and the ever-present construction scaffolding. Tommy made his way down W. 37th towards 6th Avenue. Sure, he could have crossed the street as he left Vivid, but he liked to take in some of the NYC scene before he went home for the night. He turned right on 6th Avenue and headed north towards Bryant Park. Past

Chick-fil-A, In & Out Deli, Yi Fang Taiwan Fruit Tea, and a pizza place. As touristy as it can be, he always enjoyed the gardens and the majesty of the nearby New York Library. The library was closed now, but he has spent hours inside reading—he preferred the grandeur of the Rose Main Reading Room.

Philosophy became a passion over the past couple of years, especially the transcendental teachings of Emerson and Thoreau. He spent hours poring over their texts along with the works of Margaret Fuller. He had always relied on himself and viewed himself as an individual. Not anti-government, as some individualists have become, but a person who relies on his own abilities. The writings of the transcendental club reinforced and refocused those thought and behavior patterns. Two of Emerson's quotes are always top of mind for Tommy:

To be yourself in a world that is constantly trying to make you something else is the greatest accomplishment.

And:

Our greatest glory is not in never failing, but in rising up every time we fail.

Whether Emerson or Confucius said that is debatable, but Tommy reminds himself of it daily.

As he walked through Bryant Park, he recalled his many trips to visit William in Salem. Every time he traveled there, he stopped at Walden Pond near Concord. Sometimes alone, other times with William. He considered one such conversation that set him on his current path.

"So what you're saying is that transcendentalism encourages us to trust our own intuition and follow our own path in life." Tommy said as they made their way along the dirt packed trail that weaved around the famous pond. "Reject conformity. Break free from the chains of societal expectations. Embrace our individuality and live authentically."

"Absolutely!" William said. "It's all about finding our own unique voice and expressing it freely. By doing so, we can tap into our true potential and lead a more fulfilling existence. We're all part of a greater universal consciousness, and by embracing our individuality, we contribute to the diversity and richness of the whole."

"I get it. And self-reliance plays a huge role here. We need to trust ourselves and our abilities. We need to be independent and self-sufficient. Given where we are, Thoreau is a great example of demonstrating this trait by living in solitude here, cultivating his own food, and relying on his own skills."

"Yes. Thoreau's *experiment* of living deliberately, as he termed it, exemplified self-reliance in action. By living simply and minimizing his material needs, he freed himself from the constraints of a conventional lifestyle. He found that by relying on himself, he could live a more meaningful and deliberate life, in tune with nature and his own inner truth."

"Exactly! That is me, William. Self-reliance is not just about physical survival, but also about relying on our own minds and intuition. It encourages us to think critically and question the status quo, rather than blindly accepting the beliefs and values imposed upon us. It empowers us to make our own choices and live according to our own principles."

William continued, "It's about finding the balance between self-reliance and interconnectedness. While we strive for individuality and self-sufficiency, we also recognize our interconnectedness with nature and the world around us. Transcendentalism teaches us to appreciate the beauty of the natural world and to recognize that we are part of a larger whole."

"I have learned that we must constantly seek personal growth and enlightenment. By trusting ourselves, connecting with nature, and embracing our individuality, we can lead lives that are more meaningful, fulfilling, and in harmony with this world."

As they made their way towards the swimming beach, William said, "Absolutely, my friend. I believe we must live authentically while finding our own unique path in this vast universe. Through transcendentalism and self-reliance, we can truly tap into the boundless potential within ourselves and experience a deeper connection with the world."

• • • • • • • • • •

Tommy walked past the pair of marble lions—Patience and Fortitude—standing guard in front of the library's east side on 5th Avenue, then headed back to W. 37th. The street buzzed with energy, and the aroma of a food cart from the Halal Guys wafted through the air, mingling with the scent of car exhaust and warm asphalt. People hustled along, eager to escape the confines of their offices and indulge in the nightlife that New York City offered.

Just before leaving Vivid, he had received a text from an old friend inviting him to a late dinner at Frankie & Johnnie's restaurant downstairs from his loft. Besides the now ubiquitous outdoor dining area taking over a lane of W 37th Street's traffic, it would be tough to find Frankie and Johnnie's just walking down the street. It wasn't a spot where trendy health-conscious city dwellers could grab a quick bite. That would be Pokeworks across the street. No, this was an old school Manhattan steakhouse.

The building that now houses Frankie & Johnnie's has been a lot of things over the years from a little jazz club, Red Blazer Hideaway, to a townhouse home to Shakespearean actor John Barrymore, to another restaurant, The Hideaway. But to look at the restaurant's exterior today, tucked between a women's clothing store and an Asian massage parlor that advertised its services with Asian-inspired posters and neon lights that flickered like a faulty heart monitor, it's nothing special from the outside. The building's façade showed the wear and tear of decades of city life. It wasn't glamorous, but it had character, much like Tommy himself.

He walked in the restaurant where the hostess guided him to a table on the second floor where Josh and Darby were at a fireside table waiting for him. The table was neatly set with a white tablecloth, and Tommy watched as Josh snacked on the bacon and calamari appetizers in the center.

"Tommy, it's so good to see you. It's been way too long!" Josh said.

They embraced with a bro hug and Josh introduced him to Darby—her hair was crafted into a crown braid that wrapped elegantly around her head—who stood up and shook his hand.

"I've been looking forward to meeting you, Tommy. Josh and William are big fans of yours."

They sat at the table. As always, Josh was impeccably dressed in a perfectly tailored suit, managing somehow to look elegant even while reaching for another handful of garlic bread. His constant snacking had become such a part of him that his colleagues had learned to expect the rustle of food packages whenever he entered a room.

"So Darby, now that Tommy's here, welcome to Frankie & Johnnie's! This place has some of the best steaks in the city. Tommy practically lives above the restaurant, so he's our resident expert."

"You must have a permanent aroma of deliciousness surrounding you all the time," Darby said.

"Haha, you're not wrong. Sometimes I wake up in the morning and think I'm still in a carnivorous dream. But hey, it beats waking up to the smell of exhaust fumes like most

New Yorkers. And you know what they say, if you can't beat the smell, join the feast! So what's your steak preference, Darby? Are you a ribeye lover, a filet mignon connoisseur, or do you like to venture into the realm of porterhouse?"

"Well, I must confess, I'm a bit of a steak aficionado. I usually go for a juicy ribeye, but I'm open to exploring new flavors. Any recommendations for a steak lover like me?"

"Their bone-in ribeye is legendary here. It's cooked to perfection, with just the right amount of marbling to ensure that buttery texture and flavor. Trust me, once you taste it, you'll be hooked."

"Tommy's right," Josh said. "You won't find a better ribeye in the city. It's like a flavor explosion in your mouth. And don't forget to pair it with their classic garlic mashed potatoes and asparagus. It's the perfect combination."

"Alright, you two have convinced me. Bone-in ribeye it is, with all the delicious sides. I'm ready for this carnivorous delight to begin!"

"You won't regret it," Tommy said as he finished a drink of his water.

"If we're lucky, Tommy might share a few secrets about living above a steakhouse."

"Well, I'm all ears for those stories," admitted Darby. "Living here must come with some interesting tales. And hey, after this amazing meal, I might consider finding a loft above a bakery. Imagine waking up to the smell of freshly baked croissants!"

"Now you're onto something! We'll have to start a food-themed loft community!"

After their meals arrived, Tommy caught Darby and Josh staring at the wine closets and second floor stained glass skylight. "Right now," Tommy said, "we're in what used to be John Barrymore's study. He was famous for playing Richard III and Hamlet on Broadway in the 1920s."

"It's stunning," said Darby. "I knew nothing about this Manhattan neighborhood. I usually stick to the Upper East Side or a few blocks away in Chelsea. Even when I played in Madison Square Garden in college, I missed this part of town."

"The Garment District . . . it does get overlooked. Eleanor Roosevelt lived across the street. Mark Twain's funeral was held at the corner up there," pointing towards 5th Avenue.

"And just a little further on 7th Avenue between 35th and 40th Streets is the Fashion Walk of Fame."

"I see why you and William are friends," offered Josh. "He went on and on about the history of Salem when we were there."

"Next time you see him, ask him why so they paint so many houses in Salem black. Interesting story. But yes, I live next door up a couple of floors. Even though we occasionally get lines of people snaking down the sidewalk as they wait to audition for the next tv hit, it's a pretty cool part of town and I love living here."

"I love the history Tommy," Josh said, "and I notice Vivid across the street . . ."

"Vivid. That's where I landed after Afghanistan. Being a vet who left the Marines in the way I did . . . let's just say companies weren't begging me to join them. Things were tough for me when I got back. I tried my family in West New York. I moved in with friends in Miami and even stayed with William for a time. All good people, all willing to put me up. But I couldn't find a job out there. Until Vivid. They gave me a chance 18 months ago and I've been there ever since."

Tommy paused, looking thoughtfully out the windows.

"I don't like what I do. I see some truly disgusting things, and I know there's a lot more illegal stuff going on than just guys paying the dancers for sex. But let's save that for another day."

His two dinner companions nodded with an implicit understanding.

"This is not at all what I imagined my life would have in store for me. But like all of us, I needed some way to pay the mortgage. It always comes down to that, doesn't it?"

Even seated, Tommy was an imposing figure at 6'4" with broad shoulders and arms that looked like they could bench press a Mini Cooper. His military background was clear in his stance. He held himself with confidence. There was an intelligence and a dark edge lurking behind those deep black eyes.

As they continued chatting, Darby couldn't help but wonder what sort of secrets hid behind Tommy's confident yet vulnerable demeanor. There's something about him that made people feel both drawn to him and slightly wary at the same time. This quality, Darby mused, would make Tommy a valuable asset in their upcoming operation.

Tommy inquired with a smile, "Anyway, as happy as I am to see you Josh and meet you Darby, what brings you here, besides the great steak and free history lesson?"

"Yes, alright then," Josh said, clapping his hands together. "Time to get down to business." He cast a glance at Tommy, gauging his reaction. "What if we told you we have a way that we can do some good while also helping you—and our team—pay that mortgage?"

An imperceptible gleam crossed Tommy's eyes. At his core, Tommy cheered for the underdog and disadvantaged. He cheered the individual. And he wondered where this was going.

Josh leaned in with a mischievous smile. "We're putting together a little operation, and your unique set of skills would be invaluable."

Tommy's curiosity piqued as he raised an eyebrow. "Oh, you've got my attention now. What kind of operation are we talking about here?"

Darby chimed in, adding to the suspense, "Let's just say we need someone who can navigate security systems and personnel with finesse and composure."

Tommy chuckled, playing along. "Ah, I see. So you need a primary security chief who can keep their cool under pressure. Well, besides a couple of one-off jobs here and there, I've been out of that world for some time now, but yes, I used to specialize in sticky situations."

Josh grinned, appreciating Tommy's confident response. "That's exactly what we were hoping to hear. We've got a task that requires a mix of quick thinking, resourcefulness, and a touch of daring. It's going to be . . . well, explosive."

Darby's eyes gleamed with excitement. "And from what I've heard, your expertise will allow you to handle any curveballs that come our way. This mission calls for someone who thrives in the face of challenges."

Tommy leaned back, crossing his arms with a nod of approval. "Well, consider me intrigued."

They began telling Tommy about Justine and what she'd been through. About CAYA and how they use their actors and are planning worse. About Lolita and the heavy-handed, domineering way in which she uses people. She continued with what they'd all been through. How he's in the world right now.

Darby, taking a last bite of her mashed potatoes, chimed in, "Most of us entered the *underworld* willingly, but it tore us down. I know how that makes me feel. And I know how it's made others feel. The thought of a company taking advantage of the weakest out there leaves more than a sour taste in my mouth. I feel compelled to do this. And we're hoping you feel the same way."

Tommy sipped his soda. "Sounds like a noble cause. Tell me more."

They talked while finishing their steaks. Ideas, stories, and background information bounced around, frenetic at times, thoughtful at others. The three began to better understand what they needed to do. And why they needed to do it.

• • • ● • ● • ● • • •

As the group exited Frankie & Johnnie's, the busy streets of Manhattan greeted them like the booming base of a techno dance club. The sun had long since dipped below the towering skyscrapers. The air was crisp, a harbinger of the autumn chill that would soon envelop the city.

"Alright," Darby said, adjusting her leather jacket. "Herald Square is just a few blocks from here. Care for a little stroll?"

"Works for me," Tommy said, taking one last glance at his apartment building before he and Josh fell into step beside her.

The trio made their way down West 37th Street. They passed Paris Baguette, McDonald's, and Happy Socks along the way to the Square, named for the sensationalist newspaper headquartered there until 1966. The hum of traffic and chatter of pedestrians filled the air, a cacophony of noise that was uniquely New York. Though not as lively and bright as Times Square, countless signs flickered above the stores, delis, and coffee shops, while the tantalizing aroma of food wafted from nearby restaurants.

"God, I love this city," Josh remarked, taking in the sights and sounds around her. "There's just something about it that makes you feel alive, you know?"

A sardonic smile playing at the corners of Darby's lips. "Maybe it's all the crime and corruption."

"Or the fact that we're plotting to take down a major player in the porn industry."

"Either way, I wouldn't trade it for anything," Tommy chimed in, his eyes scanning the bustling street with a practiced ease.

Tommy took a seat across from Darby, his muscular frame dwarfing the delicate bistro chair. He glanced around at the busy square, observing the tourists snapping photos and the businesspeople hustling by, completely unaware of the trio's clandestine meeting. They all turned to face the iconic Macy's department store, and Tommy focused on the small building on the corner. As imposing as its façade is, Macy's history is a little more interesting and is yet another testament to the city's rich history. The flagship of the retailer had been at Herald Square since 1902. Macy's bought most of the buildings here when they moved from W. 14th to S. 37th Street. But the owner of this one small building at that corner refused to sell to them. So Macy's built around the holdout building to spite the corner store; the holdout building sold to another buyer in 1911 for $1,000,000 and became known as the Million Dollar Corner. The big red sign? It is a leased billboard in the shape of a shopping bag on the Million Dollar Corner building.

"But how do you plan on doing that?" returning them to their original conversation. "We can't just waltz into their headquarters and start smashing cameras and computers."

"True," Josh said, rubbing his chin thoughtfully. "But what if we could dismantle their operation from both the inside and the outside? We've got some pretty unique skills that make us perfectly suited for this job. You, Tommy, know your way around security systems. The studio held Justine there for three years. She has insider knowledge that can help us get our foot in the door. William and Darby? They just know things. And me? Well, I know how to follow the money."

Looking off toward Greeley Square Park and Koreatown beyond, he said, "this is our chance to make a real difference. To strike at the heart of an industry that preys on the weak and vulnerable. And I'll be damned if I'm going to let that opportunity slip through my fingers."

There was a moment of silence as the group weighed the gravity of the job. Tommy could feel the adrenaline coursing through his veins, his pulse quickening with anticipation. Finally, Josh looked back and met Tommy's gaze.

Tommy cracked his knuckles nonchalantly. "I think we need more people and intel than you've described, but I've been itching to put my skills to good use again."

Darby leaned in, her eyes dancing with mischief. "Like what?" she asked Tommy, teasingly challenging him. Her comments conflicted with her demeanor. She had an intense desire for justice and her redemptive nature was palpable, determination etched into every line of her face.

"We have some other things in the works," Josh interjected, thinking of William and Justine. "Their main headquarters has state-of-the-art security systems and a small army of goons on site. We need to infiltrate, triggering no alarms or arousing suspicion."

"Already one step ahead of you," Darby chimed in, flipping open a slim black notebook filled with names, numbers, and cryptic abbreviations. "I've been doing some reconnaissance on my own."

"Of course you have," Josh said under his breath, admiring her resourcefulness with pride.

"Excuse me?" Darby raised an eyebrow, catching his quiet remark.

"Nothing. Just impressed with your initiative, that's all."

She looked at him for a beat, her lips quirking into a self-satisfied smile. "You should be."

"Alright, you two," Tommy intervened with a smile, sensing the tension building between them. "Let's focus on the task at hand. We need to neutralize their security force without arousing suspicion."

Tommy rubbed his chin thoughtfully. "I've got no problem taking care of the security force, but it's their surveillance system that worries me. I could disable it, sure, but if they catch on, our entire operation goes down the drain."

"Easy there, soldier boy," Darby said, her eyes twinkling with mischief. "You forget that you're not alone in this. We've all got our own talents to bring to the table."

"True," Tommy conceded, a hint of a smile creeping onto his face. "But let's not get too cocky. This will require a ton of work. And luck."

"Agreed," Josh chimed in. "We need to be methodical about this. If we mess up, we won't get another shot at it."

"Okay, so we infiltrate, neutralize security, and then what?" Darby asked, her brow furrowed in concentration. "How do we actually take down CAYA? It's not like we can just waltz in and hit the delete button on all their smut and evildoing."

"Darby's right," Tommy nodded. "We need something more permanent, something that'll cripple their operations and send a message."

"Leave that to me," Josh said with a sly grin. "I've got an idea that should do the trick. And I know William's got a person in mind for the computer stuff. But first, we need to get past those security measures. We have to gather intel on their security system and any possible weak points," Josh said. "Then we'll devise a plan to exploit those weaknesses and slip in undetected."

"Sounds like a good start to a plan," Darby said, her eyes meeting Tommy's as they shared a moment of unspoken determination.

As the trio continued discussing their strategy, their thoughts raced with the possibilities and potential pitfalls of their daring endeavor.

Tommy leaned back in his chair, surveying the group around the table with a mix of amusement and apprehension. "You know . . . I never thought I'd be teaming up with a porn star, a banker, an author, and a disgraced athlete to take down an empire."

"Ex-porn star," Darby corrected, rolling her eyes. "And don't forget about our computer genius friend of William's."

"Right, right," Tommy conceded, raising his hands in mock surrender. "My bad. But seriously, this has got to be one of the strangest, most eclectic group of vigilantes ever assembled."

"Eclectic?" Darby arched an eyebrow. "That's just a fancy word for *fucked up*, isn't it?"

"Maybe," Tommy grinned, "but I think it's kind of poetic. We're all damaged goods in one way or another, yet here we are, trying to do something good."

"Speaking of doing something good," Josh interjected, "we need to iron out the details of our plan. We can't afford any slipups once we're inside CAYA's headquarters."

"Agreed," Darby nodded. "We've got one shot at this, so let's make it count."

Tommy's gaze shifted between his newfound allies. He could sense the weight of their pasts hanging heavy on their shoulders, driving them to seek redemption through this audacious mission.

"Alright," Tommy said, clapping his hands together. "Let's get to work."

As the group rose from their seats, Tommy said, "I guess there's something to be said about being *eclectic*. Maybe we're just the right kind of messed up to pull this off."

Three Years

Her first few weeks at CAYA felt like a dream—or perhaps a dream's dark reflection. Justine found herself surrounded by bright lights, designer clothes, and the constant click of cameras. The compliments flowed like honey, sweet and intoxicating.

"You're a natural, Justine," the photographer praised as she moved through poses with fluid grace. "The camera absolutely loves you."

But beneath the glittering surface, something darker lurked. It started small—suggested wardrobe changes that left her feeling increasingly exposed, scenes that pushed against her stated boundaries, subtle threats wrapped in velvet words.

"Now, now, Justine," Tony would say, his voice dripping with false concern. "You wouldn't want to disappoint your fans, would you? After *all* we've invested in you?"

Lolita's methods were more direct. Her towering presence and sculpted physique served as constant reminders of the power dynamics at play. "The contract is very clear," she would say, her voice cold as winter. "You agreed to fulfill all performance requirements. Unless you'd prefer to deal with our legal team?"

The *living quarters* slowly revealed themselves as the prison they were. Phone calls were monitored, then restricted, then forbidden. Outside contact dwindled to nothing. Guards—though they were called security staff—watched their every move.

But Justine wasn't ready to surrender. Her first escape attempt came three months in, a desperate dash through an unguarded door that ended in bruising failure. The second, a month later, got her as far as the compound's outer fence before Lolita's team caught her.

The punishments were never physical—Tony was too smart for that. Instead, they employed a sophisticated form of psychological torture. Isolation. Sleep deprivation. The steady erosion of identity.

"You belong to us now," Lolita would whisper, her breath hot against Justine's ear. "The sooner you accept that, the easier it will be."

But deep inside, a spark of defiance refused to die. During a carefully monitored shoot in San Francisco, Justine managed to slip a note to a sympathetic crew member. The message reached her father, and within weeks, his legal team had found a loophole in her contract.

The day she walked out of CAYA's gates, Justine felt reborn. Free. The California sun had never seemed brighter.

Freedom, however, came with its own price. Her reputation was tainted. Legitimate acting roles were all but impossible to land. She scraped by on small independent films and modeling jobs, but the bills kept mounting. Each rejection pushed her closer to the edge of desperation.

That's when Tony's call came. He knew exactly how much she was struggling and, honestly, had engineered much of it. His proposal boiled down to a straightforward choice: go back to CAYA and take on her previous responsibilities, but this time without any legal loopholes.

"You'll always be one of us, Justine," he said, his voice almost gentle. "Why fight it?"

The day she walked back through those gates, Lolita was waiting, a triumphant gleam in her ice-blue eyes. "Welcome home, Justine," she purred. "We've made some improvements since your last stay."

The *improvements* became apparent. Her new quarters were more heavily monitored, her movements more restricted. The psychological manipulation intensified, a constant barrage designed to break her spirit.

But this time, Justine was ready. She began keeping careful records of everything she witnessed—the abuse, the exploitation, the web of corruption that kept CAYA's empire running. She wrote in code, hiding her notes in places even Lolita's thorough searches wouldn't find.

She also formed bonds with her fellow captives, a network of shared suffering and quiet resistance. Together, they found small ways to maintain their humanity, to keep hope alive in the darkness.

"We have to stay strong," she would whisper during their brief moments alone. "Someone will notice what's happening here. We just have to survive until then."

For three long years, Justine endured. She played her role, kept her head down, and gathered evidence. She learned every detail of CAYA's operations, memorized security patterns, mapped out potential escape routes.

Every night, as she lay in her room planning her eventual escape, Justine felt that spark of defiance grow stronger. She wasn't just fighting for herself anymore. She was fighting for every soul trapped behind CAYA's walls, every dream they'd twisted and corrupted.

"I'll expose them," she whispered to herself in the darkness. "I'll burn their empire to the ground."

Standing at her window, watching the guards patrol below, Justine finally understood. Sometimes you have to lose everything—your dreams, your freedom, your very self—to find your true purpose. Her childhood dream of changing the world through acting hadn't died; it had transformed into something harder, darker, but no less powerful.

She just needed to find her way out first.

She was still going to tell stories that changed lives. But first, she had a different role to play—that of the avenging phoenix, rising from the ashes of her cage to rain fire on those who had imprisoned her.

This time, she wouldn't just escape.

This time, she would make them pay.

Interview: Tommy

Inspector: *Good evening, Tommy. Let's get right to it. Can you confirm or deny any involvement in the heist that took place at CAYA?*

Tommy: *Inspector, I categorically deny any involvement in the heist at CAYA. While I have a complicated past, I have turned my life around and strive to uphold the law. I cannot and will not take part in any illegal activities.*

Inspector: *Tommy, we believe your skills and knowledge of security systems were instrumental in planning and executing the heist. Can you explain why your expertise seems to align with the events that unfolded?*

Tommy: *I understand why you might suspect me, given my background. However, I want to make it clear that I've moved on from my troubled past. My skills in security systems come from my prior experiences and the knowledge I gained during my time in the military. But I assure you, I would never employ those skills for criminal purposes.*

Inspector: *Tommy, we have received information suggesting that you had connections with individuals involved in the heist and that you were privy to their plans. Can you shed light on these connections?*

Tommy: *I assure you, Inspector, that any connections I may have had with those individuals were purely coincidental and unrelated to the heist. I've encountered various people throughout my life, and while some may have questionable backgrounds, I have distanced myself from any illegal activities. My priority is to live a law-abiding life.*

Inspector: *Tommy, we possess evidence showing that you provided critical information regarding the security systems and vulnerabilities of CAYA. How do you explain this evidence?*

Tommy: *My knowledge of security systems is based on my professional experience and training. Any information I may have shared would have been for legitimate purposes, such as consulting or advising on security improvements. I am committed to upholding the law, and I would never knowingly aid in criminal acts.*

Inspector: *We have reports that place you at the scene. What do you say about this?*

Tommy: *I was not there. I know nothing about this.*

Inspector: *You didn't drive onto their property?*

Tommy: *No.*

Inspector: *You didn't help to steal from the studio?*

Tommy: *No.*

Inspector: *Do you know any of the others we have been talking to?*

Tommy: *Who, exactly?*

Inspector: *Darby. William. Justine. Josh. We believe they are involved in this theft.*

Tommy: *They are my friends, of course. But I have no knowledge they did this.*

Inspector: *What about those who worked there? Tony? Lolita?*

Tommy: *I don't know them.*

Inspector: *So you don't know if they were involved?*

Tommy: *No clue.*

Inspector: *Tommy, it's crucial that you cooperate fully with our investigation. We need to uncover the truth and hold accountable all those involved in the heist.*

Tommy: *Inspector, I want to assure you I am cooperating fully with your investigation. I have nothing to hide, and I will provide any information within my knowledge that may assist in your pursuit of justice. I am dedicated to helping bring the real perpetrators to light and ensuring that they face the consequences of their actions.*

Inspector: *Tommy, we will continue our investigation, and I urge you to reflect on any information that may be of significance to us. It's in your best interest to be forthcoming and transparent.*

Tommy: *Inspector, I appreciate that, and I want to reiterate my full cooperation.*

M's

Omaha has hosted the NCAA College World Series since 1950. First at Rosenblatt Stadium in South Omaha, now just north of downtown at the still gleaming Charles Schwab Field.

William gazed out the window of the rented SUV as they cruised past the baseball stadium. The golden hue of fading sunlight painted the neighboring old brick buildings a warm shade of orange. He glanced at Justine in the driver's seat, her red hair glowing like fire under the setting sun. She was focused on the road, her lips pressed into a determined line.

He fondly remembered attending the College World Series at Rosenblatt every year from First Grade through his days in college. The struggle to find parking. The Dingerville RVs. Hiding in the concourse during weather delays. The many seats with obstructed views. The cheers when the ball boys and girls caught the foul balls behind the plate and the boos when they dropped them. He missed the charm of the old but understood the need for the new.

"Ever been to Omaha before?" William asked, trying to break the silence between them.

"Can't say I have," Justine said, her green eyes flicking toward him briefly. "I'm sorry that this has always been part of flyover country for me."

"Fair enough," he said, rubbing his clean-shaven head. He couldn't help but feel a twinge of nostalgia as they drove through the familiar west Omaha neighborhood where he had once lived, back when Ella and her family were his neighbors. That was years ago, before everything went to hell. Before he became the man he was today—a recovering gambling addict and author, trying to make amends for his past sins in every way possible.

"You know, when I come back here, I'm always reminded of Emerson's quote about moving on from mistakes. It's guided me for many years now."

Finish each day and be done with it. You have done what you could. Some blunders and absurdities no doubt crept in; forget them as soon as you can. Tomorrow is a new day. You shall begin it serenely and with too high a spirit to be encumbered with your old nonsense.

Justine took a moment to reflect on William's words and Emerson's quote, her expression softening as the words sank in. She leaned back in her seat, a wistful smile tugging at the corners of her lips.

"I used to dwell so much on my past mistakes and the things I couldn't change," she began, her voice carrying a hint of nostalgia. "It felt like an anchor weighing me down, preventing me from moving forward. But those words . . . they speak to something deep within me."

She paused, her eyes drifting off for a moment as she gathered her thoughts. "I've come to realize that I can't undo the choices I made or the pain I endured. But I can choose how I respond to them. I can choose to let go of the regrets and the self-blame. I can choose to embrace each new day as an opportunity for growth and redemption."

Justine's gaze returned, her eyes meeting William's with newfound determination. "I may have been trapped in a dark industry, but I refuse to let it define me. I'm ready to leave the past behind and build a better future for myself, free from the shackles of my previous life."

She straightened her posture, a spark of resilience in her eyes. "Emerson is right. Today is a new day, a chance to rise above the mistakes and blunders. Let's seize it with a spirit that's too high to be encumbered by the old nonsense."

· · · · ● · ● · · ·

Pulling up outside Crane Coffee—a local chain coffee shop—across a steeply graded parking lot from Big Fred's Pizza, William spotted a tall, dark-haired man sitting alone at an outdoor table. He recognized him instantly—Jim, Ella's father, and his old friend. It was strange how life could bring people back together after all these years.

"Wait here. Or better yet, drive around. I will call you when we're done," William said, as he exited the car. With a deep breath, he approached Jim, who looked up at him with a smile.

"Jim!" William called out, a grin spreading across his face as he approached his old friend. Despite the near constant heartache, he years had dealt him a gentler hand than expected; his salt-and-pepper hair and laugh lines only added to his distinguished appearance.

"William!" Jim said, standing up to greet him with a firm handshake. "It's been too long, my friend."

"Tell me about it." William took a seat opposite Jim. He ordered a cappuccino, the frothy concoction reminding him of the foam that used to tickle his mustache during his gambling days.

Jim greeted him warmly. "What brings you back to Omaha?"

"Thanks for agreeing to meet, Jim. I wanted to catch up, and I was hoping to talk about Ella," William began, his voice faltering slightly with concern.

He was thinking of his move to Salem after Ella's disappearance. It was heartbreaking for him that she was gone. He was thinking of how he tried to remain in contact with her family once he moved to Salem, but the family rejected his overtures. He was thinking of how he learned of her return last year . . . via this text message from Jim:

We got her back.

He was thinking of how he repeatedly reached out to their family over the past year . . . texts, emails, phone calls, cards, even one visit; but he still learned nothing. He was thinking of how the loss he experienced years ago remained.

"I was hoping to see her. To let her know I'm here."

Jim's smile faded, replaced by a mixture of curiosity and worry. "Ella? Why? What's going on?"

William stared into his paper coffee cup. "For so many years, our families were close. Once she was gone, that relationship seemed over. I moved away. Communication didn't happen as I'd hoped. I don't know what it was like for you. And I'm not trying to compare your experience with mine, but I felt I lost something, too. I lost your friendship, and I lost my buddy, Ella."

Jim sat, staring off at the chain restaurant across the street. He knew this day would come. Someday. With William. He and Ella had been close. Not creepily so. More like a favorite uncle and niece. He knew his care for Ella was genuine and deep. So yes, he knew this conversation would happen one day.

And that day was here now.

"It was hard, William. We struggled a lot. Jenny and I nearly divorced at least twice while Ella was gone. And we're still not in a great place. We hurt. A lot. And we didn't handle it in a way that helped anyone."

William nodded sympathetically, sadness the only feeling his face expressed.

"And then when she returned . . . we were so happy. We tried to repair the damage done, to put back together the broken pieces of our family. It's there—our family—some days. But most days it's not. So I'm sorry, William, but that's the *why* of the past seven years."

William uncharacteristically grabbed his old neighbor's hands and looked at him through eyes blurred with tears. "Jim, there's no need to apologize. I'm glad she came back to you, and I hope the healing continues."

"I know you'd like to see her, William; but I don't know how to tell you this. She's not the same, sweet girl you used to know. A lot has happened since she left and returned."

"Jim. I get it—"

"I don't think you do get it," Jim said, rubbing his temples as if trying to massage away the heavy weight of his daughter's past. "She's not the person you remember. A sex trafficking gang took away from us when she was only twelve years old. Twelve years old! She survived only God knows what—I can't bring myself to ask her. She somehow escaped weeks before she should have been graduating high school."

"Jesus, Jim," William said, pain etched on his face as he imagined the horrors Ella must have endured.

"The physical Ella is here, but part of her remains with the experiences of the past seven years. Your name comes up from time-to-time, but I don't honestly know how she'd respond to seeing you."

They sat in silence for several minutes, each thinking of the carefree girl they once knew.

"Listen," Jim said, his voice strained with emotion. "She lives alone in a loft apartment in the Old Market. She's not as trusting, she has an edge to her, her lifestyle has changed, but I have her back. Not the little girl I used to know, but I have her back. Oh, and that gang that took her? They were brought down in a fiery blaze of gunfire. They say someone stole all their money . . . the rumor is that Ella did it."

"Good for her," William said, a fierce pride swelling in his chest at the thought of his young friend fighting to take back control of her life.

"Look, I don't want to put her in any more danger," Jim said, leaning forward and locking eyes with William. "But if you want to reach out . . . it might help her . . . I'll give you her number."

"Thank you, Jim." William felt the weight of responsibility settle on his shoulders. "I promise I won't let anything happen to her."

"See that you don't," Jim warned, downing the last of his coffee as if the bitter liquid could purge him of the memories that haunted his every waking moment.

As William left Crane Coffee, his thoughts tangled in a whirlwind of emotions. One thing was certain: he would protect Ella at all costs, even if it meant walking through fire himself.

Back in the SUV, he filled Justine in on the conversation he had with Jim. She listened intently, nodding in agreement when he mentioned their plan to contact Ella. As they drove towards the Old Market, William couldn't help but feel anxious about seeing her again. The innocent girl he once knew was now a tormented young woman shaped by her tragic past. What would she think of him now?

"Are you sure about this?" Justine asked, her voice low and cautious.

"Positive. Regardless of if she helps us, I owe it to her to reach out again. I will never stop trying."

Justine nodded, turning onto West Dodge Road, heading east.

"Ella may be our only chance to bring down those bastards in the porn industry and save others from the same dark path we've all walked. And maybe doing something like this will help her heal. And Justine, that part is more important to me."

"Or if she doesn't heal, maybe she can exact some revenge on an industry that hurt her. That hurt me."

As they passed the University of Nebraska Medical Center, Justine said, gripping the steering wheel tightly, "Let's hope she agrees."

"Me too," William said, staring at the phone as he prepared to call the brilliant young hacker who held the key to their success—or failure.

• • • ● • ● • ● • •

With Ella's number in hand, William found himself strolling through Omaha's newly renovated and redesigned Gene Leahy Mall, gathering the courage to make the call. He remembered the sweet girl who used to play in the yard next door and couldn't help but feel a pang of guilt for not being there when she needed someone most. His thumb hovered over the call button, hesitating for just a moment before he pressed it.

"Yeah?" came the guarded voice on the other end.

"Hey, Ella. It's William. Your dad gave me your number and told me you were living in the Old Market. I'm staying at *The Farnam* by the Mall and thought maybe we could catch up," he said, trying to sound as casual as possible.

"William? It's been . . . years. You're just now getting around to catching up?" she said, her tone edged with a mix of nostalgia and suspicion.

"Better late than never, right?" he responded, attempting to inject some humor into the conversation. "I'm walking around the Mall right now. If you're free, I'd love to see you."

"Fine. Give me 15 minutes. M's Pub." The line went dead, leaving William to wonder what kind of woman he'd meet.

• • • ● • ● • ● • • •

In the cozy Skyline neighborhood filled with spacious yards and mid-century modern homes built in the 1960s, a nostalgic scene re-enters William's mind. Ella, around eight years old and wearing a dog t-shirt and jean shorts, eagerly hops on her shiny red mountain bike. She adjusts her black helmet, her long brown hair escaping its hold as she glances across the street at William, who is preparing to join her on a biking adventure.

William, with a gentle smile etched on his face—the smiles came easier and more frequently then—emerges from his attached two-car garage. He dusts off his hardtail mountain bike, dirt caking its blue frame as it whispers stories of countless memories. With a glint in his eyes, he secures his helmet firmly on his head and pedals to Ella's driveway. William recalls the brief banter with Jim and Jenny before he and Ella head out.

The two pedal side by side, a gentle breeze carries their laughter and the occasional sound of changing gears. The wide neighborhood streets, lined with blooming flowers and swaying trees, provide a picturesque backdrop for their journey.

As they approach 119th Street, a tantalizing aroma drifts through the air, leading them to a small cupcake bakery nestled in a well-worn strip mall. Its yellow and white-striped awning and windows adorned with whimsical decorations beckon them inside. With a chorus of excited giggles, Ella and William prop their bikes against the brick wall outside.

Entering the bakery, a warm and inviting atmosphere quickly greets them. An array of delectable cupcakes filled the glass display cases—tuxedo, twirl for me, pink champagne, wedding cake, white frosted with chocolate, and so on—each one a miniature work of art, adorned with swirls of frosting, plastic decorations, or delicate sugar flowers. The sweet scent of freshly baked goods permeates the air, adding to the anticipation that fills the room.

Ella's eyes widen with delight as she surveys the assortment of cupcake flavors, her imagination running wild with possibilities. William rests his weathered hands on the counter as he encourages Ella to make her selection. They carefully choose a cupcake, each representing a unique taste and color, ensuring they have the perfect assortment for their delightful treat.

With their mouths watering and the cupcakes carefully boxed, they find a find a tree-shaded picnic bench nearby to savor their well-deserved indulgence. As they bite into the cupcakes, their eyes light up with pure delight. Sweet laughter fills the air as they exchange stories, their hearts brimming with joy and contentment.

Time seems to slow down in this moment of simple bliss, as Ella and William strengthen a bond that transcends generations. Their shared love for cycling and cupcakes unites them, creating memories they will cherish forever. With smiles on their faces and a dear friendship in their hearts, they finish their cupcakes, bid farewell to the bakery, and set off on their bicycles, embarking on more adventures waiting just around the corner.

This scene would play out in different ways over the years. Playing catch in the backyard, heading to the local public pool, sledding down the St. Robert's church hill, stopping by the local Dairy Queen.

Before cheer tryouts when she was 11, they practiced back walkovers in his backyard. He had a gentle downhill grade that helped get her over. He carefully spotted her back and helped her legs finish the motion. She made the team, and he recalls going to the competitions with Jim and Jenny on countless occasions. He was always so proud of her.

William and Ella were buddies.

· · ● · ● · ● · ● · ·

As he stepped into M's Pub, the dim lighting and warm atmosphere did little to calm his racing heart. Dressed in jeans and a black and blue oxford shirt he left untucked, William chose a booth near the back, scanning the room for any sign of Ella. M's Pub has been around for 50 years, but not continuously. During one cold Omaha winter, a gas explosion caused the restaurant to close for a year or so. Though he was settled into Salem by then, William can still see the news pictures of the frozen water clinging to the sides of the building as it burned.

When the door finally opened and she walked in, he noticed the change in her immediately—gone were the shapeless hoodies and worn jeans of her youth. Ella had developed her own sense of style, her outfit choices now as bold and distinctive as her coding skills. At 5'5", the tight black sweater and black cargo pants showed she was still rail thin. Her hair was longer now, but still straight, though perhaps a darker shade of brown, if that was possible. Her skin was close to olive, offering a warm complexion, but that appeared to be the only warmth she offered. Ella approached the table. Her posture was guarded and her once carefree deep brown eyes penetrated all they saw with an unmistakable sense of bitterness. She didn't even try to mask the smoldering anger beneath. She slid into the booth across from him, crossing her arms defensively.

"Hey, William. Long time no see," she said, her voice dripping with sarcasm.

"Hey, Ella. You look . . . different. Good, but different."

"Life does that to people," she shot back, her eyes narrowing.

"I can't believe they made this place look almost the same after the fire a few years ago. It feels as though it's always been here. Remarkable."

"I guess. We never came here when I was younger, so I don't know what it was like back then." Ella leaned forward, her eyes locked on his. "So why are we here, William? To talk about reconstructed buildings?" She let out a small, sarcastic laugh, her lips curving into a wry smile.

"Partially," he said, matching her gaze. "But there's more, too."

"Go on," she said, feigning disinterest as she scrolled through her phone.

"Put that away," he said gently, nodding at her device. "I need your full attention."

"Fine," Ella said, setting her phone down and folding her hands on the table. "You have my undivided attention. For now."

She locked eyes with him, her piercing stare conveyed what she couldn't articulate.

William tried to keep the conversation light. "Can't I just want to catch up with an old friend?"

"Cut the crap, William. I know my dad sent you," she said, her voice laced with bitterness. "What do you want? Are you going to lecture me on how I should live my life?"

"Nothing like that," he assured her, raising his hands in surrender. "We talked, yes. But he had nothing but loving things to say about you. He cares about you and updated me as best he could."

She just stared at him, her face blank. Even her eyes, that gave away so much, were without expression.

"Ella . . . you know I looked for you every day for a year after you disappeared. I tried getting information from the police and FBI and used that to look here. In Iowa. In Kansas City. South Dakota. Even in Dallas."

He paused to look at her and caught her eye. Perhaps a hint of . . . something. She offered a look that suggested the warmth she used to feel for William was still there somewhere.

"I moved to Salem after that year. A part of me was gone, and I thought moving would help. It didn't, but I pretended it did.

"I continued to look for you in different ways and lost count of the sleepless nights I spent searching for you online. I came back here and looked again. Maybe you left a clue. Maybe I passed something I should have seen."

He paused and looked down at the glass of water he held in his now trembling hands.

"When I heard you came back, I was thrilled. I called your parents. I texted. I emailed. But I got no response. I didn't know how to contact you. I even came back to Omaha, but your mom refused to let me see you. Said you needed time to heal. She was probably right. Maybe I should have asked again. And again. And again. But I figured your parents needed time, too. So I let all of you be."

Tears filled his eyes as he lowered his glass.

"Ella, you were—you are—my friend. You're a daughter to me."

The tears escaped his eyes and freely flowed down his clean-shaven cheeks. "I'm so sorry I wasn't here to help you. I'm sorry I wasn't smart enough to find you. I'm sorry I couldn't help you after it ended. I'm sorry."

"William, you know what? It's never ended. Sure, I got away, but the pain won't end. It's always there and I'm afraid it will never leave." Ella turned to stare out the window.

Their food came, and they both picked at their dishes. Floyd's Skinny Plate for him, Thai Lahvosh for her.

In between her small bites, Ella looked up and held William's gaze for a minute, before returning her distracted focus to grab a piece of chicken with her fork.

Walls

After what seemed like an hour without conversation, William asked, "do you remember Jim Rissler, your 5th grade PE teacher?"

"I think of him at least once a week. He, along with so many others, hurt me and tried to steal my . . . essence."

Ella and her family moved to Omaha, and she started school at the beginning of fourth grade. As happened to Darby many years earlier in a town far from Omaha, Mr. Rissler began giving extra attention to Ella. He looked at her with lust but tried to mask it with caring. The looks became playful touches on her shoulders or arms or head. And then he caressed her arms. And then he touched her backside.

"As soon as he started touching me, I told you—and only you—about it. And then you . . . you did something I never would have guessed."

William let a small smile escape him.

"You wanted revenge. To punish him for what he did to me. For what we learned he did to others."

Ella avoided Mr. Rissler while she and William plotted. She was always good with computers, so she began using those skills. She hacked into the school's computers using a password he left taped to the side of his computer monitor. And what did she find? There was a journal detailing all his conquests. Mostly fourth and fifth-grade girls. A few were younger. A handful were boys. But in total, the journal had over 20 entries. The last two names were hers and her friend Sidnie's. They were blank so far.

But Ella didn't stop there. She accessed his home computer and could get the data from his phone. She found hundreds of images that she couldn't bear to look at. Videos she couldn't unsee. Never one for emotion, she cried when she saw them.

"Once I told you what I saw, you got really mad. I had never seen you like that."

William nodded along, "what he did to you, what he was planning to do with Sidnie, and what he did to all those other kids . . . Ella, it still makes me mad. Having you trap him like you did was brilliant."

Ella put down her glass. "I knew we could just send what we found to the police, but I didn't know if that would help, and I thought he deserved more."

William and Ella hacked into his bank accounts, emptied them, and then anonymously sent the photos, videos, journals, and other materials to the police. Before they hit send, however, they sent a summary of their findings to the Omaha World Herald, the school, Mr. Rissler's church, his family . . . anyone they could think of.

They humiliated him and their efforts got him sent to prison for life. Last either of them heard, he was a favorite toy for many of the inmates.

"Sending that money—while not millions—to the other families was a great idea, Ella. It was a good plan, and it went off without a hitch. No violence, just simple revenge for a trusted person's evil acts."

Precocious Ella had the grand idea to repeat this same plan with others in the community. Some of their targets borderline pedophiles, others stole from those in need, others still were violent and abusive. In total, William and Ella targeted nearly a dozen people during her 5th grade year and the summer that followed. Their capers ended when Ella was snatched. Did their actions put a target on her back? She was the hacker. She was online. She may have unwittingly exposed herself. They would probably never know.

The pair let that simmer for a few minutes and got up to leave. As they walked into the brisk air of the evening, William said, "I'm actually working on something big, and I think you could help."

"Help with what, exactly?" she asked, her curiosity piqued despite her best efforts to return to her aloof affect.

"Working with a team to do something good. Like what we did to Mr. Rissler. Using the computer skills I'm certain you still have," he said, watching as her eyes widened in shock. "But we don't have to talk about that now. Let's just enjoy each other's company for a bit, okay?"

Ella hesitated, clearly weighing her options. Finally, she stopped walking and looked him in the eye. "Fine," she said, her voice softening ever so slightly. "But don't think this means I'm going to help you. And don't expect me to tell you about what happened to me."

"Deal," William said, a small half-smile tugging at the corner of his mouth. "But I expect you to know that I will always care for you, Ella."

A hint of a smile came to her, but just as quickly as it came, it left. To further mask the emotion, she said, "Look, it's been a lot seeing you after all this time. Can we catch up tomorrow or something?"

"Of course. I'm going to bring a friend . . . ok with you?"

"Sure, if it's a friend of yours, I know it's ok."

He walked her to the door of her loft and then walked the two blocks to his hotel. During his walk, he couldn't help but wonder if he'd made the right decision to approach her. But one thing was certain: there was no turning back now.

• • • ● • ● • • •

They met at Block 16 the next day for lunch. Block 16 is designed in the popular loft-style with two rooms; the first allows customers to order from a large chalkboard menu of farm to table offerings. Next to that room, the second area has several tables with a combination of white walls and horizontal wood planks. A large black and white drawing of restaurant-goers dominated the largest wall.

William and Justine entered and found Ella sitting at a table. William was again wearing jeans but had a blue V-neck cashmere sweater with a gray undershirt. Justine was dressed in faded jeans with several holes and a black sweater. Ella wore a black skirt, tight white crop top and a white oxford shirt left unbuttoned.

"Ella, this is Justine, the friend I mentioned last night."

They shook hands, but Ella did not smile and did not stand to greet them.

"Ella, it's so great to meet you. William has told me so much about you."

"And I know almost nothing about you," Ella said. "So, we caught up yesterday, William. Why are both of you really here? In Omaha. Together. To see me."

"While I was running this morning, I tried to think of how to start this conversation," William said, leaning in. "As I crossed over the pedestrian bridge from Council Bluffs, I decided to just lay it all out there.

"You know I've spent years battling my own demons, so I perk up when I hear the story of someone struggling. I like to help others."

"Because you can't help yourself?" said Ella.

"Well, I suppose yes. Thanks for noticing Ella. Justine and two other friends—Darby and Josh—met with me a couple of weeks ago in Salem. I recall I had just finished a 16-mile run to Nahant and back when they were waiting for me near my home. They explained the situation and asked for my help."

"What situation?"

Justine spoke, "Ella, I know you don't know me. But a ruthless Los Angeles company coerced me into a working relationship. William and the others would like to help . . . well, let's just say they'd like to exact revenge on a nasty pair of individuals."

"Coerced?"

"Yes. I was a porn actress and this company—Cum As You Are—enticed me with grandiose visions of what my life would become. I eventually agreed. And then I couldn't leave."

Almost imperceptibly, Ella nodded along.

"I did get out, but only just. And I know they're still looking for me. Ella, I only know a bit about you, but from what William tells me, you can help."

"Do you know what happened to me?" asked Ella.

"No, not really. I only know it was impactful. That it tore William up. He told me he felt he let you down. Beyond that, no. And I didn't ask."

They all stared at their food, nibbling on their Croque Garcon Burger, Duck Duck Goose Fries, and B16 House Salad. Three kindred souls. All still hurting.

William jumped in. "Ella, we're working on something that could make a real difference for Justine and the many others this company is ruining. I think you're the missing piece to this puzzle."

"Is that so?" Ella asked, her voice dripping with skepticism. "And what makes you think I'd be interested?"

"Because I know you, Ella." His tone softened. "And I know that underneath that tough exterior, you want to make a difference, too."

"Careful, William," she warned, her eyes narrowing. "Don't try using my past for any other gain. You're treading on thin ice."

"Understood," he conceded, leaning back. "I'll bluntly and openly cut to the chase. We've put together a team to take down the porn industry, or at least this part of it. And I need your brilliant mind and digital expertise."

Ella's eyes widened for a moment, then she burst into laughter. "You can't be serious. The entire porn industry?"

"Deadly serious. And I believe we can do it. But we need you, Ella."

Ella looked away, her fingers absently tracing patterns on the tablecloth. She was silent for a moment before turning her gaze back to him. "I'll think about it," she uttered, her voice heavy with uncertainty.

"Take your time," William assured her. "Just know that when you're ready, we'll be waiting."

"Thanks," she said softly. "But I'd like to know more first. Let's talk about this so-called team of yours."

William and Justine talked about their team—Darby, Josh, and Tommy (Darby sent a text late last night confirming Tommy's involvement)—and summarized each team member's role.

Darby is the planner.

Josh is finance.

Tommy is security.

William is more of an advisor ("The old guy with lots of opinions.").

Justine is the inside woman.

"We just need someone to help us get past their firewalls and computer defenses."

"Just," Ella said, the word dripping with a combination of sarcasm and the dismissive mention of the challenge. As if hacking a company was easy and straightforward.

"Ella, I don't know all that's happened to you. And I don't really need to," Justine caringly reflected.

Ella stiffened at the mention of her past, her fingers tightening around the glass. Hearing her past discussed openly made her uneasy. She glanced at William, who offered a reassuring smile. "Yeah, well, we've all got our sob stories, right?"

"True," Justine said, her voice softening. "But not everyone uses their pain to fuel something greater. You're a fighter, Ella. I can see it in your eyes."

"Great, you can read people," Ella shot back, her defensiveness manifesting as sarcasm. "What do you want from me?"

"We want you to join us," Justine said, leaning in closer. "We're going to take them down, and we need you to do it. Someone who knows what it's like to be hurt by that world."

Ella hesitated, her bravado wavering. She had spent years building walls around herself, protecting her heart from further anguish. The thought of diving headfirst into such a dangerous mission terrified her.

I survived once. But can I really risk everything again?

"Look," Justine said, sensing Ella's uncertainty. "I know it's scary. But think about all the people we could help. All the lives we could change."

Ella swirled the remnants of her Dr. Pepper. "Or all the lives we could destroy. You're asking me to wade back into the darkness. What if I don't come out the other side?"

"Then we'll be there to pull you back," William interjected, his voice firm yet gentle. "You won't be alone, Ella. We'll face this together."

Ella stared at the liquid and ice in her glass, her mind racing. The weight of the decision pressed heavily upon her, threatening to crush her resolve. With one last sigh, she drained her drink and slammed the glass onto the table, rattling the ice within. The soft murmur of conversation around them created a white noise backdrop that did little to numb the chaos inside her head.

"Joining this team won't erase your past," Justine said, her voice gentle yet strong. "But it could help you reclaim what they took from you. Power. Control. A chance to say, *no more.*"

"Revenge is a hell of a drug," Ella said, trying to hide her trembling hand. "But is it worth risking everything I've managed to rebuild?"

"Depends on how much you value what you have now," William chimed in, his gaze never leaving Ella's. "And how much you want to make those bastards pay?"

"Since when did you become such a vigilante?" Ella asked, eyebrows raised, even though she recalled the retribution she meted out when she was younger.

"Things change, Ella," William said, a hint of sadness in his eyes. "What you and I did before you were taken . . . well, it inspired me. I think we can do that on a larger scale. Look, we've all got our demons, and sometimes fighting for something bigger helps keep them at bay."

And with that, the trio fell silent, each lost in their own thoughts as they weighed the risks and rewards of their impending crusade. For Ella, the decision loomed like a storm cloud on the horizon—dark and terrifying, yet oddly enticing.

Interview: William

Inspector: *Good afternoon, William. Let's get right to it, shall we? Can you deny any involvement in the heist at CAYA?*

William: *Inspector, I have no idea what you're talking about. I'm focused on my books and writing. And occasional teaching. I am not involved in any criminal activities.*

Inspector: *William, I've come across individuals like you before. The ones who try to distance themselves from their past but find themselves dragged back into it. We have evidence that suggests your knowledge and experience could have been valuable in planning this heist.*

William: *Inspector, I understand your doubts, but I assure you, I had nothing to do with any heist. I've been trying to overcome my past and move forward. My involvement with gambling was a dark chapter in my life that I'm trying to leave behind.*

Inspector: *Do you know a woman named Darby?*

William: *Darby? Yes.*

Inspector: *Did the two of you plot and plan the theft of money from CAYA?*

William: *Steal? Absolutely not.*

Inspector: *Did you plan and execute a hack of this studio's computer network?*

William: *No.*

Inspector: *Do you know an individual named Ella?*

William: *Yes.*

Inspector: *What is your relationship?*

William: *We are longtime friends.*

Inspector: *For how long?*

William: *Since she was around eight, I suppose.*

Inspector: *So you're aware of her abduction?*

William: *One of the very saddest things I've ever experienced. But my pain pales in comparison with all she went through.*

Inspector: *Yes, it was quite a lot.*

William: *Whatever you think you know, double it. Triple it. It was—and is—the worst imaginable.*

Inspector: *Did you visit her recently?*

William: *I traveled to Omaha to see her, yes. We hadn't talked for seven years. So I reached out to her dad, and he helped us reconnect. She's been through a lot, but our meeting made me happy. And I think it made her happy, too.*

Inspector: *Was your real reason for traveling there to get her to hack for you?*

William: *What? No.*

Inspector: *To avenge herself and the horrible life they forced her to lead?*

William: *No.*

Inspector: *Fine. We also have information that shows your expertise in identifying vulnerabilities and exploiting them. Given your connections and friendships, it's hard to believe that someone with your background wouldn't have played a role in this heist. I strongly advise you to reconsider your position.*

William: *I can't help you with something I know nothing about, Inspector. I've dedicated myself to self-improvement and finding a fresh path in life. I have no involvement in any criminal activities, including this heist. As Emerson said, "Trust thyself: every heart vibrates to that iron string." I have confidence in my own judgment, and I am following my own path.*

Inspector: *Well, William, I don't really know what that means, but I do hope you're being honest with me. But remember, the truth has a way of catching up with us. Make sure you're on the right side of it.*

William: *"Rather than love, than money, than fame, give me truth." Thoreau said that.*

Inspector: *Thanks for the philosophy lesson. We're done here. For now.*

Instant Ramen

A late autumn evening found Ella in her preferred spot—a quiet corner of a coffee shop in Omaha's Old Market. The warm glow of Edison bulbs cast a gentle light over her workspace as her fingers flew across the keyboard. Her laptop's screen reflected in her dark brown eyes as she concentrated, the faint aroma of coffee and pastries filling the air.

The contrast between her current life and her childhood couldn't have been starker. She had grown up just a few miles from here in a picturesque suburban home, surrounded by caring neighbors and block parties. Her childhood had been filled with piano lessons, soccer practices, and family game nights. Now here she was, using her skills to right wrongs in ways her parents could never have imagined.

As she typed away on her keyboard, flashes of her past flickered in her mind. Sunday morning cartoons in her pajamas, bike rides with her friends, fishing with her dad, and baking cookies with her mom. And yes, cupcakes with William. Those memories felt like they belonged to someone else—a different version of herself that had disappeared long ago.

"Can I get you anything else?" the barista asked softly, respecting the quiet atmosphere of the late hour.

Ella glanced up from her laptop. "Just a refill on my green tea, thanks."

She couldn't help but smile faintly as she returned to her work. The coffee shop staff had grown used to her presence during these late hours, never questioning why someone so young spent her nights staring intently at lines of code.

"You must be some kind of programmer," came a voice from the next table. A guy about her age with a laptop of his own was looking over with what he probably thought was a winning smile. "I'm learning Python at the University. Maybe we could talk code sometime?"

Ella glanced at his screen—a basic coding tutorial website was open. "Thanks, but I'm not the study group type."

"Come on, you're here every night working on something. And I've seen some of the command line stuff you do—it looks way more advanced than my intro class." He started to slide his chair closer.

"If you can see my screen, you're sitting too close," Ella said without looking up, her voice flat. "And I prefer to work alone."

"Geez, just trying to be friendly," he said, returning to his tutorial.

"I get enough friends through my laptop," Ella said under her breath, a small smirk playing at her lips as she dove back into her work.

The truth was, she was hacking into systems that enabled trafficking and exploitation, searching for information that could help make the world a little safer. It was a personal mission, one that consumed her every waking moment.

Her focus remained unbroken as she typed. She could feel the weight of her past pressing down on her, driving her forward. It was a burden she had learned to carry, but one she was determined to use for good.

As midnight approached and the cafe began to empty, Ella continued her work, her resolve unwavering. She knew that somewhere in the digital realm, the key to helping others lay hidden in streams of data. And she wouldn't stop until she found it. With each line of code, she was making a difference, piece by piece.

"We're closing in fifteen minutes," the barista called out gently.

"Thanks," Ella said, beginning to pack up her equipment. She stood, stretching her thin frame and adjusting her oversized sweater. As she stepped out into the cool night air, she thought about her old neighbor William, wondering what he would think of her now.

Ella allowed herself a small smile. She may have lost her innocence along the way, but she had found something far more powerful.

Purpose.

And as she walked home through the cobblestone streets of the Old Market, her steps steady and sure, she knew she would never again be just another face in the crowd.

· · · ● · ● · ● · · ·

Ella, once a wide-eyed, innocent girl from Nebraska, had her world turned upside down in a matter of moments. She was now one of the prized girls in a large sex network. There were boys there, too, but she was one of the top prizes regardless of gender.

Taken from an amusement park in Iowa, she had been gone for two years. She had no hope. They had beaten her down.

"Hey, you. Don't just stand there with that deer-in-the-headlights look," a gruff voice yelled as Ella stood frozen, unsure of where to turn or what to do next.

"Sorry," she mumbled, her dark eyes darting around the dimly lit room filled with leering faces and the pungent stench of sweat mixed with stale smoke. She tried to ignore the gnawing fear that clawed at her insides, attempting to feign an air of confidence.

"Get it together, sweetheart. Time is money," the man said, shoving her forward into the waiting hands of yet another stranger.

Whatever.

Ella buried the growing rage deep within her.

As the days blurred into weeks and then years, Ella's innocence was stripped away, replaced by a steely resolve and an ever-growing determination to escape her captors. She used her sharp wit and sarcastic humor to shield herself from the horrors she endured.

"Wow, you're quite the charmer," she'd quip with a forced smile after enduring another degrading encounter. "But really, don't go feeling too special. I've seen more impressive things in a petting zoo."

She spent five years being treated like an animal. Eventually, she became more confident. And she began doing other jobs for the gang that held her. They noticed her aptitude with computers, so they had her fix them. Then performing other random jobs like updating antivirus software, building firewalls, and so on.

One of her early loves—computers—was back. And it was like riding a bike. The feeling was familiar, comfortable, and a little bit of heaven. There was a sense of relief and familiarity in the pulsing glow of the screen, the sound of hard steel and plastic clicking, the feel of the familiar keyboard and mouse against her hands and fingers.

The gang took her to some of their other sites to do more advanced work for their satellite locations as well. Miami, Phoenix, New York, Dallas, Los Angeles; they took her all over from their base in Chicago. Sure, they still had her seeing their clients for sex, but they had her doing more and more for them computer-wise.

Harnessing her innate talent for hacking, Ella managed to secretly access her captors' computers, gathering valuable information about their operations. She knew her chance to break free would come eventually, and when it did, she wanted to ensure they paid dearly for what they'd done to her.

"Ah, my dear friends," Ella said to herself as she navigated through the traffickers' digital underworld, her fingers flying across the keyboard. "You may have stolen my innocence, but you've also unleashed a beast."

Finally, the opportunity presented itself. In one swift, calculated move, Ella brought their entire operation to a halt. By re-routing or turning off cameras and by introducing malware to override the security system, she could slip out into the night.

She was gone.

"Step One, complete," she said with a wry smile before disappearing into the shadows of the night.

• • • • ● • ● • ● • • •

Now Ella was a far cry from the innocent girl she once was. The scars of her past still lingered, fueling her drive to use her hacking skills for good—or at least, for her own brand of justice.

Ella's fingers flew across the keyboard, the clacking of the keys echoing through the dimly lit motel room. The neon sign outside flashed red and blue lights intermittently, creating a hypnotic effect on the walls. She stared at her laptop screen, the reflection of her gaunt face warped in the monitor as if mocking her anger. She chewed on her bottom lip, her dark eyes narrowed in concentration.

"Gotcha," she said under her breath as lines of code danced across the screen. Another scumbag was about to get what he deserved.

Ella—wearing an ivory cropped crochet tank with rust-colored acid wash smocked shorts and white cowboy boots—leaned back in her chair for a moment, stretching her arms over her head. A faint smile played on her lips as she thought about the impending chaos that would engulf the man's life. It was sweet justice, served with an extra helping of payback.

"Hey, Ella!" came a voice from her laptop speakers. She rolled her eyes before turning her attention to the video call.

"Hey, Zack," she responded, her tone dripping with sarcasm. "What do you want?"

"Nice to see you too," Zack said, feigning hurt. "I just wanted to check up on my favorite hacker vigilante. How's the whole *bringing down evil politicians* thing going?"

"Swimmingly. Just putting the finishing touches on this one now."

"Ah, the anticipation is killing me. You know, I'd offer to help, but I don't think I've quite reached your level of skill yet."

"You got that right. Now, if you don't mind, I've got a career to ruin."

Zack relented and held up his hands in surrender. "Alright, alright. Just remember to take a break every once in a while, okay? You're going to burn yourself out at this rate."

"Thanks, mom," Ella said, rolling her eyes again. "I'll be fine."

"Hey, I'm just looking out for you," as he ended the call.

Ella sighed and rubbed her temples, feeling the weight of exhaustion pressing down on her. A sudden flash of memory hit her—the sound of laughter and the smell of freshly baked cookies filling her childhood home. The contrast between her past and present life was jarring, sending a shiver down her spine.

"Focus, Ella," she said to herself, shaking off the memory. She couldn't afford to dwell on the past when there was still so much work to be done. She turned back to her laptop, determination etched into her face as her fingers resumed their dance across the keyboard.

"Alright, you slimy bastard . . . time to pay the piper."

Ella's current lifestyle was far from glamorous. She lived in a loft in Omaha's Old Market area but traveled to cheap motels in various cities—tonight she was in Chicago—surviving on a diet of instant ramen and coffee. Her only company was her laptop and the occasional video call with her friend Zack, a fellow hacker who shared her passion for justice.

But despite the hardships, Ella wouldn't trade her life for anything else. Each victory against the corrupt and powerful was a balm for her soul, healing the wounds left by her traumatic past. And she would continue to fight, one keystroke at a time, until the world finally saw the change it needed.

"Sweet dreams, Senator," she said as she hit *Enter*, sealing the man's fate. A wicked grin spread across her face as she watched the chaos unfold on her screen.

She was Atlas, carrying the weight of the world on her slender shoulders, and each victory seemed to add another layer of burden.

"Score another one for the good guys."

· · • · • · • · ·

"Hey, Zack," Ella said, her fingers tapping against the keys with impatience, "you still there?"

"Yup, still here, Miss Vengeance. What's next on your hit list?"

"Something big, something that'll make them all squirm," she said, her dark eyes narrowing in determination. "I want them to fear me like a freaking hurricane."

"Any ideas?"

"Maybe . . . but I need time to think." Ella said, running her hands through her raven hair. She imagined herself as a puppet master, pulling strings to topple the mighty from their pedestals, forcing them to dance to her tune.

"Take all the time you need, El."

"Thanks, Zack."

Ella's lips curled into a small smile. She appreciated his support, but there was only so much he could understand. He hadn't lived through the hell she had experienced. Her past clung to her like a serpent, coiling around her neck, threatening to choke the life out of her.

Over time, Ella learned to cope with her traumatic history. She channeled the pain and rage into her digital crusade, striking back at those who perpetuated the suffering of others. It was a delicate dance of fire and ice—her cold logic tempered by the blazing fury of her past.

Ella knew that to continue her quest for justice, she had to evolve, to adapt like a chameleon in the shadows. And so she embraced her dark side, transforming herself into a force to be reckoned with.

As she dove into the digital realm, seeking their next conquest, Ella felt the serpent of her past loosen its grip ever so slightly. The dance continued, but each step forward carried her further from the darkness that had once threatened to consume her.

"Ready, El?" Zack asked, his voice full of anticipation.

She answered, her fingers poised over the keys. "Let's make some waves."

· · · · ● · ● · · · · ·

Ella stood on the rooftop of an abandoned warehouse, the wind teased her hair and the smell of grime almost overwhelming. The city sprawled beneath her, each flickering light representing a potential target. She couldn't help but smile.

"God, I love this view," she said, feeling the thrill of heights and danger course through her veins.

She had been tracking a corrupt CEO in Atlanta who was not only funneling corporate money into personal accounts for his own gain, but he was also dabbling in underage sex arranged through an intermediary in New York. This is the kind of person Ella has been conditioned to hate. She had to act.

Mr. CEO was hosting a charity gala at his Buckhead mansion tonight. The perfect opportunity to make a statement.

"So here's the plan; I will infiltrate the event as a guest, access his private office, and plant some incriminating evidence. Then, I will expose him during his big speech. Simple and sweet."

"Simple, maybe, but definitely not sweet . . . at least not for him."

As she descended from her perch, Ella couldn't help but reflect on her journey. She had found purpose—not only in seeking justice for herself, but for all those who had been wronged by powerful predators. She had become a symbol of hope in a world beset by shadows.

Zack's voice snapped her back to the present. "Still with me, El?"

"Always," she said, before slipping into the night like a specter.

Throughout the evening, Ella moved through the gala, weaving in and out of conversations like a snake slithering through tall grass. She was the embodiment of grace and cunning, her experiences molding her into a formidable force.

"Alright, El," Zack whispered in her ear. "He's about to make his speech. It's showtime."

Ella slipped into the private office, her heartbeat thrumming like a hummingbird's wings. As she planted the evidence on his computer, she couldn't help but revel in the irony of it all: using the tools that had once been used against her to dismantle the lives of those who preyed on the weak. The hack was easy and straightforward.

"Done," she said, her excitement palpable. "It's like there was no security watching over his system at all."

"Excellent! Now, let's bring this bastard down."

As the CEO began his self-congratulatory speech, Ella felt a strange sense of pride swelling within her chest. She knew that tonight's events would send shockwaves through Atlanta.

In that moment, amidst the turmoil and the noise, Ella realized she didn't always need to fight alone. She had found an ally in Zack, someone who understood her desire for vengeance and her need to protect others from suffering the same fate.

"Thank you, Zack," she said, surprising tears welling in her eyes. "Thanks for everything."

"My pleasure, El," he said, his voice warm and comforting. "And let me know when you're ready for another one."

"Oh, I'm ready! Trust me. There's a lot more where that came from."

Interview: Zack

Inspector: *Thank you for agreeing to speak with me, Zack. I understand that you and Ella are friends and have a background in hacking. I wanted to ask you about her involvement in the theft at the CAYA studios that recently took place in California. Are you familiar with this?*

Zack: *Only what I read in the papers.*

Inspector: *Can you shed some light on her role in all of this?*

Zack: *Wait, what? I've known Ella for a while, and we've collaborated on a few projects in the past. But I played no part in this thing. What are you calling it, a 'heist?' Further, I have no knowledge of her involvement.*

Inspector: *Are you certain about that, Zack? We know the two of you are friends. And we have evidence connecting Ella to the hacking of the company's systems, which led to the theft of a significant amount of money and data. It would be helpful if you could provide some insights into her motives or actions during that time.*

Zack: *I understand, Inspector, but I assure you, I have no information regarding Ella's involvement in the heist. Those of us who do freelance computer work have our own networks and collaborations, sure. But we also respect each other's boundaries. With that being said, I can't imagine her being involved in something illegal like this.*

Inspector: *I appreciate your loyalty to your friend, Zack. However, we have sound evidence pointing to Ella's participation. We know she has the expertise to hack into systems and bypass security measures. It's important that we get the full picture here. Is there anything you can tell me about her recent activities or any conversations that might shed light on her potential motives?*

Zack: *Look, Inspector, the last time we worked together was at least six months ago. We text now and then, but we haven't discussed her projects recently.*

Inspector: *Nothing at all about this?*

Zack: *No.*

Inspector: *Did you help her hack in?*

Zack: *No way!*

Inspector: *Did you access their financial data?*

Zack: *Absolutely not?*

Inspector: *Are you sure?*

Zack: *Absolutely. Seriously, I just don't see Ella as someone who would do this, this thing . . . this kind of criminal activity. She's driven by a strong moral compass and a desire to make a positive impact with her skills. If she had any involvement in the heist, I believe there must be some misunderstanding or manipulation at play. I suggest you dig deeper, explore alternative leads, and consider other culprits.*

Inspector: *I hear your concerns, Zack, and I assure you we are conducting a thorough investigation. We value your perspective, and any additional information you can provide could help us uncover the truth. We don't want to jump to conclusions, but the evidence is compelling, and we need to explore all possibilities.*

Zack: *I understand your duty, Inspector, and I'm willing to cooperate to the best of my abilities. However, I genuinely believe that Ella is innocent. If there is any way I can help find the truth or providing further insights, please let me know. But I stand by my conviction that she would not be involved in such actions.*

Inspector: *Thank you, Zack. Again, your loyalty to your friend is commendable, and I appreciate your willingness to cooperate. If we need to follow up with you or require any additional information, we'll be in touch.*

Breathe

The sun dipped low on the horizon, casting a warm glow across the Salem green. A group of squirrels scurried between trees, collecting acorns for winter. Darby glanced at their frantic activity and smirked, thinking about how they mirrored her team's current state. "Nature always finds a way to imitate life, huh?" she thought.

The group had been busy over the past few weeks. There had been a lot of debate about where they should begin planning and then staging this daring venture. Los Angeles was an obvious choice, but Darby quickly ruled that out; their plan involved a great deal of secrecy and the worry was that Tony and Lolita would learn about their plan more easily.

They considered Tommy's place in New York City as well. It had the infrastructure, easy access to transportation, and was near other freelancers if they needed them. But they couldn't be sure how low key they could keep things, as facial recognition gear was installed and in use all over the city.

Even Omaha was an option. Under the radar. Minimal facial recognition cameras. It was the airport that ultimately made their decision. Flights in and out of town proved too big a challenge; Omaha was a medium-sized city with a small-town airport.

Ultimately, they chose William's home in Salem. William is not a Los Angeles player, so the team assumed nobody from the studio would think to have eyes and ears here. It was also close to Boston—good for travel and for letting off steam following late-night planning sessions.

As the team gathered in William's living room, the crackling fireplace cast a warm glow on their faces. Darby paced the room, her brow furrowed in concentration. "Alright, folks," she said, her voice cutting through the pensive silence, "we need to plan our next move."

The crew gathered around William's oak dining table in his charming colonial house near the Salem green. "We needed a secure location to plan this without tipping off Tony and Lolita. So welcome to Salem."

"Good thing William's got this place," Justine chimed in. She leaned against the fireplace mantel, running her fingers across its intricate woodwork. "Feels like we're on the set of *Hocus Pocus* or something."

"Without the witches," William chimed in.

"Exactly," Darby said, her long blonde hair flowing past her shoulders as she nodded. "It's off the grid enough to give us privacy, but close enough to keep an eye on our targets."

"Works for me," said Tommy, sitting back and flipping open a Swiss army knife, absent-mindedly cleaning under his fingernails.

"Great. Let's get down to business." Darby unrolled a map of CAYA's sprawling headquarters on the table. "William and I have worked on this quite a bit . . . here's our plan in a nutshell," Darby smiled, thinking of the scampering squirrels running up and down the uneven brick sidewalk outside, "we are going to wipe away everything they've ever produced—original film recordings, photos, computer files and databases, phone systems, you name it, we're erasing it. Like it never existed."

Justine's eyes welled up with tears. She was part of that history and knew relief will hopefully follow the purge.

Josh leaned forward in his perfectly pressed charcoal suit, reaching for another handful of cashews as he studied the surveillance photos. "I've been thinking," he began, his eyes darting between his teammates, "what if we target their financial infrastructure next? Hit them where it really hurts?"

"You're a step ahead, Josh . . . yes, we're also going to take all their money," Darby said. "This is not exactly blood money, but it's not clean either.

"Justine tells us there are dozens of people—actors and staff—being held there and they can't leave. The studio will say they're just providing housing. But housing that doesn't let you come and go as you please is not free, it's a prison. We're going to get them out.

"After we do all of this, they could just start up again. They may not have the financial resources or the actors or the data. But with the right investors, they could rebrand, pivot, and come out ok," Darby paused again, this time to let this possibility sink in. "So we're also going to ensure that nobody in The Valley, Los Angeles, or even the US wants to work with Tony and Lolita again."

They all stared ahead. Sure, they signed on for this, but when Darby laid it out, it seemed both much more real and much more daunting.

"Sounds ambitious," Tommy remarked, rubbing his stubbled chin. "But . . . I think I like it."

"Of course you do," Darby shot back playfully, twirling a strand of her hair around her finger. "We're going to start with a computer hack that'll cripple their infrastructure and grab all their materials. Then Josh will siphon off their funds, making it look like an inside job."

"Wait, who's handling the hack?" Josh asked, eyebrows raised.

"Still working on that," William offered. "We think we have the right person, and she'll be great. She'll be our linchpin."

"Any other info?" Tommy inquired, crossing his arms.

"Maybe . . ." Darby trailed off, a secretive glint in her eye. "Now, while all this is happening, we'll infiltrate the building and free those being held against their will. Justine, your insider knowledge of the layout will be crucial here."

"Leave it to me," Justine said, smirking. Having her on board with her knowledge of CAYA will be priceless.

"Tommy, you'll handle security. Make sure no one gets in or out without us knowing," Darby said, pointing at Tommy with a determined expression.

"Affirmative," Tommy said, his Cuban accent surfacing as his adrenaline spiked. "I'll keep them locked down tighter than a drum."

"Lastly, William and I will work on ruining Tony and Lolita's reputation. We've got some dirt on them that'll make the headlines sing."

"Can't wait to see their faces when it all comes crashing down," William said; for the briefest of moments, a small smile creeped across his face. But it was just as quickly gone.

"Let's give ourselves two weeks to prep," Darby decided, folding her arms and staring intently at the blueprint. "We need to *get our ducks in a row* before we go in, *guns blazing*."

"Quack, quack," Tommy joked, earning a round of laughter from the group. "Any other idioms you'd like to use, boss?"

Darby tried to stare him down, but she joined in the laughter. "Colloquialism and cliché are my two middle names, I guess. Maybe trope is, too!"

· · · • · • · · ·

The team continued to brainstorm and refine their schemes, each member bringing their unique skills and insights to the table. The mood was light. Almost festive. The occasional joke or moment of laughter broke any remaining tension. They moved around the space, some jotting down notes, others pouring over maps and diagrams, each contributing their unique skills and perspectives to the plan taking shape before them. Even William, the most stoic of the group, allowed himself a small smile as he surveyed his team, pride evident in his gaze. The room buzzed with energy, the weight of their task slowly sinking in.

But Darby knew the stakes were high. Failure was not an option, not when innocent people's lives were on the line. She felt the weight of responsibility heavy on her shoulders, but also the thrill of the challenge. As the meeting wrapped up, the group dispersed to their individual tasks. Darby stayed behind, looking out the window at the peaceful scene outside. The squirrels had disappeared, replaced by the occasional pedestrian strolling to and from the park. She took a deep breath, feeling the crisp autumn air fill her lungs.

Sometime after 2am, Darby stared at the blueprints, compound maps, and charts spread out on William's dining table, a sense of urgency creeping in. She glanced at her empty water glass, its shiny surface lit by the dim light of a single lamp in the otherwise dark room. She liked where the plan was, but she was concerned about Ella. Would she show?

William went on an on about her skills and was certain she would join the team. Darby believed him. But she hadn't met Ella, and Ella wasn't here now when she needed to be. Even if she was the greatest hacker the world had ever seen, time with the team and time with the plan were important. And she was giving none of that.

That was an issue, but it wasn't the only issue. Aside from taking down the innards of the company and the money, the emancipation of the staff being held there was tough. The housing complex was a three-story glass building with no balconies. Each floor had 20 individually locked apartments. There were cameras in each hallway, at every exterior door, and in the common areas like the kitchen, dining area, and fitness center. There was a floor mother on each floor as well. Like college dorm resident assistants, these floor mothers coordinate activities, mentor occasionally, and guide residents to area resources like doctors and agents. But they also combine a nightly 1am curfew with a headcount to be sure all who should be there are. In addition, a pair of guards who walked a path that encircled the building watched the perimeter.

Justine was the wild card here. She spent years as a resident of the compound, so the information she had was proving to be invaluable. But Darby hadn't known her as long as she'd known the others, so she couldn't anticipate how Justine would respond and react to being on the company's campus. Would she break down? Freeze up? Fall apart? Or would she show the strength Darby thought was in there?

And then was the reputation smearing. They had the goods, the dirt, the rumors. But would it stick? She had clients in the past who ran large PR firms, so she understood the involved complexities. The team—she and William, really—were now creating their own PR firm built on both the nasty deeds CAYA had done along with a disinformation campaign to destroy any future prospects its leaders would have.

The documents she stared out were providing no help at this time of the morning. So Darby slipped on black leggings, a black quarter-zip top, and ASICS running shoes; she headed outside for a middle of the night run to Salem Willows Park and Salem Harbor.

· · · · ● · ● · ● · · ·

A week into their planning, Ella finally showed up at William's house.

The team was in the middle of one of their dining room tabletop exercises—this time on the money process and trail their efforts would create—when they heard the side door quietly open and close. They stopped their work to see Ella standing in the kitchen in black Doc Marten boots, a knee length black skirt with white trim at the bottom, and an oversized white Pink Floyd t-shirt with a large v-neck that exposed her left shoulder and white bra. Her face flushed with excitement but no apology, she walked in and past the seated team members. No words, no greetings, no excuses. She went right to the computers and got to work.

"I'm guessing you're Ella. Better late than never, I guess," Darby said, her tone a mix of relief, exasperation, and frustration. "We'll fill you in on everything—"

"No need, I've got it," Ella remarked, her dark eyes shining as much as she allowed them. This is what she loved. What she lived for now. She wanted to say, *I won't let you down*, but her brain wouldn't make those words come out.

The team gradually returned to their banking discussion.

Ella got to work with feverishly fast typing while staring at three separate 27-inch computer monitors. William had gotten her messages and had her requested equipment set up. *Not as good as home, but it will do*, she thought as she began installing encryption tools, virtual private networks (VPNs), firewalls, and antivirus software to mask her actions and safeguard against detection. She routinely relied on a suite of specialized hacking tools and software to carry out her operations effectively. For her, this included penetration testing frameworks, network analyzers, password crackers, and programming languages for scripting and automation.

But that wasn't enough. To conceal her true identity and location, Ella employed anonymity tools such as Tor (The Onion Router) to route her internet traffic through multiple servers, masking her IP address and making it difficult to trace her activities.

She would supplement the local storage solutions with cloud storage services to ensure the safety and availability of critical information. To protect her equipment and data from physical threats, Ella also had William implement measures such as secure access controls, locked cabinets, and surveillance systems to maintain the confidentiality and integrity of her workspace.

While she was far from approachable, they welcomed Ella's presence into their fold, and they all breathed a collective sigh of relief. Darby's sigh was the loudest.

This might work.

· · · ● · ● · ● · · ·

"So Tommy," Darby began, drinking a post-workout recovery aid, "What type of security surveillance measures are we looking at?"

Tommy began:

"Given the size of the operation, we can expect comprehensive security measures throughout the entire area.

"They've stationed two-man guard teams at each access point, and those teams regularly walk the grounds surrounding the building to maintain alertness. Once they move, we have a narrow window of only 45 seconds until they arrive back at the front door."

"This timeframe is tight," Justine offered.

Tommy continued, "The monitoring system, consisting of 127 motion-sensitive 8K cameras, covers the entire area with overlapping fields of vision, ensuring no blind spots exist."

"So we can't hide in the corners," Josh quietly observed.

"Correct. They maintain constant vigilance through continuous surveillance and audio monitoring, resembling a version of Siri on steroids.

"Now, here's where it becomes challenging. They had the doors leading to the dorm constructed with military-grade biometric technology. The only way to open it is through facial and voice recognition. However, only a few specific faces and voices can activate it. Lolita and Tony, of course, plus each of three house mothers and the security shift leaders."

"How can we get one of those voices and facial features?" William asked.

"Let's not get too negative here. I've been working with Ella; we can use advanced deep-fake technology. It's a bit unsettling, but if someone has more than eight images available on the internet, it's possible to create a manipulated video that acts just like them."

The team looked at each other, getting worn out at the level of detail being presented.

"But that's not all. There's a randomly generated 24-digit passcode that changes every ten minutes. This code can only be found on phones given to those I mentioned earlier."

"So not a simple task," Josh signed, standing up to look out the window onto Winter Street.

"Oh, and one more crucial detail," Tommy concluded. "We'll need a thumbprint since the special phones use that, not facial recognition, to unlock them. So if we don't get a thumbprint, accessing the building will be impossible."

· · ● · ● · ● · ● · ·

"Ella . . ." Darby said under her breath as she paced around William's living room. It was 11am. The team had been waiting for over an hour, and their young hacker was nowhere to be found. Again. It was becoming a pattern, one that was causing considerable concern among the group. They needed an update on the accessibility of the banking information. Josh was ready to begin his deep dive into the company's financial infrastructure. He needed to carefully examine their relationships with banks, patterns of transactions, and vulnerabilities. He wanted to look at their cash flow so he could identify weak points in their financial management systems to uncover potential avenues for exploitation. But first, he needed access.

Ella's department.

"Maybe she's just stuck in traffic?" Tommy suggested, only half-seriously. He knew as well as the others how unlikely that was. They'd all heard the rumors of Ella's late-nights in Boston and Providence.

"Traffic? Well it is horrendous, nearly as bad as that in Los Angeles," Justine said, rolling her eyes.

"Guys, let's not jump to conclusions," Josh said, his brow furrowed with concern. "She might be going through something. We should try to be understanding."

"Understanding?" Justine said, folding her arms across his chest. "We're on a tight schedule here, and we need her. If she can't pull it together, then what's the point of having her on the team?"

"Because we care about her," William said, casting a stern glance at Justine. "And because without her, our chances of success drop significantly. But you're right—we need to have a backup plan in case she doesn't pull through."

The team mulled over their options, working out contingency plans and refining their existing schemes. Though they were growing increasingly concerned about Ella's reliability, they couldn't deny the genuine affection they felt for the troubled young woman. They wanted her to succeed—not just for the sake of the mission, but for her own sake as well.

"Alright," Darby said, clapping her hands together as she refocused the group. "Let's work on training one of us to handle the hacking if necessary. It won't be as good as Ella, but it's better than nothing."

"Agreed," Tommy nodded, pulling out his laptop. "I've dabbled in cybersecurity before. I'll start brushing up on my skills."

As the team dove back into their scheming . . .

. . . in walked Ella.

Interview: Big Mike

Inspector: *Thank you for agreeing to speak with me, Mike. I understand that you and Darby are friends and that you workout together, is that correct?*

Big Mike: *Yes. Well, we don't exactly workout together. But yes, I consider us friends.*

Inspector: *Meaning?*

Big Mike: *We're at the gym. Same time. Both working out. But not together.*

Inspector: *I see. I wanted to ask you about her involvement in the theft at the CAYA studios that recently took place across town. Have you come across this?*

Big Mike: *Saw something online.*

Inspector: *Any idea what Darby's role is in all of this?*

Big Mike: *Seriously? We workout at the same place. Chat a bit from time-to-time. She doesn't tell me what she does outside the gym.*

Inspector: *Nothing at all?*

Big Mike: *No.*

Inspector: *Not even a little slip up like, 'I traveled to New England last week?'*

Big Mike: *No.*

Inspector: *Nothing at all about this?*

Big Mike: *No. Look, I like Darby, she's pretty cool. We're what I'd call 'gym friends.' But our personal lives are our own. Nothing more, nothing less.*

Inspector: *Got it. We need to investigate every possibility.*

Big Mike: *I understand, and I'm trying to help. I just don't know anything.*

Inspector: *I understand and I believe you. So thank you, Mike. We'll contact you if we need to follow up with you or require more information.*

Good Gray Poet

M onday mornings can be tough for many people. This day marks a close to the weekend's freedom and more personal pursuits. Dreading Mondays has become common for most in the working world. Not Chloe Jane. Sure, she loved her family and spending the weekends going from one activity to another. Rather, early Monday mornings were a treat for her. Something she looked forward to every week. It was a time to return to a job she loved. And because she arrived before any others—6:15am—the time was peaceful.

Now 42 years old with a husband and two teenage girls at home, Chloe Jane had progressed in the company over the 15 years she'd worked at CAYA. What began as per diem secretarial work ended at her current position at Executive Assistant to both Lolita and Suzanne, Vice President of Human Resources. Lolita was a demanding boss with a tough demeanor, while Suzanne possessed a gentle and compassionate nature; despite the obvious differences, Chloe Jane was unendingly loyal to both of them and they in-turn relied upon her to help organize their days.

An email came to her one day with a resume and cover letter attached. This person—Walter Whitmann—was submitting materials in application for a security position with the company. There was a fair amount of turnover with this team, so Chloe Jane wasn't shocked such a position was open. What was surprising was that the applicant sent the materials to her and didn't use the online application portal. True, the online process had some hiccups, but that's what Suzanne and her team relied upon during the hiring process.

Always wanting to help—she loved her job and her bosses—Chloe Jane opened the email and took a quick glance at the attachments; she noted that Mr. Whitmann had no security experience. There was no chance they'd consider him for such a position.

Normally the job of one of their talent acquisition staff, Chloe Jane, decided not to move Mr. Whitmann forward and sent him a polite rejection letter.

After clicking *send*, Chloe Jane didn't give it another thought and immediately moved onto organizing Suzanne's calendar for the week.

• • ● ● • ● • ● • •

Tony leaned back in his oversized leather chair behind his sleek, clear glass desk. He absently swirled a glass of sparkling mineral water with a twist of lime, an indulgence he insisted on importing from a small Italian spring. His office was a tribute to his success, adorned with gilded frames displaying photos of him shaking hands with powerful individuals from around the world. It had been quiet this afternoon—a silence that was shattered by the information Lolita had just shared with him. She came in wearing her signature outfit: a black crop top showcasing her sculpted abs, paired with tight leather pants. A sly smile parted his lips as he listened to the audio recording she played for him. As he listened, she walked from the front of his desk and confidently strode to the window. Lolita just loved this view. She stood looking out, thinking of their new AI-based film series and how it would be a topic and approach no other production company fully embraced. She remained stoic, but her eyes burned with curiosity.

"Can you believe it?" Lolita said, her spiky blonde hair casting shadows on the concrete floor. "Justine and her friends—who knew she had friends?—think they can take us down."

"How did we get this information?" Tony asked.

"When she left earlier this year, I had a tracking device put into that little bracelet she never takes off."

She described Justine's movements from Los Angeles to Salem to Omaha and back to Salem. "I thought maybe she became obsessed with witches, but something seemed off. I had some friends start to—"

"What friends?"

"You don't want to know. They began tailing her, saw her meet with some others. Quite a diverse group. They performed video and audio surveillance, intercepted some chatter about planning a heist. After she left the area, they tracked their movements from New York to Omaha and now, Salem."

"Interesting choice of locations," Tony said, his voice hardening. "What's their endgame?"

"They're after something that could ruin us," Lolita said, approaching his desk. "Something big enough to bring our entire empire crashing down."

"Ah, the old good vs. evil story. Take out the bad guy," Tony deadpanned, rubbing at the bags under his eyes. "Every hero needs a cause, I suppose."

"This is personal, Tony. It's not just about protecting our business; it's about protecting our legacy. We built this company from nothing, and I won't let a group of wannabe thieves tarnish your name."

Tony set down his water and leaned forward, meeting Lolita's gaze. "We can't underestimate them. We need to know who they are and what they're after. And we need to act fast. What's our plan?"

"I've already sent our team to gather more information. But we need to take a more hands-on approach."

"What do you have in mind?"

Lolita's lips curved into a slight smile. "Simple: we stop them in their tracks. We'll use every resource at our disposal, call in every favor we're owed. Nothing is off the table. I'll have our friends continue monitoring their movements, making sure we have eyes on them at all times."

"Good," Tony said, feeling a surge of confidence. "These fools don't know who they're messing with. Find out their next move and intercept them. No mistakes."

"None," Lolita confirmed. She turned and strode out of the office, heels clacking on the concrete floor, ready to defend the empire they had built together.

Tony sat in his chair, staring at the empty glass. He knew the real reason they were fighting—it was more than just protecting their business. It was about proving that they were still in control, that they hadn't lost their edge. This team seeking revenge, no matter how justified that vengeance might be, would not best them. Tony thought of his father just then. As a teenager, Tony's father—Arash—immigrated to the United States from Iran and settled in Los Angeles near Persian Square in Westwood. He married an American woman while attending UCLA and soon Tony and his two sisters—Sara and Mehri—were born. Arash opened a small Persian market and then a Persian bookstore, both of which remain open today. Arash loved his new country and was happy to work hard to provide for his family.

His father died when Tony was a month shy of his high school graduation. The family was crushed; he was a wonderful father and cared deeply for his wife and children.

Tony worked hard before his father passed away, but he became maniacal after his death. He started a small production company while he attended the prestigious UCLA School of Theater, Film and Television at his father's alma mater. They focused on documentaries at first; movies about old Hollywood, architecturally significant buildings, and people with interesting backgrounds. One of these biographies was of a 50-year-old actress who transitioned from commercials and small TV rolls to adult movies. These movies and her responses intrigued Tony, and he spent several more hours than necessary interviewing this woman. She spoke in glowing terms about the adult film business when she was younger; sure, there was a dark side, but she romanticized it. She loved it and was thrilled to have been a part of its history.

The thought of this encouraged Tony to create a new branch of his young production company. He wrote a screenplay, hired actors, used his regular crew, and made his first pornographic movie, "Two Girls for Every Guy." Distributed on VHS tapes. The movie was a tremendous hit and sold more copies than all his other movies combined.

Three times more.

In one month.

That sealed it for him. Gone were the documentaries he loved. Pornographic movies replaced them. He created a bit of a niche early on by signing actors and actresses to exclusive deals; part of the arrangement was that he would provide housing and medical care for them. His practices and what was then a niche exploded to allow him to become a major player in this space. CAYA was born.

Would his father be proud of his hard work? Would he be proud of what he had built?

· · · · ● · ● · ● · · ·

The door to Chase Harrison's office swung open with a creak, revealing the man himself hunched over his polished mahogany desk, papers strewn about as if he were in the middle of a tornado. An expensive cigar smoldered between his fingers, filling the room with an aromatic haze that seemed fitting for someone of his stature.

"Ah, Tony! Thank you so much for making time to meet with me," Chase said, looking up from his cluttered workspace and flashing a sly grin. "Will Lolita be joining us?"

"You've really made yourself at home here, haven't you, Mr. Harrison?" Tony said, stepping into the room and surveying the chaos with raised eyebrows. "Lolita is working on another matter, so it's just us!"

Chase—along with his company—invested in CAYA. One condition of the investment is that he would join the operations team as a sort of co-CFO. He loved numbers and while his company's due diligence had cleared the studio's books, he wanted to ensure that it continued to run efficiently. Tony quickly agreed. Lolita, however, was skeptical.

"There's something I don't like about him, Tony. His confidence. His bravado," Lolita said during a late-night discussion. "I don't know what it is, but there's something that doesn't feel right."

He heard what she said, but he had already decided. Chase had a brilliant financial mind, much greater than the company's current CFO, who was really just a glorified accountant. It was his charisma, his amiable nature, that really sucked him in. He had a way with people that could not be taught. Tony lived for the sessions he had with Chase. He longed for a mentor for so many years, now he might actually have one. Lolita was a trusted confidante, and he knew she always looked out for him. But he never had a teacher like this.

"Chase, Tony, please call me Chase," he said, puffing out a cloud of smoke. "And yes, I've really enjoyed the time I've been here. You have made me feel welcome. You've also made me feel needed. So thank you."

"What are you up to today, Chase?" asked Tony, trying to ignore the mess on the desk.

"Today's focus is productivity. Staffing and filming both. Can we maximize staff while they're here? Can we adjust the set schedules to film more scenes? Do we need to update equipment to produce higher quality? Can AI help us with editing? Tomorrow I'd like to chat about diversifying some of our investments, but today it's all about efficiencies." He tapped his cigar ash into a crystal ashtray, his eyes twinkling with excitement. "I've become quite . . . active in the CAYA operation, as you might have noticed."

"Active" was an understatement. Chase had been practically living in his office since he'd discovered the potential profit of the operation. His investment had grown tenfold, and so had his obsession.

"Tell me more about AI?"

"What an opportunity! Let's look at just scriptwriting. AI algorithms can analyze large volumes of existing scripts, screenplays, and films to identify patterns, structures, and successful storytelling techniques. I know we generally do this now, but a new data-driven approach can provide insights and suggestions to our writers, helping them refine their scripts and develop variations with current narratives."

Tony nodded along. He knew AI was going to become big. Sure, there were Lolita's AI story ideas, but there were so many other applications as well.

"It can even assist with post-production editing. Tony, AI can automate and enhance various aspects of post-production, including video editing, color grading, and visual effects. With machine learning algorithms, AI can analyze footage, identify the best takes, and assist in seamless editing, resulting in more efficient workflows and improved final outputs."

This was getting too much for Tony.

"Right, well, while you're busy making it rain, we've got a problem," Tony said, changing the subject. "Someone's planning to wipe us off the map—our money, our data, everything."

"Really?" Chase snorted, amused. "And who might this be?"

"We're just beginning to get a fix on them," Tony said, watching as Chase's face morphed from amusement to interest. "But one of them used to be one of our actors. She's teamed up with some others and we know they're planning something. We suspect they want to get into our network."

"But that's pretty secure. I know Lolita sees to all security personally," Chase offered, tapping his fingers on the desk. "What do they hope to achieve?"

"We assume it's revenge," Tony spat, his voice hardening. "The actor left on less than friendly terms, so we suspect her bitterness is driving her to bring us down."

"Ha!" Chase barked out a laugh. "Good luck to them. You've built an empire, and it'll take more than a group of misfits to tear it apart."

"Perhaps," Tony conceded, his expression darkening. "But if there's one thing I've learned in this business, it's never to underestimate your enemies."

"True enough," Chase said, leaning back in his chair with a thoughtful frown. "So what do you propose we do about this little thorn in our side?"

"Simple," Tony said, a wicked gleam in his eye. "We outsmart them. We beat them at their own game."

Tony couldn't help but feel a surge of adrenaline coursing through his veins. It was time to put an end to this threat once and for all, and he was eager to prove that he and Lolita still had what it took to protect their empire.

Challenge accepted Justine.

Chez Tortoni

"What's up with the field trip, William?"

Tommy enjoyed learning as much as anyone, but he was locked and focused on their current plan. He wasn't in the mood for culture right now.

Darby allowed herself a sly smile. She knew their true purpose of the visit before William spoke.

Walking through the museum's main entrance in what is now known as the auxiliary wing, William spoke.

"Who has been here before?" asked William.

No replies.

"Just as I expected. OK, an easier question. Who knows about the heist?"

All their hands shot up.

"Again, no surprise."

Darby described the infamous theft of art from the Isabella Stewart Gardner Museum in Boston over thirty years prior. Thieves posing as police officers gained entry at 1:30am on March 18, 1990, tying up the guards and making off with 13 pieces worth over $500 million. Though authorities never recovered the stolen art, the brazen heist captured the public imagination.

"The early investigation focused heavily on the guards and other museum insiders," William said. "But they never found concrete proof."

Tommy nodded thoughtfully. "So if I'm following you, when we hit the studio in California, at first, they'll suspect inside people like Tony. Or Lolita."

"OK, sure," Justine said. "But so what?"

William was ready. "When that goes nowhere, they'll start looking outside. With the Gardner heist, over time, suspicion shifted to the New England mob and even an international art smuggling ring. The focus never returned to the guards or other Gardner employees because those responsible did nothing to deflect the focus back to those employees. That was their mistake."

"It won't be ours," Darby said, finishing William's point.

· · · ● · ● · ● · ● · ·

They made their way to the Fenway Court building of the museum. Nearly everyone pictures the Fenway Court building when thinking of the Gardner Museum. It is a large, imposing brick structure; inside, four balconied walls surrounded a lush courtyard filled with seasonal displays. This being October, chrysanthemums of all colors were the focus. Though not as dramatic as the springtime Hanging Nasturtiums display, the effect was a beautiful, peaceful place to visit and for quiet contemplation.

They made their way to the Dutch Room on the 2nd floor, where they found several empty frames hanging on the walls. The empty frames were a haunting reminder of the art that was once there. To see the elaborate gold-colored frames hung bare, the effect was dramatic and pointed to the loss that remained.

"The selection of stolen works puzzled police. A couple were quite valuable and rare—like the Rembrandt and the Vermeer—but other works in the museum were even more valuable. The thieves took 13 pieces in total, including, oddly enough, a decorative bronze finial—just an ornamental eagle from the top of a flagpole. These pieces will always be connected to this heist.

"Many thought that if they found one painting, the rest would soon follow. The FBI pursued countless leads: they were buried in Tupperware containers, they were hung in bedrooms, they were stored in warehouses. But as we all know, the art was never found."

The team left the Dutch Room and returned to the first floor. They wound their way through other rooms, including The Blue Room and the Chinese Loggia, before exiting and sitting in Café G's outdoor patio section.

"One last thing before we leave this beautiful place. Are you familiar with String Theory?" asked William to no one in particular.

The blank faces told him no.

"In string theory, the fundamental building blocks of the universe are not particles, but rather tiny, one-dimensional strings. An interaction between these strings occurs as they propagate through space in the cracks we either cannot see or that we ignore. In the spaces between one destination and the next, between sunrise and sunset, between one room and the next, between love and abuse, these strings vibrate imperceptibly, unheard and unseen. Strings then pull all this together.

"The porn industry is like a tangled web of these strings, but if we can find one strand to pull—like CAYA—the whole thing will come undone. We can rip it apart."

***

The crew settled into the large corner booth just inside Champion's Pub's entrance, the worn leather seats creaking beneath them. The brick walls and dim lighting of the Peabody institution created the perfect atmosphere for plotting their next job, though tonight was more about tradition and camaraderie. Sports memorabilia and neon beer signs cast a soft glow over their table as the familiar sounds of clinking glasses and animated conversations filled the cozy space.

"The steak tips here are legendary," William said, not bothering to open his menu as he adjusted his position in the booth. "The marinade is apparently some closely-guarded family secret." Darby rolled her eyes but couldn't hide her smile—William's enthusiasm for local institutions and their histories was oddly endearing. Tommy and Josh were already debating between the buffalo chicken fingers and wings, while Ella sat quietly studying the menu with her usual intensity.

"I don't get why you two always argue about this," Darby said, watching Josh and Tommy's animated discussion. "You're going to order both anyway." Tommy grinned sheepishly while Josh just shrugged, popping a piece of bread into his mouth.

Their server approached with a practiced cheerfulness, notepad ready. "The tips," five voices said almost in unison, causing Justine to laugh. "I'll be different—give me the turkey tips," she said with a wink. "Rebel," Darby muttered under her breath. They ordered a round of drinks—soft drinks and water—and settled into the comfortable rhythm they'd developed over their previous jobs together.

"You know," Josh said, reaching for another piece of bread, "for a crew about to pull off something huge, we sure do spend a lot of time eating."

Tommy snorted. "Says the guy who always has snacks in his pockets."

Ella glanced up from her phone long enough to add, "At least three kinds at all times. I've counted."

When their food arrived, conversation died down as they dug in. The steak tips were indeed everything William had promised—perfectly charred on the outside, tender and flavorful inside. They shared bites of french fries and onion rings, the casual family-style dining belying the complexity of what they were about to undertake.

"Anyone want to trade a few tips for some turkey tips?" Justine asked, eyeing everyone else's plates.

"Should've ordered what everyone else did," Tommy teased, but still slid a few pieces of his steak onto her plate.

"Next time," William said, "I'm ordering two plates. One for me, one for Justine to steal from." The table erupted in quiet laughter, drawing a few curious glances from nearby patrons that they skillfully ignored.

For these moments, they weren't master thieves or vigilantes—they were just friends sharing a meal, finding comfort in each other's company before the chaos that would soon follow. The Red Sox game played quietly on the mounted TVs, providing a perfect backdrop to their easy conversation and comfortable silences.

Arnie the Mason

The sun dipped low in the sky, casting a golden-orange hue across Venice Beach as if Mother Nature herself had applied an Instagram filter. Five bodybuilders—three men, two women—were working out under the still warm sun at the landmark Muscle Beach Venice, an outdoor gym situated along Ocean Front Walk. Tourists and eclectic residents strolled past on the bustling boardwalk, many stopping to watch the athletes train.

There are actually two muscle beaches in California; the older of the two is just over two miles north in Santa Monica. Dubbed the Original Muscle Beach, the Santa Monica outdoor gym has been around since the early 1930s. With parallel bars, rings, and ropes, the Original caters more to gymnastic and acrobatic-type activities.

Muscle Beach Venice is a little newer and perhaps not as popular, but it may be more famous. Bodybuilders like Arnold Schwarzenegger, Franco Columbu, Ed Corney, and Lou Ferrigno helped put the small gym on the map and helped influence its focus on building and sculpting muscles. It's said that they liked to do some of their workouts outdoors as it allowed them to get an allover tan to prep for their bodybuilding shows.

Today, most bodybuilders use spray tan products instead of outdoor tanning. There are several reasons they tan—it evens out skin tone and enhances muscle separation, definition, and shape—but regardless of the reason, a strong tan helps to showcase body size more effectively when competing and may give an edge over other competitors. It was also an excellent way to generate hype for the relatively young sport of bodybuilding. The exercise area is now gated off and beachgoers can watch the lifters while sitting on newly erected bleachers.

A few blocks away from Muscle Beach Venice stood an impressive three-story home, its brown stucco exterior and red-barred windows belying the architectural marvel within. Behind a stucco-covered brick wall—one that Arnold Schwarzenegger himself had helped build during his early days in America—the house revealed its true character: a central courtyard surrounded by industrial-modern design elements, ocean-view windows, and a rooftop terrace. This perfect blend of unassuming exterior and luxurious interior would serve as their forward operating base for the weeks ahead. Not a bad spot.

"Ugh, did someone leave a dead fish here?" Justine asked, scrunching her nose at the pungent mix of saltwater and disuse as the front door creaked open.

"Ah, the sweet smell of success," said Josh, rubbing his hands together in anticipation. "Or maybe it's just that sushi place next door."

"Alright, folks, let's get cracking," Darby said, clapping her hands together. With her hair crafted in a sleek ponytail and simple metallic hair pin, she looked around the house with a critical eye. Despite its impressive bones—the exposed wood beams above and the Italian tile floor beneath them—the space needed some attention after sitting empty. Everyone was here. And they were all ready for this next-to-last step.

"Nothing screams *temporary safe house* like a luxury home that needs a good airing out," Justine said, clearing off the dining room table.

· · · ● · ● · ● · · ·

Despite the salt air and casual setting, Josh's bespoke suit remained immaculate as he paced the room, absently munching on pistachios while reviewing the timeline.

"Guys, I know we're all committed to this plan, but we need to be smart about it," he said, his brow furrowed with concern. "If we're not careful, we could end up on the FBI's radar. They have resources and expertise we can't even begin to imagine."

Ella nodded, her fingers tapping anxiously on her laptop. "Josh is right," she said, her voice low and serious. "I'll route all our communications through encrypted channels and bounce our digital signatures through multiple servers. We can't afford to leave any breadcrumbs for the feds to follow."

"Speaking of that, Ella," Darby began as the team gathered round Ella's workstation, "Will you show us what you've been up to since you've been here?"

Ella came to Venice Beach two days ahead of the team to allow time for her to set up her power computer system. Her three 27inch monitors came to life and their black screens filled with lines of neon green code. Her dark hair braided into two pigtails and wearing a light green button-down shirt over a midriff-revealing white tank and light denim jeans, Ella began, "I cracked the CAYA computer system by combining social engineering, spear phishing, and my personal favorite: good old-fashioned brute force."

"Sounds like my last date," Josh smirked.

For the past few weeks, she used her deep understanding of computer systems and unique skill set to exploit the vulnerabilities of the company's sophisticated infrastructure, by-passing firewalls and encryption layers with uncanny ease.

Sitting in front of her computer each day, her nimble fingers executed intricate commands with lightning speed. Lines of code flowed before her eyes, and she effortlessly navigated through the digital labyrinth that guarded the secrets of CAYA.

Identifying a potential weakness, Ella exploited a known vulnerability in the company's database management system. Using a carefully crafted sequence of commands, she bypassed the intricate web of authentication protocols that guarded the gates of the database.

Typing furiously, she injected custom-crafted SQL queries into the system. With each line of code, she cleverly manipulated the database's logic, tricking it into revealing its closely guarded secrets.

Ella's expertise in data manipulation came to the fore as she skillfully exploited administrative oversights. The access control settings allowed her to elevate her privileges—another flaw in the system's design—granting her unrestricted access to confidential files and information that had long been off limits.

With the database's virtual doors now open to her, Ella navigated its labyrinthine structure with ease. She deftly bypassed additional security layers, bypassing firewalls and intrusion detection systems designed to identify and repel unauthorized access attempts.

Within the vast expanse of the company's database, Ella's search narrowed in on the files and information that held the key to their mission's success. She swiftly located hidden directories and encrypted files, employing her mastery of encryption algorithms to decrypt and extract the valuable data concealed within.

Protected by layers of encryption, the confidential files revealed a trove of incriminating evidence—the dark secrets that the company had fought so hard to keep hidden. Financial records detailing illicit transactions, communication logs exposing connections to criminal networks, and damning evidence of exploitation and abuse came to light under Ella's relentless pursuit.

Her actions went undetected, her presence masked by her expertise in covering her digital tracks. She left no trace of her intrusion, meticulously erasing any evidence of her presence in the system's logs.

Through her exploitation of security loopholes, bypassing complex authentication protocols, and navigating the intricate maze of the database's defenses, she armed the team with crucial information. She became a vital linchpin of the operation, her ability to exploit vulnerabilities, bypass security measures, and extract incriminating evidence showcased the full extent of her brilliance as a hacker. With each keystroke, she wielded her digital prowess; the team forgot their early misgivings and gave her some latitude in how she worked.

"Seriously, Ella, nice work," beamed William as he paced the floor. He even cracked a tiny smile. "As Emerson said, *It is easy in the world to live after the world's opinion; it is easy in solitude to live after our own; but the great man is he who in the midst of the crowd keeps with perfect sweetness the independence of solitude.* You've kept this sweet."

She blushed—no smile—but she appreciated the thought. "Thanks. It's what I do and it's what I've become."

• • • • • • • • • •

There was one other problem they would need to solve. Money. CAYA had vast sums of money. Some in cash, some in cryptocurrency, still more in other assets like paintings. "Team, we need to discuss the issue that none of us have taken on," Josh stated in a serious and collected manner. "We've got a massive amount of money here, and we need to make sure it's untraceable. Ella, tell us what you've got in mind."

Ella leaned forward, her eyes gleaming with excitement. "I've been doing some research," she began, her fingers tapping on the table. "We need to start with the bank transfers—multiple small transactions through a series of shell accounts before we even think about crypto. The trick is making it look like legitimate business."

Josh nodded as he passed a bowl of roasted almonds around the table, his Italian wool suit somehow looking even crisper after hours of planning. A slow grin spread across his face. "I can help with that," he said, his mind already racing with possibilities. "I've got contacts in Switzerland, the Caymans, and Panama. Once we've layered the transfers enough, we can convert some to crypto—but we'll need to be careful about how we eventually cash out. That's where most people get caught."

Tommy's expression darkened in concentration. "That's a good start," he said, his voice gruff. "But we'll need to go further to really obscure the trail. What if we used some funds to purchase untraceable assets, like real estate or artwork? We could use front companies to make the purchases, then sell them later. Old school money laundering still works best for large amounts."

Darby's eyes widened, a slow smile spreading across her face. "That's brilliant," she said, her voice filled with admiration. "And I know just the person who can help us with that. An old friend of mine from my art thief days—he's got the connections and expertise to handle transactions like that without leaving a trace."

As the team continued to discuss and refine their plans, a sense of excitement and purpose filled the air. They knew that laundering such a vast sum of money would be a challenge, but with their combined skills, expertise, and network of contacts, they were confident that they could pull off the impossible and ensure that their hard-won gains would be safe from prying eyes.

• • • • • • • • • •

Night had fallen over the old house, casting the space in a moody chiaroscuro of shadows and lamplight as the team pored over the information Ella had gathered. Justine sat apart from the others, her flaming red hair spilling over her shoulders like blood. Her face, usually a canvas for her cunning and charm, was etched with vulnerability.

"Hey, Justine," Darby said softly, approaching her. "You've been awfully quiet. What's on your mind?"

Justine stared at her hands, as if they held the answer to the question she wasn't sure how to ask. "It's just . . . I never thought I'd be back here, facing this world again."

"What's going on?" Ella asked, setting aside her laptop and joining them.

"Alright," Justine began hesitantly, "but it's not a pretty story. You're all risking every-thing to help me, so you deserve to know the whole truth. Darby, I've told you some of this, but certainly not all." She took a deep breath, steeling herself. "When I was younger, I was desperate for money and fame," her voice cracked, eyes welling with tears as she recounted her painful past. "I started in legitimate acting, but when that didn't work out, I thought porn would be my ticket out of anonymity and teenage angst."

Justine paused to take a drink as the rest of the crew gathered around.

"Once I got in, I realized how wrong I was. They didn't care about me—I was just a piece of meat to them. But I stayed. After working for one company for a couple years, I went independent. That freedom felt amazing—I could choose my roles, my co-stars, set my boundaries. For several years, I thrived. But then the industry started turning its back on me. With no long-term contract, nobody really wanted me."

"That's when CAYA stepped in. Tony promised me everything. He'd help rebuild my career. I'd be able to accept—and reject—any role I chose. I'd be able to help guide the careers of younger actors. This move rejuvenated my career. I wasn't the young starlet anymore, but I became as popular as I'd ever been."

"Then it changed. Lolita—who I had minimal interaction with—demanded that I act in more movies. She required me to perform acts I had never allowed before and I was in movies with subjects I previously spurned."

She paused again, taking a deep breath to steady herself. The memories weighed heavily on her, but she was determined to share her truth. "I tried to leave, but they wouldn't let me," she said, her voice quivering with a mix of anger and sorrow. "They threatened me, blackmailed me, even sent people to hurt me. So they imprisoned me. I'm the reason the living quarters exist there. They built it to keep me—and others like me—there. Sure, they said we could leave, but we couldn't. I felt trapped, like there was no way out of the darkness that surrounded me."

Justine's gaze hardened, her determination shining through her tears. "But now I have a chance to fight back. Because of you," she said, her voice filled with newfound resolve. "With this team and our plan, I can finally reclaim my life and put an end to the suffering they inflicted upon me and countless others. This isn't just about revenge. It's about stopping them from destroying more lives."

Her words echoed with the pain of past experiences and the unwavering determination to seek justice. Justine's desire to begin a new life fueled her motivation to dismantle the industry that had ensnared her. The heist they were about to undertake would not only serve as an act of retribution but also as a steppingstone towards a brighter future, where Justine could pursue her dreams on her own terms.

Darby listened, her eyes full of empathy. "You're strong, Justine. You fought your way out of that hell, and you're standing here with us now. We'll make sure you never have to go back."

"Darby's right," Josh said, his usual smirk replaced by a look of genuine concern. "You've got us now, and we won't let anything happen to you. We're in this together."

Justine looked at her new friends, their faces etched with determination and support. She felt a spark of hope, like a phoenix rising from the ashes of her past.

"Thank you," she said, tears of gratitude filling her eyes. "I don't know what I would do without you guys."

"Hey, no need for tears," Tommy said, trying to lighten the mood. "We're a team, remember? And together, we're going to take down the people who hurt you and make them pay for what they've done."

Josh chimed in, snacking on roasted cashews as his smirk returned. "And when we're done, they'll rue the day they ever crossed Justine and her band of merry misfits."

The laughter that followed was tentative at first but grew stronger as the weight of Justine's story lifted. They knew there was still a long road ahead, but tonight, they stood united by a shared desire for revenge on the porn industry—and a newfound camaraderie that would see them through whatever challenges awaited them.

Running Hills

William paused to take a drink at one of the road's many turnouts. And to catch his breath. It's rare that William's respiratory rate increases this much, but after running over two miles up Rambla Pacifico Road—with its elevation gain of over 1500 feet, an average of over 9% gradient—he allowed himself this break. Along this residential road is the CAYA campus. The complex sits majestically atop the Malibu mountain and offers unobstructed views stretching from Santa Monica Bay, across the iconic Malibu Pier, all the way to Point Dume. Though it is in Malibu and not in the San Fernando Valley, the location allows easy access to the porn film mecca via the PCH, the 10, and the 405.

Though able to talk his way past the guards at the road's lower entrance gate, he knew this would need to be addressed the night of their operation. He ran further up the road and just before the guarded entrance gate to the studio, he found an old shed set back from the road behind a couple of trees and some scrub brush. It did not appear to be in use and likely hadn't been in years. He removed his phone from the armband and took photos of the road, the shed, and the studio gate. He replaced the phone and approached the gate, the running-induced sweat caking a salty residue on his cheeks. The studio guards politely handed him a bottle of water and, after taking a last look at the shed, William began making his way back down the hill.

"Yes," he thought as his quads burned from the run down the long descent, "this shed would work as an ideal place to house our stakeout."

• • • • • • • • • •

When William returned and showered, he gathered the team to discuss the plan in detail. They reviewed the layout of the compound, the security measures in place, and the contingency plans.

"What's our goal here?" asked Justine.

Tommy was waiting for this question. "A few things, really. 1.) We need to gather operational information. Who comes and goes? How are they allowed entry? And exit? Is it something like a garage door opener? Do they need a badge or other identification? How many guards are there? Does that change depending on the time of day or shooting schedule or other circumstances? 2.) We need to identify vulnerabilities. Are the gates fully operational? What about any phones or cameras at the front? Do all guards work with the same set of rules or procedures? Or are some stricter—or less strict—than others? How many guards are there at once? How many different guards rotate through? And 3) We need to see how they treat our specific targets. In other words, are Tony and Lolita granted special access? If so, how does that work?"

Tommy ensures they have all the necessary surveillance equipment, including binoculars, night vision goggles, high-resolution cameras with long-range lenses, and audio recording devices. Ella sets up a secure communication network to share real-time information. While Tommy is the primary team member at the shed, to maintain alertness and prevent fatigue, the team establishes a rotation schedule. Each member takes shifts of a few hours, during which they maintain surveillance and document any unusual activity. They communicate through secure channels and Ella's secure network to update each other. Justine, with her background in deception and disguise, provides the team with different outfits and disguises. They change their appearances periodically to avoid suspicion, posing as maintenance workers, delivery personnel, or even tourists.

While on watch, team members document all incoming and outgoing vehicles, noting license plate numbers, descriptions of occupants, and any unusual behavior. They also monitor security personnel movements and routines. Ella uses her hacking skills to access security camera feeds and disable them temporarily to create blind spots. They use codenames and coded messages to relay information. Ella also monitors security frequencies, intercepting and decrypting relevant conversations.

In the event of an unexpected incident, like a security breach, they have multiple escape routes to withdraw quietly or change their stakeout strategy to avoid detection. Above all else, however, these stakeouts require patience, often involving long hours of waiting. Waiting for the right moment is crucial, and they remain focused on their mission.

• • • ● ● • ● ● • • •

Besides the shed near the compound's entrance, the team placed a Jeep Wrangler near the gate that crossed lower Rambla Pacifico, close to its intersection with the PCH. Though the gate is staffed and operational, it remains open throughout the day, with guards providing minimal scrutiny to those entering.

"We need to watch multiple locations and we need to watch them at the same time. To learn patterns, rhythms. To see if their teams connect with others." Tommy was in his element here. He lived for this. "Josh and Justine, I want you in our Jeep on lower Rambla Pacifica, near the gate. Darby, you and I will take the shed. William, you are going to provide mobile surveillance. I want you running and biking and driving this road. Get a feel for it. Ella is in charge of communications and logging our reports and cataloging the video."

They're practicing simultaneous surveillance, said Tommy. "We want any reference to another person to the other spot at the base of the road."

"How long do we do this?" Darby wanted to know.

With confidence born of experience, Tommy said, "two weeks. Longer would be better, but I don't think we have the time."

• • • ● ● • ● ● • • •

The shed was a derelict building, sun-bleached, unpainted barn wood. The structure—a classic studio dormer shed customized with two double-hung windows facing the road and a door and window facing the shed's property—was surrounded by withering palms and tan-tinted gravel. Despite its worn exterior, the inside was unexpectedly cozy and inviting. Sure, the roof sagged in spots and had at least one leak the team could see, but there was a concrete floor and built-in cabinets that lined one wall.

Tommy and Darby pried open the door for their first full day of watching. The smell of fertilizer lingers on the bare shed floor. At the window, Tommy raises a pair of binoculars. The entrance to the studio's compound dominated his view.

Tommy watched traffic and the people coming and going from the compound: women with kids in strollers walked up and down the road, men in dark green jackets and matching pants coming out with lawn equipment. Trucks and cars pulled up at least four times an hour. Some were obviously carrying deliveries, most of the others had unknown passengers.

"They have two guards out front. With the heavy traffic, they don't hide that the place is more than just someone's home," Tommy radioed his report to Ella as he looked at the stunning late afternoon sun.

Beyond the gate was the driveway—an interior road, really. Extensive Southern California landscaping separated the driveway from the sidewalks. The paved sidewalks were a spidery network of concrete that surrounds and crisscrosses the compound. To the right, just past the gatehouse, was another road that travels down. The gate provided a good view, but they could only see a single building beyond. They knew there were more.

They knew most of this already—Justine's descriptions were quite accurate—but they needed to know more.

• • • ● • ● • • •

A small smile tugged at the corners of Tommy's mouth as he felt a twinge of excitement. His drone had been up to monitor the compound a few times now. They'd piloted it so it circumnavigated—but didn't cross—the borders to prevent detection. Even though it hadn't passed across the interior of the compound, the elevation provided them with a superb view. Tommy watched a box truck's crew as they lifted and maneuvered the heavy, shrink-wrapped plastic bales onto the dollies and carts; even from this height, he could see the sweat glistening on their foreheads in the bright sunlight as they rolled them into the interior of what was obviously a warehouse. He recorded this video and sent it to Ella.

"What do you have?" Darby asked, looking out the window on the far side of the shed.

On the monitor with the drone's video feed, Tommy scanned the loading dock. "Two armed guards are flanking the truck. And each has a shotgun."

He panned and zoomed; in the shade just outside the warehouse's large overhead door, another guard was stationed with a pistol sticking out from the waistband of his jeans. He was sitting in a plastic chair watching something on an iPad.

The walkie talkie app on Tommy's phone came to life. Justine. "A police car with two officers is coming your way."

Darby crossed to the windows overlooking the street. A minute passed and a police car cruised up the hill and turned into the compound's gated driveway. At the gate, they stopped and put down their window. One of the armed guards ambled over to speak to them. Men continued unloading the box truck at the warehouse. After a minute, the police car entered and began a slow tour of the compound. One guard acknowledges them with a salute.

After 10 minutes, the car re-appeared at the gate; the guards opened the gates, waved them through, and both Tommy and Darby watched them drive back down the hill.

Tommy radioed Josh and Justine. "The cops are gone. Move from your current location in case they notice you. Return in 15 minutes. We'll watch to see if they patrol the street and the compound on a schedule."

Tommy sent a message to Ella with the time it took to unload the truck and the time of day the cops drove by on their check-in. He kept watching and counting: two men from the box truck; two guards at the compound's gate; unknown number of guards inside. Justine had described two per building, but Tommy couldn't confirm that.

One guard, the one who waved to the cop, got in a white Ford Bronco and headed out to patrol the neighborhood. Maybe because the cops told him they saw a suspicious parked Jeep near the bottom of the street. Or maybe this was just part of his routine. The studio's crew was alert and connected . . . wired in with their eyes trained on the street and every move covered. Tommy knew that tight teamwork and precision timing would be essential to getting in.

· · · · ● · ● · ● · ● · · ·

Darby needed a break one day, so she headed on a run from the shed up the rest of the Rambla Pacifico hill and past CAYA's front gate. She waved to the guards—who did not wave back—and continued until she reached Hume Road. This was near the area Justine ran to when she escaped the compound those many months ago. She looked south and west, past the small forest of trees and scrub brush to see the rooflines of Tony and Lolita's empire before heading back down. Darby waved to the guards as she passed the gatehouse again and smiled inwardly as she received a reluctant wave from them.

"Oh, how lovely," she thought, her inner voice dripping with sarcasm. "A *warm* welcome from my favorite studio guards. I feel so special."

She kept running, her pace steady and measured, as if she were just out for a casual jog. She glanced back to the gates and the guards surprisingly waved again, their enthusiastic greetings following her down the street.

Thank you, kind sirs, for your unwavering support, she said to herself, resisting the urge to roll her eyes. *Your friendly waves are the highlight of my day. Truly, I'm touched.*

As she rounded the corner, leaving the studio gates behind, Darby couldn't help but chuckle to herself. *I should send them a fruit basket*, she said, her thoughts still laced with sarcasm. *A token of my heartfelt appreciation for their diligent service and warm hospitality.*

She shook her head, focusing her attention back on the task at hand. There would be time for more witty remarks later. Right now, she had a job to do, and she couldn't afford any distractions, even if they came in the form of overly friendly security guards.

She had little to report to Tommy or Ella, but it was nice to get out and have a different perspective of the mountain.

· · · · ● · ● · ● · ● · ·

A guard approached the shed. He examined the tire treads in the dusty asphalt on the road; he looked up at the building and back at the ground as he crouched to read the footprints.

Tommy moved swiftly to the back of the building and out the door. He ran silently down the hill, checking that he had left no footprints, or so he hoped. He found a tree, squatted behind it, and waited. When he heard the young guard enter the shed above, he descended to a tall cluster of coastal scrub. He rolled behind the soft leaves and flattened himself. The plants emitted a stronger fragrance as the wind picked up.

Five minutes later, Tommy heard the man slowly walk to the studio's guard shack.

Tony and Lolita's guards were highly skilled . . . they're cautious and don't ignore the little things. He lied back, knowing that this would be a difficult undertaking, one that would test all of his abilities. But he was fixated on achieving this takedown. For Justine. And for the victory.

Interview: Justine

Inspector: *Good morning, Justine. Let's get straight to the point. Do you deny your involvement in the heist at CAYA?*

Justine: *Inspector, I have no idea what you're talking about. I've been trying to distance myself from that world, and I certainly haven't been involved in any criminal activities.*

Inspector: *Justine, I've seen it all before. The innocent act, the denial. But let's not waste each other's time. We know you were connected to the studio, and the people involved in this heist. It's in your best interest to cooperate and tell me what you know.*

Justine: *I swear, Inspector, I've been trying to move on from that life. I don't have any information about whatever you're talking about, and I certainly didn't take part in it. I heard about it on KTLA, I think. Yes, I still watch the news on tv.*

Inspector: *So you're the one.*

Justine: *Ha ha.*

Inspector: *Anyway, you can keep denying your involvement, but we have evidence that suggests otherwise. Again, we know you were connected to CAYA. And . . .*

Justine: *I worked there, yes, but in our industry, that's common knowledge. But it was only for a few years. That's it.*

Inspector: **. . . and we know you are friends with those who did it. Now, it's up to you to decide whether you want to help us or hinder the investigation.**

Justine: *I get what you're asking. I really do. But I genuinely don't know anything about this thing. I've been trying to rebuild my life and put that dark chapter behind me.*

Inspector: *Justine, the evidence doesn't lie. You were part of that world, and we understand that you—and many other actors—were treated rather poorly. So it's highly unlikely that you didn't have some vendetta. That you didn't have some knowledge of what was going on. I urge you to reconsider your stance and cooperate with us.*

Justine: *I hate them. With an intense, burning passion. I promise you got that right. Spot on. They did things to me you couldn't imagine. Held me hostage. Withheld wages. Emotional abuse that got awfully close to physical. It may have even been physical. They forced me to act much more than I should have been. It was horrible.*

Inspector: *I'm sorry that happened . . .*

Justine: *But I also promise you that beyond telling horror stories of my captivity, Inspector, I have nothing further to offer. I can't wait until that chapter of my life has finished. Until I have truly distanced myself from that world. Until I find that new path forward. I can't help you with your investigation.*

Inspector: *Well, Justine, I hope you find that path. And I hope for your sake that you're telling the truth . . .*

Justine: *Whatever really happened to them . . . whatever was stolen, I can't say I'm sad. I'm not a vindictive person, but I can say that their fall is music to my ears.*

Inspector: *I get it. I do. And I meant it when I wish you well. Just remember, the truth has a way of revealing itself. Don't let it catch up with you.*

Breadcrumbs

The California Scrub Oak tree—trimmed as a bush—and Hollyleaf Cherry tree obscured the small "Cum As You Are" sign as Justine and Tommy pulled up to the studio's main entrance. Justine glanced over at Tommy, her flaming red hair whipping around her face in the breeze, and smirked. "Ready to dive back into the miasma?" she asked, her voice dripping with sarcasm.

"Only if you promise to hold my hand," Tommy joked, his muscular frame barely contained by the tailored suit he wore for his role as Justine's agent. He flashed a grin that would have been charming if it wasn't for the dark edge behind it—an edge that had only grown deeper since his dishonorable discharge from the military.

The rest of the team remained at the Venice Beach house to monitor the situation. Justine and Tommy both had tiny earpieces that allowed two-way communication with each other and the team. Both also had tiny front-facing HD cameras embedded in buttons on their shirts. Instead of Ella's three 27inch monitors, the team was relying on two large wall-mounted 80inch OLED TVs to follow the events.

Stepping out of their car, Justine felt the familiar tug of apprehension in her chest as they approached the door. She knew every filthy secret this place held, and the thought of returning to its grasp sent shivers down her spine.

"Welcome back, Justine! I was so excited to hear of your return!" Lilly, her former house mother, greeted them with a saccharine smile as they entered the lobby of the main building. Her eyes flicked over Tommy, sizing him up like a piece of meat. "And who is this delicious specimen?"

"Meet my new agent, Tommy," Justine said, feigning excitement. "He's going to make me a star. Again."

"Tomás, actually," Tommy corrected, slipping into a flawless Cuban accent as his excitement grew. "It's a pleasure to meet you."

Lilly blushed and led them into the conversation pit for an introductory meeting with Brittany, the head of Talent Relations. They spoke for nearly an hour, giving both personal and business updates, bouncing ideas off each other at a rapid-fire frenzy. Brittany was excited and her big smile showed it.

Her smile turned fake the moment Lolita appeared to greet Justine and Tommy. Her presence immediately put Brittany on edge.

Wearing a black classic wide leg suit pant with pintuck detailing and tan crop top—to show her abs, of course—with no jacket, Lolita shook hands with both Justine and Tommy.

Justine forced a smile, trying to ignore the way Lolita's eyes seemed to linger on Tommy's broad shoulders. "Hello, Lolita. It's been a while."

Lolita's lips curved into a wicked grin. "Yes, it has. But I'm glad you're back. We have big plans for you."

Tommy narrowed his eyes, sensing the tension between the two women. "What kind of plans?"

Lolita's gaze flicked over to him and back to Justine. "Oh, just some exciting projects we want Justine to be a part of. Nothing for you to worry about, Tommy."

Justine could feel the hairs on the back of her neck stand up. She had a feeling that Lolita was up to something, and she didn't trust her one bit.

As the meeting continued, Justine couldn't shake the feeling that something was off. She caught whispers of conversations between Lolita and Brittany, both of whom seemed to be planning something behind her back. Tommy noticed it too, his hand subtly gripping Justine's under the table in a silent show of solidarity.

After what felt like an eternity, the meeting finally ended. Brittany and Lilly led Justine and Tommy back to the building's lobby, both lost in thought.

Tommy said smoothly, his eyes never leaving Brittany. "We'll be in touch about any upcoming projects." He gave Justine a hug. "I will leave you now."

He left the building and drove away. A huge part of him—most of him, really—didn't want to leave Justine with these evildoers, but he knew it was part of the plan. He drove the black Mercedes AMG G-Class SUV—The *G-Wagen*—out the gate and back to Venice Beach.

· · · · ● · ● · ● · · ·

Lilly led Justine down a brightly lit hallway lined with doors on either side; each one concealed a world of depravity. As they walked, Justine couldn't help but notice the way Lilly's hips swayed with practiced sensuality. It made her stomach churn—how many times had she used that same walk to appease the lustful gazes of the men who controlled her life?

"Before we get you settled, Lolita wanted to meet with you again."

They stepped back into the conversation pit. "Lilly, you may leave us now; I will send for you when we have finished."

Lilly's face turned red as she turned and walked away. Not going far as she knew she'd be called right back.

"So welcome back, Justine," Lolita said dryly and completely devoid of emotion. "We're so happy you had a change of heart."

"I knew this is where I belonged. I missed the—"

"Cut the crap, Justine. I know you're not here for movies. I know you're planning to rob us of all we've built. Don't worry, sweetie, we've upgraded our security and our systems. You and your team have no chance to do whatever it is you are going to do. We will be ready for them and will make all of you pay for daring to hurt us. We're too big for you and we know your plan. You and your little team are finished."

Justine's jaw dropped. She sat in silence, staring into the face of her greatest tormentor.

"No, your plan won't work. But you will. For us. We have a new line of movies and you fit the main character perfectly. So settle in, Justine, you're ours until we say you're not. By then, you'll be too old to work anywhere and too worn down to execute any revenge you and your little tribe have in mind."

With that, Lolita strode out of the room and pushed a button as her heels announced her exit. They left Justine to sit and sob. She just made a huge mistake, and her team was walking into a trap.

"Your old room is still available," Lilly said, returning to the conversation pit.

Justine wiped away her tears, her mind racing with thoughts of how to warn her team. She couldn't believe she had fallen right into Lolita's trap. She tried to keep it together as she began walking out of the headquarters building. The walls seemed to close in on her, and every door they passed made her feel sick to her stomach. She knew Lolita was right, that her team was walking into a trap.

Lilly, of course, knew what Lolita could do—heck, she enforced it—but she did not feel sadness for Justine. She actually had a slight gleam in her eye.

She led Justine onto the grounds and to the dorm. Using the facial and voice recognition Justine was all too familiar with, Lilly entered the building. They walked down a long hall, opening a door at the end. "I'm sure you'll find your old room . . . comfortable."

Justine forced a smile as she stepped inside, memories flooding back like a tidal wave. She could almost hear the echo of her own moans and cries in the small, dingy space.

"Before I leave, I'll need your phone. And I'll need to search your body."

Justine handed her the phone and removed her clothes.

Lilly grinned, her gaze lingering on Justine for a moment longer before she closed the door behind her. "God, I hate this place," Justine said to herself, her voice thick with disgust.

Justine paced the confines of her old room, the worn carpet beneath her feet a tangible reminder of her tainted past. "Hey, I'm only here long enough to bring it down," Justine reassured herself. "Josh and Ella are already working on the money and the data. I just need to play my part until everything is set."

• • • ● ● • ● • ● • •

Tommy returned to the Venice home and immediately asked Darby, "You got anything from our resident prodigy?"

"Yep. She just started the takedown."

He recalled the importance of timing here based on a conversation he had two days ago. Ella's job was to cripple the company's data infrastructure, ensuring that they could never rebuild and continue their operations. With meticulous planning, she devised a multi-faceted approach to unleash havoc on their digital realm.

"I've located their data centers—their servers, backups, and cloud storage. Taking down these key elements will throw CAYA into disarray, making recovery nearly impossible. The security measures are on a standalone system, so that will still run when you're there. But neither of us can begin until the other is ready; if one of us jumps the gun, we might tip them off to the plan."

As she texted with Tommy, she was firmly planted at her workstation, executing a series of complex commands and deploying custom-designed malware. She infiltrated their servers, implanting destructive code that would systematically corrupt and erase their data. Like a digital wildfire, the malware spread through the company's networks, obliterating files, wiping out databases, and rendering their systems irreparably damaged.

But Ella didn't stop there. She anticipated the company might have implemented robust backup systems to safeguard their information. To counter this, she targeted their backup servers, employing sophisticated techniques to undermine their redundancy and integrity. She meticulously deleted or corrupted backup files, leaving the company with no viable means of recovering their lost data.

Realizing that the company might still attempt to salvage their operations by relying on cloud-based resources, Ella shifted her focus. She manipulated their cloud infrastructure, systematically deleting crucial data from their virtual storage and rendering it inaccessible.

With each carefully orchestrated move, she dismantled their digital backbone, ensuring that the company would face insurmountable challenges in rebuilding their operations.

To add a final blow, Ella planted digital traces, intentionally leading future investigators to believe that the destruction was an inside job orchestrated by disgruntled employees or rival factions. Remembering William's Isabella Stewart Gardner field trip and lesson, she left a digital trail of breadcrumbs pointing away from the team, deflecting suspicion, and covering their tracks.

Ella's destruction was a symphony of precision and cunning. She left no room for recovery, decimating their digital presence and ensuring that their reign in the porn industry would come to a permanent and irreversible end. Her expertise and determination sealed the fate of the company, leaving behind a hollow shell of what was once a thriving enterprise.

· · · ● · ● · ● · · ·

Josh had been busy, too. He orchestrated a series of calculated moves, his mind focused solely on the success of their audacious plan. With Ella's early help accessing CAYA's accounts and drawing upon his banking expertise, he devised a strategy that would drain their resources and render their operations impotent.

When they first arrived at their Venice house two weeks ago, Josh immersed himself in a thorough analysis of the company's monetary structure, carefully examining their banking relationships, transaction patterns, and vulnerabilities. He spent countless hours tracking money flows, identifying weak points in their accounting systems, and uncovering potential avenues for exploitation.

Armed with this intelligence, over the past several days, Josh began executing a masterful game of economic sleight-of-hand. Employing his industry connections and discreet channels, he orchestrated a series of clandestine transactions designed to empty the company's accounts while leaving a misleading digital trail.

He initiated a complex web of transfers, shifting funds through a labyrinth of offshore accounts, shell companies, and digital currencies. He strategically timed each transaction and meticulously executed them to avoid suspicion and detection.

To further conceal his tracks, Josh employed sophisticated money laundering techniques. He layered transactions, obfuscating the source and destination of funds, making it nearly impossible to trace the money back to its origin.

Throughout this elaborate operation, Josh remained one step ahead of any potential alarm bells that might have alerted the company or law enforcement. He manipulated financial records, creating a mirage of stability and normalcy while siphoning off substantial amounts of capital.

Panic spread within CAYA's financial ranks as the company's accounts dwindled gradually. The company's financial division initially attributed the surprise depletion of funds to internal errors and discrepancies, providing Josh with a crucial window of opportunity to execute the final blow.

In the culmination of his meticulous plan, Josh orchestrated a series of simultaneous withdrawals and transfers, draining the company's remaining resources in a swift and devastating blow. The company's financial infrastructure crumbled under the weight of their financial losses, leaving them teetering on the edge of bankruptcy.

By strategically dismantling the company's financial foundation, Josh effectively rendered them financially crippled and unable to operate. The carefully calculated moves he employed, coupled with his deep understanding of financial systems and his ability to exploit vulnerabilities, resulted in a windfall for the team and dealt a significant blow to the porn movie industry's empire.

Mercedes Sprinter

Justine's heart raced as she peered around the corner of her CAYA room, her flaming red hair contrasting with the shadows that enveloped her. She was ready to begin.

All the resident rooms had locks on them, but there was a single master key that unlocked them all. Lilly had a key, of course. So did Lolita and probably Tony. They needed a key like that to allow easy access, she guessed.

Tony having easy access to her room?

Gross.

Whatever the reason, Justine took advantage of the lock-picking skills Tommy taught her to escape her room and go from room to room, telling the residents of their plan. In two hours, Tommy would return with his security *force* to liberate all of them. They would be free.

Every resident—no exception—was ecstatic. Nobody fell victim to Stockholm syndrome; there was no love lost between residents and captors.

All the residents were women; interestingly, the studio didn't force men to stay. Was there no fear they would leave? Were men expendable? Easily replaced? Did the men not really matter? Were the women the genuine stars?

The women—there were 47 in all—ranged in age from 18 to 61 and they really covered all types of performers. Some were very thin, others were quite large. Some looked to be in high school, while others were obviously grandmothers. Some played kids, others played moms. Some had large breasts, others seemed to have no chest development yet.

Justine learned in her short time that the building under construction next to theirs was intended for two new projects. One involved transgender actors, the other project—if rumors were true—involved underage actors.

Justine was repulsed and angry—not by the transgender actors—but by the thought of children being brought into this world. She was even more motivated to bring this company down. She just couldn't let CAYA destroy kids as they had destroyed her.

Anger aside, all she and the rest of the residents needed to do was wait. This was, of course, draining. The outcome of this emancipation would determine the next steps for all. Given the heightened stress and anxiety that enveloped all of them, time seemed to move more slowly and makes waiting seem longer.

• • • ● • ● • ● • •

The team huddled together, their eyes fixed on the blueprint of the building they were about to infiltrate. The formidable security measures painted a daunting picture, but they were determined to overcome every obstacle and free the residents held against their will. Ex-military operators—*guns for hire*—joined Tommy for the emancipation.

"We have four primary tasks here," said Tommy. "Get past the gate and immobilize the guards. Enter the building while overcoming their computerized security. Get all residents out of the building. Leave."

He stood and reminded all present, "We will not be using guns or knives. If you have those, leave them here. We do not intend to inflict serious physical harm on anyone. We're here to free people. And we'll do it without lethal actions."

Ella let those words sink in, then offered a plan to exploit weaknesses and outsmart the surveillance network. "I can hack into their monitoring system," she stated, her voice filled with confidence. "By gaining control of their 8K cameras, I can manipulate the video feeds, creating temporary blind spots and masking our—your—movements. You'll need precise timing and coordination to take advantage of these gaps in surveillance."

Tommy nodded approvingly. "Once we have our window of opportunity, we'll move swiftly and silently. We'll neutralize each guard team using takedowns, tasers, or tranquilizers to avoid alerting their comrades. With our synchronized actions, we can incapacitate them within seconds, rendering them unable to raise an alarm."

William interjected, "And what about those biometric doors? How can we bypass facial and voice recognition?

Ella's eyes sparkled with determination. "I've developed a sophisticated facial recognition spoofing algorithm and voice modulation technology. We'll create convincing replicas of the authorized personnel's facial features and voices. With those replicas in our possession, we can trick the system into granting us access."

Josh, letting his banking hack work in the background, chimed in from across the room, "We'll need to ensure that the replicas are flawless, down to the smallest detail. We can't afford any suspicion or hesitation from the security system. It must believe that we are the permitted individuals."

• • • ● • ● • ● • •

Tommy and his crew of nine operators traveled to the complex two miles off the PCH in Malibu in five black, long wheelbase Mercedes-Benz Sprinter vans. Each van has four rows behind the driver and passenger and can hold up to 15 passengers.

As they approached the gates of the complex, they saw two guards in a heated discussion with a couple. While they couldn't hear the words being said, they could see that their distraction was in progress.

Darby and William left the Venice house before the crew, drove to Malibu, up the steep Rambla Pacifico, and approached CAYA's front gate. They told the security guards that they wanted access to the land so they could birdwatch. The California Scrub-Jay was a favorite of theirs and the couple learned that the company's land was a haven for this rare bird.

While the California Scrub-Jay isn't actually rare—its population is quite stable and not at risk—the guards didn't know this. They looked at the photos of this blue, white, and grayish bird William was showing. But they refused to let them in.

This request and subsequent conversation between the guards and Darby and William became heated. The two implored the guards to let them in and threatened legal action if such access wasn't allowed. Though they strongly refused to bend their rules, the volatile discussion offered Tommy's crew the perfect distraction. The vans pulled up and the crew immediately went about their tasks.

Tommy and Sabrina, an operator from his days in the Middle East, swiftly moved in to deliver non-lethal takedowns. They incapacitated the guards with expertly executed strikes and holds, while Fran, shooting with a crossbow from the passenger seat of the second van, ensured their immobilization using tranquilizer darts. True, these darts are commonly used to incapacitate animals, but in this case, the team used them to deliver a sedative to the guards.

They returned to the vans and headed to the residential dorm and prepared to enter. Darby and William quickly left the area and returned to Venice.

Ella signaled that she temporarily disabled the cameras' feeds and manipulated the audio monitoring system, creating temporary blind spots and silence within the security network. To do this, she exploited weaknesses in the cameras' firmware, injecting her custom-designed malware that disrupted the communication between the cameras and the central surveillance hub. By having Tommy enter during a brief network maintenance window, she could create a temporary blackout of the cameras' footage and audio data, giving the team precious moments to move undetected.

Weeks before, Tommy and Ella worked on a solution to use deepfake technology to bypass the biometric security system. These algorithms created realistic audio and visual simulations to allow entrance to the dorm. When Tommy escorted Justine to the compound earlier, he covertly recorded Lilly's voice and took several photos during the visit. Ella found a dozen other photos online on the California DMV, Instagram—three accounts, one real, two fake—Facebook, and even TikTok. For someone in such a sensitive position, Lilly wasn't shy about being out there.

With the fabricated facial image in hand, Tommy imitated Lilly's authorized voice and closely matched her biometric profile using a voice modulation device as he approached the dorm's front door.

It worked.

Tommy fooled the system into granting access, and the doors leading to the restricted dorm opened, allowing the team to proceed without raising suspicion.

With practiced precision, the team moved through the building, systematically neutralizing each guard team they encountered. They moved with silent efficiency, their synchronized actions and well-choreographed movements—honed through training and trust—allowed them to swiftly incapacitate the guards within seconds, preventing them from raising an alarm or posing a threat to their mission.

As they progressed deeper into the building, the neutralized guards were discreetly secured and restrained to ensure they would not pose a risk later. The team remained focused and disciplined, knowing that the success of their mission relied on maintaining control and minimizing any potential complications.

The team cleared a path toward their end goal: freeing the residents held against their will. Each team member was at a door, ready to open and begin the evacuation. They waited for Tommy's signal.

Two of the four tasks complete, each operator was thrilled. Their journey was far from over, but it was a perfect start.

Tick Tock

Through a barely visible earpiece, Ella guided Tommy to Justine's room. She was on the second floor, room 24. Knowing the studio would confiscate her phone, Tommy had hidden a tiny tracking chip in Justine's hair clip earlier that day. Ella had the chip's information and could track Justine's movements and positions to within an inch of her location.

Tommy slipped into Justine's room; she threw her arms around him with pure joy. He stood beside her in his best impersonation of a stealthy soldier, though he couldn't help but slip into his Cuban accent as he whispered, "OK, we're in position. Let's do this."

"About time," Justine whispered back, ready to help free the others.

"Go!" Tommy spoke into his earpiece, giving the signal for his operators to move into action. Then, turning back to Justine, he said, "Let's start with this floor—take the north wing while I handle the south."

Justine nodded and moved swiftly down the hallway. Suddenly and all at once, the team members spread throughout the building and began opening doors, quickly explaining the escape plan to the residents before ushering them out. They avoided the front door; if any guards had alerted the CAYA security force, that's the first place they'd check. The meeting place was the gym, which had a door leading directly to the waiting Sprinters.

As they guided more residents to the gym, the tension mounted. Whispers and murmurs grew louder, threatening to alert the security guards. A cacophony of footsteps and panicked voices shattered the silence, and a scene that bordered on pandemonium erupted.

"Whoa, easy there, cowgirl!" Justine called out to a wild-eyed young woman sprinting toward the escape route. "We're trying to avoid an all-out stampede!"

"Sorry," she said as she joined the others, her face flushed with fear and embarrassment.

Are we losing control here? Justine thought to herself, feeling her own panic rise. She glanced over at Tommy, who seemed to choreograph the madness like a conductor guiding an orchestra. *I guess it's just another day in paradise for him.*

"Keep it together, people!" Tommy barked at the frantic residents, his voice strong and steady. "We've come this far, and we will not let a little chaos ruin our great escape!"

"Great escape?" Justine said under her breath. "More like a hot mess express."

Despite the mayhem surrounding them, Justine couldn't help but admire Tommy's focus as he managed the situation with precision. She shook her head, a smile tugging at the corner of her mouth. "Who knew a strip club bouncer could have such a talent for crowd control?"

Scratch that . . . it makes perfect sense.

"Stay sharp, Justine," snapping her out of her thoughts and back to the present. Tommy's eyes never left the tumultuous scene before them. "We're not out of the woods yet."

"Understood, Captain Chaos," she said, her sarcasm thinly veiling the concern that clouded her thoughts. As the last of the residents bounded into the gym, Justine crossed her fingers and prayed they'd all make it out unscathed.

"Let's hope our luck doesn't run out now."

• • • ● • ● • ● • •

With the last of the residents safely escorted from the gym to the Sprinters, Justine and Tommy re-walked the hallways to be sure they had rounded all of them up. Finding no stragglers, they made their way to join them. The adrenaline that had fueled them throughout the confusing scene ebbed, replaced by a cautious optimism. Behind them, the remnants of their grand escape plan lay scattered like confetti after a wild party.

"Is it just me, or does it feel like we're forgetting something?" Justine asked, her eyes darting around the room as if a hidden threat might reveal itself at any moment.

"Relax, Justine," Tommy said, his voice tinged with amusement. "We've got this under control."

"Under control? I wouldn't go that far," she said, her flaming red hair catching the dim light as she shook her head in disbelief. "But hey, at least we didn't burn the place down . . . yet."

As they approached the gym door to freedom, Tommy's hand on the industrial handle, a sudden chill ran down Justine's spine. She thought she heard voices inside, but before she could express her concern, they opened the door and found Lolita and four security guards waiting for them.

"Going somewhere?" Lolita said, her sculpted abs glistening with sweat. She was a haunting sight, her spiky blonde hair casting eerie shadows across her gaunt face.

"Finally joining the party, Lolita . . . how nice of you," Justine said with her heart pounding in her chest. "A bit of a surprise, if I'm being honest. I always suspected you were more of a wallflower."

"Enough chitchat," the security guard said, grabbing Justine's arm with a vice-like grip. "You're not going anywhere."

Justine winced from the pain shooting up her arm. "Tommy, do something!"

"Hey, let her go!" Tommy demanded, taking a step forward, but Lolita quickly blocked his path.

"Try anything, and I'll break her like a twig," she threatened, her eyes devoid of emotion. "Now, just walk away."

"Tommy," Justine said, her voice strained with fear and determination. "Don't let these two ruin our plan. Get them out of here."

"Is this your grand plan?" Lolita asked. "You really think this little escape plan will hurt us? You're delusional. We'll have this place full again in no time."

"Be that as it may," Tommy said, his eyes locked on Justine's. "I'm not leaving without her."

"Fine," Lolita said, "but you'll have to go through me first."

"Bring it on, blondie," Tommy said, his Cuban accent slipping out as he lunged forward.

In the ensuing scuffle, Justine felt the guard's grip loosen ever so slightly. Seizing the opportunity, she kicked him in the shin with all her might, causing him to howl in pain and release her. She stumbled back, watching as Tommy managed to evade Lolita's grasp and sprint toward the exit.

"Go, Tommy!" she shouted, her heart swelling with pride at his resourcefulness. "I'll be ok. Get them out of here!"

"Don't let her leave," Lolita ordered the security guard, her voice venomous. She rushed to the door and saw all five Sprinters leaving.

Returning to the gym, she said to no one in particular, "We'll make sure she regrets ever stepping foot in this place again."

As Lolita began barking orders, Justine steeled herself for whatever fate awaited her. She knew the odds were against her, but she refused to back down. After all, she was a survivor—and survivors never gave up without a fight.

· · ● · ● · ● · ● · ·

"Tick Tock, Justine," Lolita taunted, her emotionless face betraying a flicker of malicious enjoyment. "Your time is running out."

Justine's wrists were bound tightly behind her back, her red hair falling over her eyes as she struggled against the restraints. The room they'd locked her in was dimly lit, casting eerie shadows on the walls. She could feel the cold concrete floor beneath her bare feet, reminding her that escape would not be easy.

"They're not coming back for me," Justine said defiantly, trying to hide the fear creeping into her voice. "They're smarter than that. Our goal was to free those you wrongfully kept here. Those you imprisoned."

"Really?" Lolita said, circling Justine like a predator sizing up its prey. "I think they're just as dumb as you are. And when we find them, all of you will pay for what you tried to do here."

"Good luck with that," Justine said, her voice dripping with sarcasm. "You can't keep us down forever."

"Is that so?" Lolita said, leaving the room and slamming the door shut behind her.

As hours ticked away, Justine's thoughts raced with plans and strategies. If Tommy couldn't make it back, she needed to find her own way out. Her captors had underestimated her before—she wouldn't let them make that mistake again.

Alone in the darkness, Justine's resolve solidified. She braced herself for the worst, her mind racing with thoughts of her team and the uncertain outcome of their heist.

• • • ● • ● • ● • •

Justine sat on the cold, hard floor of the dingy room. The only light came from a single bare bulb hanging from the ceiling, casting eerie shadows on the grimy walls. She had to admit that this wasn't exactly how she'd imagined spending her evening.

"Of all the dark, rat-infested rooms I've been locked in, this one's definitely in the top five," she said to herself. "At least there's no company."

She glanced down at the frayed rope binding her wrists together, sensing an opportunity. With a wry smile, she thought, *Well, it's not like they had time to stop by the hardware store for some quality restraints.*

As Justine worked at the knots, she couldn't help but think about her team and wonder what their plan was. *Were they safe? Did all the actors escape? Would they be able to outsmart their enemies long enough to mount a rescue?*

The sound of approaching footsteps interrupted her thoughts. For a moment, her heart raced with hope—but then she recognized the icy, measured gait of Lolita.

"Ah, the Wicked Witch of the West Coast returns," Justine said, unable to resist a smirk. "What do you want now? To give me decorating tips for my new digs?"

"Your sense of humor is truly admirable," Lolita said, unimpressed. "But it won't save you. Tony has just informed me he's offering a reward for your friend's capture. It's only a matter of time before someone turns him in."

Justine scoffed, refusing to let Lolita see any hint of fear. "You really don't know us, do you? We've got more tricks up our sleeves than a Vegas magician. By the time you find them, they'll all be long gone."

"Keep telling yourself that. In the meantime, I suggest you get comfortable. You're going to be here for a while."

As Lolita left the room and locked the door behind her, Justine returned her attention to the ropes around her wrists. With each twist and tug, she felt the knot loosening ever so slightly.

"Come on, Justine," she said, pushing herself to stay focused. "You've escaped worse situations than this. Just keep your wits about you and trust in your team."

She paused, chuckling darkly at the absurdity of her predicament. "God, if someone had told me a year ago that I'd be breaking out of a porn mogul's secret lair with a ragtag team of misfits, I would've laughed in their face. But here we are."

Stay strong. We're not done yet. Not by a long shot.

Interview: Chloe Jane

Inspector: *Thank you for agreeing to speak with me this morning, Chloe. You worked at CAYA, is that correct?*

Chloe Jane: *It's Chloe Jane. But, yes, I worked there.*

Inspector: *Sorry, Chloe Jane. What was it like to work there?*

Chloe Jane: *I loved it. It was like my home away from home.*

Inspector: *You worked there for quite some time, is that correct?*

Chloe Jane: *Yes, nearly 16 years now. I began there shortly after my oldest daughter was born and never left.*

Inspector: *Have you always done the same thing?*

Chloe Jane: *No, over the years I began doing more and more. The company was wonderful to me.*

Inspector: *And who specifically did you work for?*

Chloe Jane: *Suzanne and Lolita. Suzanne is in charge of Human Resources, Lolita—I'm sure you know—is the COO.*

Inspector: *In this role, did you have access to sensitive data?*

Chloe Jane: *I suppose so, yes.*

Inspector: *Like what?*

Chloe Jane: *Personnel files, strategic initiatives, communications.*

Inspector: *Finances?*

Chloe Jane: *Well, I suppose so, but I never looked at that information.*

Inspector: *Never?*

Chloe Jane: *Not once.*

Inspector: *So you didn't grant someone access to banking and financial data so they could take all the company's money?*

Chloe Jane: *What?!?!? No, I would never do that.*

Inspector: *Did you take the money?*

Chloe Jane: *No way.*

Inspector: *Do you know a 'Walter Whitmann?'*

Chloe Jane: *I don't think so, should I?*

Inspector: *He applied for a security job with CAYA and sent an application that you opened.*

Chloe Jane: *If you say so. I get a lot of emails, but we routed most applications through our online portal. Because I don't really see a lot of applications, I seem to recall a recent resume sent to me, but I don't remember the name.*

Inspector: *It was 'Walter Whitmann.' We were able to reconstruct many of the network connections and files and emails and found this one.*

Chloe Jane: *Ok . . .*

Inspector: *It wasn't a real application for a job. It was actually an elaborate phishing email. When you clicked on the attached resume, you granted hackers access to your system. Specifically, financial and banking information.*

Chloe Jane: *Oh my goodness, I had no idea! Is that how they took all the company's money?*

Inspector: *It is, yes.*

Chloe Jane: *I am shocked. I just don't understand how a resume could do this.*

Inspector: *When 'Walter Whitmann' had his email opened, and the resume reviewed, that set off a cascade of events that ultimately allowed access to the company's systems.*

Chloe Jane: *But how?*

Inspector: *CAYA had their data and finances stored and accessed in two separate locations. We don't yet know how they grabbed the data, but we know about the finances.*

Chloe Jane: *And?*

Inspector: *Well, the team used a blackhat AI tool to—*

Chloe Jane: *Blackhat? AI?*

Inspector: *Criminals who have malicious intentions and break into computer networks are known as blackhat hackers. One of the common tools they use is malware. They release this malware which can lead to file destruction, computer hostage-taking, and theft of personal information. The hackers augment their programming with AI to appear even more convincing. It is so much more effective than what was done years ago with PlayStation or Yahoo.*

Chloe Jane: *But I deleted that email, I think.*

Inspector: *You did. We have a record of that, too.*

Chloe Jane: *Creepy.*

Inspector: *Once you opened the email and clicked on the resume attachment. That's all the team needed to get in. It's not your fault. I looked at the email and had our security experts do the same. It appeared legitimate on its surface. But the team that hacked the computers was good, and this was a sophisticated attack.*

Chloe Jane: (Beginning to sob) *Am I in trouble?*

Inspector: *No, I do not believe you were involved.*

Chloe Jane: *I'm so sorry this happened to Tony and Lolita. Tony was always kind to me and Lolita . . . well, she was tough but treated me with as much respect as she could probably muster.*

Inspector: *Thank you for your honesty, Chloe Jane. Do you think either of those two would have orchestrated this?*

Chloe Jane: *What . . . steal from themselves?*

Inspector: *Yes.*

Chloe Jane: *Why on earth would they do that?*

Inspector: *Insurance fraud because of a false claim.*

Chloe Jane: *People do that?*

Inspector: *Every day. Did you ever hear either of them—or anyone else, for that matter—talk about doing something like this?*

Chloe Jane: *No, never. I wasn't in all their meetings—some, but not all—so I wasn't privy to all they discussed.*

Inspector: *Understood. And I believe you Chloe Jane. What about Lilly?*

Chloe Jane: *I barely ever talked to her. Thankfully, I had no reason to.*

Inspector: *'Thankfully?'*

Chloe Jane: *I didn't care for her. Nasty. Mean. Didn't treat anyone right, except maybe Lolita. Sorry for gossiping, but I'm not the only one who didn't like her. Nobody really did.*

Inspector: *I see. Did she never discuss something like this?*

Chloe Jane: *Never.*

Inspector: *I appreciate your honest, transparent responses, Chloe Jane. We may need to contact you again at a later date, if that's ok.*

Chloe Jane: *Of course, whatever you need.*

Interview: Lilly

Inspector: *Thank you for agreeing to speak with me, Lilly. You worked at CAYA, is that correct?*

Lilly: *Yes.*

Inspector: *What was it like to work there?*

Lilly: *It was a job.*

Inspector: *So you didn't love it?*

Lilly: *It helped me pay the bills.*

Inspector: *I understand. And how long did you work there?*

Lilly: *Oh, ten years, I guess.*

Inspector: *What did you do there?*

Lilly: *I was something like a den mother, I guess.*

Inspector: *'Den mother?'*

Lilly: *Or like a dorm diplomat…floor fairy…house navigator. I guess I helped coordinate and organize the residents.*

Inspector: *At the dorm?*

Lilly: *Yes.*

Inspector: *Did you help Tony and Lolita steal the money?*

Lilly: *No way!*

Inspector: *How about destroying proof of what happened here? Did you help disable and erase all the computers?*

Lilly: *I would have no idea of how to do that, so no.*

Inspector: *You weren't the only 'den mother,' correct?*

Lilly: *No. Each of us had a floor and there were four people in charge of each floor. So three floors, four people each, there were twelve of us.*

Inspector: *Can you explain what that job entailed?*

Lilly: *I thought of it as a den mother, like I said. Or maybe a scout leader. You know, like the boy or girl scouts?—*

Inspector: *Warden?*

Lilly: (Stares ahead blankly)

Lilly: *Whatever. Anyway, I was there to be a mentor. To get the actors what they needed. To be a go-between for the actors and the producers and administrators.*

Inspector: *Did you live there?*

Lilly: *Each of us had a room we could use, but most of us stayed off campus and used our dorm rooms just now and then.*

Inspector: *Have you always done the same thing?*

Lilly: *Basically, yes. I suppose I was the head of all the monitors—that's what we were called.*

Inspector: *Why 'monitor?'*

Lilly: *I don't know. Lolita used that term, and it stuck.*

Inspector: *Is it because you watched their every move?*

Lilly: *Uh . . .*

Inspector: *From calls made to websites surfed to visitors to where they might go?*

Lilly: *Well, you see—*

Inspector: *Just so you know, we have all the records of these things. Logs, recordings, all of it.*

Lilly: *We just wanted to be sure our actors were safe.*

Inspector: *Is that why you locked them in their rooms, and they weren't allowed to leave?*

Lilly: *What? No, no, no. We didn't . . . I mean, they were—*

Inspector: *Lilly, we just want to know what happened.*

Lilly: *We locked the doors and monitored them to protect them. There was nothing else. No other reason. Safety. Yeah . . . safety.*

Inspector: *So they were prisoners.*

Lilly: *No. They weren't prisoners, more like protected guests.*

Inspector: *Who couldn't leave . . .*

Lilly: (Silence.)

Inspector: *And the security guards patrolling the dorm?*

Lilly: *They were there to keep people out. To guard our assets, I mean actors. Our employees.*

Inspector: *Guard?*

Lilly: *Not like that. Kind of like the bouncer at a nightclub. They're there to keep the bad people out.*

Inspector: *And in your 10 years at CAYA, how many illegal entry attempts have you had in the dorm? How many times has someone tried to break in?*

Lilly: *Well, none.*

Inspector: *Let's move on.*

Lilly: *We probably had nobody try to get in **because** of our security. Right?*

Inspector: *Sure Lilly. Moving on . . . did you torture the actors?*

Lilly: *No. We protected them.*

Inspector: *No abuse? No withholding food or medicine?*

Lilly: *Not that I ever saw, no.*

Inspector: *Did you like the actors, Lilly?*

Lilly: *It was my job to help guide them—*

Inspector: *But did you like them?*

Lilly: *Well . . .*

Inspector: *Or were you jealous that they got the attention you wanted?*

Lilly: (Silence.)

Inspector: *I'll assume that's a 'yes.' Who specifically did you work for?*

Lilly: *Lolita.*

Inspector: *Not Tony?*

Lilly: *I suppose ultimately, yes. But Lolita is who I reported to.*

Inspector: *What was she like?*

Lilly: *I'm sure you've heard. She was tough. Fierce.*

Inspector: *Did she treat you well?*

Lilly: *I guess so. She was demanding, but I thought she was fair.*

Inspector: *Did you ever see her abuse the actors? Or anyone else?*

Lilly: *Not that I can think of no.*

Inspector: *Did she ever force actors to act in too many movies?*

Lilly: *Well, some of them did work a lot. And they seemed pretty tired.*

Inspector: *Did you notice anything else about those actors?*

Lilly: *Hmmm . . . I guess they seemed to be in the medical building more than others.*

Inspector: *Any idea why?*

Lilly: *I just assumed they got hurt . . .*

Inspector: *Or they were exhausted from working too much?*

Lilly: (Silence.)

Inspector: *Last couple questions, Lilly. Did you check the IDs of the actors?*

Lilly: *What do you mean?*

Inspector: *You know, names, where they were from, how old they were?*

Lilly: *No, I just used the portfolio given to me by Lolita.*

Inspector: *So the binder of IDs in your room was . . .*

Lilly: (Gasping for air.)

Inspector: *Yes, we know about the binder, Lilly. So I'll get right to it: Were any of the actors underage? Were they all at least 18?*

Lilly: *Um. You see. I mean. I don't know. I guess I didn't look at that part. I just kept the IDs until later. Like until they left.*

Inspector: *Really?*

Lilly: *Yes, really.*

Inspector: *We know that at various times, some actors were underage. Some were quite a bit younger.*

Lilly: (Silence.)

Inspector: *What was the fourth floor for? You mentioned there were three floors of actors, but the building has four floors. What happened up there?*

Lilly: *I . . . I don't know.*

Inspector: *Isn't it true that minors stayed there while they were not filming?*

Lilly: (Silence.)

Inspector: *We know they did, Lilly. If you help us with this, we will go easy on you.*

Lilly: (Sobbing.)

Inspector: *Take your time.*

Lilly: *Yes.*

Inspector: *Yes, to what?*

Lilly: *Yes (sob), there were kids there. Yes, they filmed them.*

Inspector: *How many? In your 10 years, how many minors?*

Lilly: *None for the first five or six years. Then a few would come, stay for a short while, and then leave. Then we'd go months without seeing kids. But it became more frequent lately.*

Inspector: *Go on.*

Lilly: *Up until three months ago, we had at least three minors staying on the fourth floor at all times. They moved in and out. But yes, there were kids staying there. Oh, my . . . I'm so sorry. I knew it was wrong, but I—*

Inspector: *You could have stopped them, Lilly. But you didn't.*

Lilly: *But I didn't.*

Inspector: (Silence.)

Lilly: *What's going to happen now?*

Inspector: *We are going to place you under arrest, Lilly. Your cooperation may help you eventually, but you are going to jail. This is never ok. You and CAYA crossed a line. Kidnapping. False imprisonment. Trafficking. And there's no coming back from that.*

Crisscross Applesauce

In Venice, CA, stands a building that seems plucked from a Gothic fantasy. The El Bordello Alexandra Apartments rises like a fever dream against the California sky, its façade a mesmerizing carnival of mythological excess. The building is painted in bold strokes of midnight blue and sunshine yellow, with ornate golden railings and balconies that seem to float like metallic lace against the dark backdrop. Atop the roof, an eccentric parade of life-sized statues stands sentinel—winged angels brandishing swords, fearsome gargoyles crouched and ready to pounce, and various mythological creatures frozen mid-motion against the coastal sky.

The building's face is a masterwork of controlled chaos. Oval medallions painted with ethereal scenes punctuate the walls, while ornate lanterns cast mysterious shadows across the intricate metalwork. A massive mural depicts a scantily clad warrior-woman astride a dragon, her hair wild in an imaginary wind. Demons lurk in corners while nymphs dance across panels, and a proud centaur rears beneath one of the many baroque balconies. Ivy creeps up one side of the building . . . nature's attempt to join this supernatural revelry.

Once a bordello and heroin den left to decay by an indifferent slumlord, the building has been transformed by a free-spirited couple into something between a haunted mansion and a Renaissance painting. Every inch tells a story, from the devil sculptures grinning at passersby to the classical statues standing guard at the entrance. The result is both beautiful and bizarre—a fever dream rendered in stucco and steel that has become one of Venice's most striking architectural characters, proving that sometimes the most re-markable beauty can rise from the ashes of neglect.

Two blocks away stood the team's Venice Beach house; its brown stucco exterior and red-barred windows masking the sophisticated space within. Behind the historic wall Arnold helped build, the three-story structure stood tall and proud like a sentinel overlooking the waves. Its design masterfully balanced rustic and industrial elements, featuring a large central courtyard with rooms on the upper levels that offered views of the ocean, while hardwood floors and steel accents added a contemporary edge. The spacious interior boasted six bedrooms, a state-of-the-art kitchen, home theater, and an impressive rooftop terrace, perfect for entertaining or simply watching the sunset over the Pacific.

They gathered on that terrace, but they weren't there to admire the view. They weren't done. Yet.

Darby lounged on an outdoor sofa, a small, conflicted grin etched across her face as she toyed with a strand of her ever-changing hair, today styled into an intricate fishtail braid. The adrenaline from their caper still coursed through her veins—$4.6 billion dollars they had collectively taken. Plus, all the data from CAYA's systems was now theirs. She couldn't help but feel a sense of pride in their accomplishment, but the lingering uncertainty surrounding Justine's fate tempered all of that.

"Can you believe we actually pulled this off?" Darby said aloud, her eyes gleaming with a mix of excitement and sadness.

Josh, impeccably groomed as always, leaned against the terrace wall with a bag of oven baked chips in hand. He exhaled slowly, his dark eyes reflecting a mix of satisfaction and concern. "I knew we could do it, but I'd be lying if I said I wasn't worried about what's next," he admitted, taking another bite thoughtfully.

"Speak for yourself," Tommy said. The towering ex-military man paced the deck, his muscular frame casting imposing shadows on the walls. "The money's fine, but we left someone behind. I don't do that. I'm ready to go back now. To take on whatever comes our way. Bring it on!"

Ella sat cross-legged—*crisscross applesauce*—on the floor amidst a sea of electronic devices. The young hacker's eyes were lit up with determination, her mind racing to secure their newfound fortune. As she did this, she scanned the news headlines on a second monitor with growing unease. "Guys, listen to this," she said, her voice strained. "*FBI Cyber Crimes Division Investigating Massive Data Breach at Adult Entertainment Studio.* They're not messing around."

Darby leaned over her shoulder, her face etched with concern. "We knew this was a possibility," she reminded him, her voice low. "That's why we have contingency plans in place. We stay off the grid, avoid any unnecessary risks, and let the heat die down. The FBI may be good, but we're better."

In the corner of the roof deck, William stood near the edge, his gaze fixed on the ocean beyond. The grizzled philosopher shook his head and said something about a marathon, not a sprint, before quoting Thoreau: *The price of anything is the amount of life you exchange for it.*

"William's right," Darby said, her face turning serious. "We've won this battle, but there's a lot more at stake here than just the money. We need to make sure Justine is safe and that Tony and Lolita don't come after us."

A heavy silence settled over the group as they each contemplated the weight of their actions. They had struck a massive blow against CAYA, but their work was far from over.

Darby changed the subject. "We've got a lot to do . . . get Justine back, worry about Tony and Lolita, distract the police and FBI. But our most pressing issue is taking care of the actors we freed from Tony's clutches; they're in the courtyard downstairs. We need to make sure they have everything they need to start fresh. We will give them a way to communicate, as we know their involvement in our plan isn't over yet."

The team headed downstairs and, one by one, warmly greeted each of the freed actors with a genuine smile and a caring embrace. There were tears, there was joy, there was relief, there was hope. Each actor received a new phone and a sincere request from Darby: "Keep this with you for further instructions. We hope you won't return to your previous lives, but there are no guarantees in this world. Just remember that you have a choice now."

With that, the actors slowly left the safety of the beach house, each entering a ride share car that took them to different hotels in nearby Marina del Rey and Santa Monica. This was the first true step on their journeys to rebuild their lives.

Darby turned to face her team, her eyes blazing with a fierce determination. "Alright, everyone. We've got work to do. We need to plan our next move and figuring out how to keep Justine safe. But first, we need to take care of ourselves. Let's all take a moment to decompress and recharge. We'll meet back here in two hours to plan."

With that, the team dispersed, each heading off to their individual rooms to relax and unwind. Josh retreated to the rooftop terrace, where he nibbled on a bowl of pistachios and watched the sun slowly set over the ocean. Ella dove headfirst into her hacking setup, working to secure their newly acquired data. Tommy hit the home gym, his muscles rippling as he pushed himself to the limit, channeling his anger and frustration into his workout. William retreated to his room, where he sat on the floor with one leg tucked under him, meditating and reflecting on the events of the day. And Darby, ever the leader, retired to the central courtyard where she sat, her eyes closed in meditation, her mind clearing itself and preparing for what was to come.

As the sun set over Venice Beach, the El Bordello Alexandra Apartments stood tall and proud, an architectural marvel that had seen its fair share of history and strife. But tonight, it was a sentinel, a protector for those the world had left behind. And as the team gathered once more, their spirits renewed and their resolve unbroken, they knew they would stop at nothing to see their mission through to the end.

• • • • ● • ● • • •

Tony paced the concrete floor of his office, his eyes darting from the desktop monitors to the darkness outside. The air was heavy, and it felt like a suffocating shroud around him. He clenched his fists, feeling the weight of defeat bearing down on him. Lolita stood in the corner, her icy demeanor unbroken despite the chaos that surrounded them.

"Damn it," Tony said, running a hand through his thinning hair. "All our data, our movies, our financial resources . . . gone. Nothing on our servers here. They cleaned out the backups. Our clouds of data are empty. Our bank accounts are empty. They got it all, Lolita. All of it. How on earth could such a small team . . . a team we've been trailing and monitoring for weeks . . . how could they do this?"

"It seems our adversaries were thorough in their attack," Lolita acknowledged, her voice a monotone as always, but with the slightest hint of defeat.

Security—and following this team—was her department. But she took no responsibility for any failures. She'd be damned if this fell on her. No, this was a cunning group of misfits who got lucky. Very lucky. And she would not take the blame.

"Thorough?" Tony snorted. "This is a freaking massacre."

Chase Harrison, their new financial associate and sometimes fixer, sauntered into the room with the nonchalance of someone who had seen it all before. He had been in contact with the IT team about the wreckage and raised an eyebrow. "Well, this isn't looking too good, is it?"

"Fantastic observation, Chase. I hadn't noticed."

"Hey, now . . . don't take out your anger on me. I'm just the messenger. I'm just saying, it's not the end of the world. We can bounce back from this."

"Can we, though? They've crippled us, Chase. How are we supposed to recover from this?"

"By doing what we do best," Chase said, a sly grin spreading across his face. "Making entertainment."

"Really? Just like that?"

"Maybe not *just like that*," Chase admitted, "but we can come up with a plan. A slow start, but we'll rebuild. You've got the connections, I've got the resources, and Lolita here,"—he gestured towards her—"has the unyielding determination of a cyborg."

"Flattering," Lolita deadpanned, though she seemed to appreciate the sentiment.

They headed out to the conversation pit, each grabbing a drink to sustain them. Coffee for Chase, seltzer for Lolita, green tea for Tony.

In years long since passed, Chinese scholars gathered in conversation pits to debate philosophy and literature. In medieval Spain, nobles gathered on cushioned benches set into the floor to eat and drink. But it wasn't until the 1950s and 60s that the modern iteration of the conversation pit was popularized, with plush rugs and comfortable cushions filling the sunken living spaces.

The 1970s saw the conversation pit reach its heyday, with people of all ages embracing the concept. But a decade later, the appeal had worn off—busy families found it impractical to navigate around, while others just thought the style just looked too dated.

But not here. Though populated with buildings and rooms others could only dream of, the conversation pit at CAYA really was the driving feature of the compound. Sure, it was retro. The ability to have a comfortable, central gathering place to discuss business and strategy was paramount. For Tony, it always felt like home and even in tough times, he looked forward to retreating here.

"Alright," Tony said, his resolve strengthening. "Let's brainstorm. If we're going to *bounce back*, as you put it, we'll need new talent, we may need new equipment, and most importantly, we need to get back at those bastards who did this to us."

"Agreed," Chase said, putting a foot up on the coffee table. "But first things first, we need to fund this. Without that, everything else is nearly impossible. We could look for investors, but without the catalog of movies and other active revenue streams, attracting quality money that way will be difficult at best."

Out of nowhere, Tony slammed his fist on the table, causing Lolita and Chase to flinch. "We need to act fast," he said, his face flushed with anger, frustration, and a hint of despair. "We can't let this setback destroy everything we've built."

Lolita crossed the room to the window, her heels clicking on the polished floor. She gazed out at the city below, her mind racing with possibilities. "You know we still have our contacts, our resources," she said, her voice cool and calculating. "We can leverage those to get back on our feet."

Chase leaned back in his chair, his fingers steepled under his chin. "And let's not forget the insurance payout," he said, a sly grin playing on his lips. "That'll give us a nice cushion to work with."

Tony began to pace, his hands clasped behind his back. "But we'll need more than just money," he argued, his brow furrowed in concentration. "We need to rebuild our reputation, our brand. Show the world that we're not so easily defeated."

Lolita turned from the window, her eyes narrowing. "I have a few ideas on that front," she said, her voice dripping with determination. "But first, we need to secure new talent, new locations. I'll make some calls."

As the three continued to plan and strategize, the tension in the room grew more palpable, the weight of their shared history and uncertain future hanging heavy in the air. They moved around the space, Tony pouring himself a drink, Lolita scribbling furiously on a notepad, Chase studying the documents spread before him, each working in their own way to salvage what remained of their once-powerful empire.

· · · ● · ● · ● · · ·

Following an hour of brainstorming, Tony and Lolita shared a knowing glance and nodded in agreement, their actions barely noticeable. "Chase," said Lolita, "let's meet in the data center in 15 minutes. There's something we want to discuss with you and we feel that's a better place to do it."

Chase was unsure what to make of this.

Why couldn't we discuss it here? Most important decisions were talked out here. Should I be worried?

· · · ● · ● · ● · · ·

They found a large table in one of the underground data center's glassed-in conference rooms. At 3am, they all knew they should wait until the sun rose again to begin a more thoughtful discussion and plan. The adrenaline remained high, however, so they all wanted to start immediately. They were livid at what they had lost and how they lost it. Their systems let them down. Their people let them down. There would be time to address failures later. Now was the time to return to what they knew best.

Tony leaned back in his chair, a wry smile etched across his face. "You know, it's funny. All this time we thought Justine was just another pretty face, but she turned out to be so much more."

Chase raised an eyebrow, intrigued by the sudden shift in conversation. "What do you mean?"

"Think about it," Tony said, his voice tinged with equal parts admiration and frustration. "She was our top actress for years. Her ability to . . . how should I put it? Throw herself into her roles was unmatched. She brought in more money than any other performer. Her earliest roles were playing teens. We even had her in fake braces for a couple of movies. She moved on to mainstream movies and eventually started dabbling in some of our titles featuring older actors. And now,"—he clenched his fists, suddenly angry—"now she's colluded with this group of . . . of . . . thieves. Dirty little petty thieves!"

"Her talents were undeniable," Lolita chimed in, her sculpted abs on full display as she crossed her arms. "But she wasn't just a performer; she had a mind for strategy. She knew how to play the game, and she played it well."

"And she played us," Tony said, nodding emphatically. "But we have her back now."

Chase looked at them, shocked to hear this. He thought she had escaped with the other actors.

"Yes, Chase, we have her. I grabbed her and held her so she could watch her little friends leave without her. Desert her. Abandon her. She's all alone. Locked in an unused office in the HQ building. We can chat with her later about our plans for her. So we have a start. She will be our start."

Lolita paused to let this sink in for Chase. A growing sense of unease washed over him. He didn't sign up for kidnapping. Sometimes his face gave him away, but he hoped he held in his true feelings. Until now, he had skillfully hidden this—and more. Chase knew he couldn't afford a misstep now. Not when he had come so far.

"Speaking of which," Lolita said, changing the subject. "We should probably let you in on our other little secret. You know, the one behind that door."

She pointed to the black steel barn door on the wall just outside the conference room. Chase recalled seeing it during an early tour and when he asked about it, they shut him down. His mind was spinning. First, they kidnapped Justine, and she's being held on their campus? Now there was another surprise? A secret? Behind a door? Chase had trouble processing all of this.

"Ah, yes," Tony grinned, casting a sidelong glance at Chase. "Our ace in the hole, so to speak."

"Alright, you've got my attention," Chase admitted, trying to regroup, but his curiosity piqued. "What's behind this enormous steel door?"

"Only the most valuable part of our entire operation," Tony said, his voice low and conspiratorial.

"Well, most valuable now," Lolita said, knowing the destruction of their data represented billions lost.

"Right. Well, it's a vault filled with all sorts of goodies," he paused, savoring the moment as best he could. "And the best part is, they,"—Tony gestured vaguely toward their unseen enemies—"didn't know about it."

"Goodies?" Chase inquired.

"In that room, er, vault," answered Lolita, "is our only refuge now. We have jewels . . . including a rather enormous diamond. We have some artwork. Gold. And we have some cash. If we count everything—and I do every week—we have nearly $10 million worth of items stored in that vault. We even have a dozen of our early movie masters. The originals. We're not as down as we could've been."

He and his investment group did not know about this cache. It may have changed the terms of their agreement. But this wasn't the time to bring this up. That would come later. Their foresight impressed Chase.

"Very clever. What should we do with this hidden stash?"

"Simple," Tony said, a wicked gleam in his eye. "We use it to rebuild and get our revenge."

• • • ● • ● • ● • •

The massive steel door to the vault slid open with a heavy groan, revealing the dazzling fortune that lay within. Chase couldn't help but gawk at the stacks of gold bars, cash bricks wrapped in plastic on the floor, the overly large diamond, and exquisite artwork lining the walls. The room even had a small couch facing a flat panel tv; next to the tv was a floating shelf with several items that appeared to be VHS tapes from this distance. It was as if he had stumbled upon the treasure trove of a modern-day pirate.

"Ten million dollars' worth of assets," Tony bragged, barely suppressing a grin. "All ours to play with."

"Wow," Chase said, his eyes wide as he took in the scene. "I always knew CAYA was ahead of the curve, and this is further proof of your brilliance."

"Isn't it?" Lolita chimed in, her tone almost flirtatious. "With this kind of capital, we can rebuild faster than they ever thought possible."

"Exactly," Tony said, regaining his focus.

"What's with the tv over there?" asked Chase.

"Those tapes on the shelf are the original recordings of our first 12 movies. I come down here now and then and watch them. Just to remind me of where we came from." Tony was clearly nostalgic and proud.

"So if we are to bounce back, what are your thoughts? You've answered my money question. But we need actors—though I guess you have one." A shadow of doubt had fallen on Chase's earlier, bright hope.

"We'll start by checking our equipment and acquiring new things as needed. Aside from Justine, we'll start scouting fresh talent—that isn't usually an issue," Tony began.

"Speaking of which,"—Lolita said, an idea forming in her mind—"we should implement some . . . insurance policies for our new stars. We wouldn't want another situation like tonight on our hands, now, would we?"

"Good thinking," Tony nodded, his expression turning shrewd. "We'll make sure they understand just how much they stand to lose if they decide to *go rogue*."

"Way to keep it light, Tony," Chase said under his breath, rolling his eyes. "But seriously, we've got to make movies again. The longer we wait, the more ground we're losing."

"Agreed," Tony said, clapping his hands together with finality. "We'll start immediately with no time to rest. New scripts, new actors, new everything. And,"—he glanced around the vault, a wicked smile playing on his lips—"we've got the means to do it."

"Let's get to work then. We'll meet in the HQ conversation pit at noon. We'll gather our IT, writing, filming, and security teams to begin a true inventory of what we've lost and what—and who—we need," Lolita said, her icy demeanor returning as she led the way out of the vault. "Time is money, after all."

Interview: Darby

Inspector: *Good to see you, Darby. Long time no see.*

Darby: *Inspector. Did those test scores finally lead you back to me? I'm retired from academic consulting, but I would have made an exception for you.*

Inspector: *I . . . well . . . uh . . . anyway, let's get straight to the point. Did you have any involvement in the heist targeting CAYA?*

Darby: *I miss grading papers too. Look, Inspector, I don't know what you're talking about. Besides what I read online, I have no idea what happened at CAYA. I'm just a regular person trying to live my life.*

Inspector: *Darby, let's cut the games. You've always been good at working systems—whether it's university databases or security protocols. We know you were at the scene of the crime, and we have evidence that suggests your direct involvement. Now, I'm giving you a chance to come clean and tell me what you know.*

Darby: *I'm telling you, Inspector, I have nothing to do with it. Those days of helping students are long behind me. I don't know what evidence you have, but I'm innocent. I'm retired, working on opening a small business.*

Inspector: *Innocent? That's a strong word, Darby. But here's what I think. You were part of a team, carefully orchestrated and skilled in executing this heist. You have knowledge that can help us solve this case. Now, do you really want to deny your involvement and face the consequences?*

Darby: *I don't know what you want me to say. I'm not involved in any heist, and I don't have any information to offer you.*

Inspector: *Darby, I've seen people like you before, claiming innocence until the evidence becomes undeniable. Let me remind you we have a responsibility to bring justice to those involved, and if you continue to withhold information, you'll find yourself on the wrong side of the law.*

Darby: *Look, Inspector, I understand your position, but I'm telling you the truth. I had nothing to do with it. I read they did some awful things there.*

Inspector: *They did, yes.*

Darby: *Porn is what it is; but I heard they held people captive.*

Inspector: *That appears to be a possibility, yes.*

Darby: *And kids, inspector, I heard that underage kids—KIDS!—were involved.*

Inspector: *Unfortunately, we're looking into that, too.*

Darby: *Seriously . . . lots of bad stuff happened to some rotten people, and you're questioning me?*

Inspector: *I know Darby. Look, you and I were, well, business associates—if not friends. I'm asking as someone who knows you. What went down?*

Darby: *All I know is what I heard . . .*

Inspector: *Which is?*

Darby: *I heard a crew from out-of-town came in and took all their data. And took all their money. Wiped them out is what I heard.*

Inspector: *Yes, that was mostly in the news, but how?*

Darby: *Oh, and they helped free dozens of women held against their will. That wasn't in the papers, was it? And neither was the pedophilia.*

Inspector: *No. The media glossed over that.*

Darby: *Are they being paid off?*

Inspector: *The media? It would appear so yes.*

Darby: *They can't get away with this, can they? The money may be gone, but they can re-start, can't they?*

Inspector: *I can't comment on that.*

Darby: *Of course not. Look, I don't know how it happened, but whatever happened to them, I'd say they got what they deserved.*

Inspector: *Let me be direct here, Darby. Did you or any of your associates plot to steal money from CAYA studios?*

Darby: *No.*

Inspector: *Did you or any of your associates hijack their computer systems?*

Darby: *No.*

Inspector: *Did you or any of your associates break into the studio's compound to emancipate staff held against their will?*

Darby: *I wish I could take credit for that, but no.*

Inspector: *Is there anything you can offer here, Darby?*

Darby: *As I said, Inspector, I didn't do this. I have heard rumors that the leaders of the company hired some people to make it appear to be what you have called it—a heist . . .*

Inspector: *Go on . . .*

Darby: *But those same rumors point to one of the c-suite—someone named Lolita?—as being the ringleader of this theft.*

Inspector: *And where did you hear all this?*

Darby: *Oh, I can't say for sure . . . here and there, I guess.*

Inspector: *Fine. For now I'll let you stick to your story. But remember, the truth has a way of coming out. Like you, I hope they go down. It's only a matter of time. And I hope you stay clean. Keep that in mind, Darby.*

Darby: *Thanks . . . 'Inspector.'*

Conversation Pit

"Tony, we'd like to meet with you and Lolita at the headquarters of CAYA," William said over the phone, his gruff voice betraying a hint of amusement. "It's time we had a chat."

"Fine. Tomorrow, 3 PM sharp," Tony said, hanging up without another word.

"Was that our favorite porn mogul?" Darby asked. William rolled his eyes but nodded in affirmation, unable to suppress a smile.

"Meeting set for tomorrow." He quoted Emerson to her, *For everything you have missed, you have gained something else*, before heading out for his daily run.

• • • • ● • ● • ● • •

The next day, as they entered the lavish CAYA headquarters, William and Darby couldn't help but marvel at the understated beauty of their surroundings. The mid-century modern esthetic, when used properly, is stunning. In this building, the vibe was perfect.

"Nice place," William said. "I guess nothing says high-class like brick walls and wood paneling."

Darby smirked, adjusting her hair, which she styled into a sleek ponytail for the occasion. She knew her height would unnerve Tony, and she wanted to use it to her advantage.

"Welcome," Tony greeted them with a false smile as he led them into the main room, where the centerpiece was the conversation pit. The intimate setting was perfect for the discussion at hand.

"Take a seat," Tony gestured towards the pit. Lolita stood silently beside him, her emotionless expression and sculpted abs on full display. Her imposing figure loomed over the group as they descended into the sunken area.

"Cozy," Darby remarked, settling into one of the plush seats. William sat beside her, silently observing the room as he thought about the next few minutes. "You know, Tony," she said, "Your office has a certain . . . decadence that I didn't expect."

"Compliments will get you everywhere, my dear," Tony said, his voice dripping with sarcasm. "Now, what is it you wanted to discuss?"

"Ah, straight to business," Darby grinned. "We'll get to that soon enough," she said, glancing over at William, who gave her a knowing nod.

"Very well," Tony said, leaning back in his seat, trying to maintain an air of indifference despite the uneasiness creeping up on him.

"Before we begin," William interjected, "I'd like to share a quote by Seneca" He paused for dramatic effect, "*The greatest wealth is contentment with a little*" His eyes locked onto Tony's, clearly sending a message.

"Are we here for a philosophy lesson or a meeting?" Lolita said, breaking her stoic silence.

"Both," Darby said with a mischievous grin, her blue eyes sparkling with determination. The atmosphere in the conversation pit grew tense, and the stakes were higher than ever before.

"Get to the point," Lolita said, her sculpted abs tense beneath her tight clothing. She radiated menace, like a coiled snake poised to strike.

"Fine," William said, his gruff exterior momentarily slipping as he met Tony's eyes. "We're here to discuss the future of CAYA."

It was time for the proper game to begin.

Darby leaned forward in her seat with a confident smirk. "Tony, Lolita, your little empire is done. Finished. Kaput."

William chimed in, his voice calm and steady. "We've taken all your data, emptied your accounts, and freed your actors. You can't make movies anymore."

Lolita sneered, her emotionless façade wavering for the first time since they entered the room. "And how, out of professional curiosity, did you manage that?"

"Trade secret," Darby said with a wink, enjoying the shock that registered on Lolita's face. "But your days of peddling smut are over."

"Or perhaps more like an insidious weed that can't be eradicated," William said, his mind wandering back to a particularly stubborn dandelion he'd encountered during one of his many runs.

"Fine, if you want to underestimate us," Lolita interjected, her spiky hair seeming to bristle with indignation, "go ahead. But once we rebuild, we will hunt down every single member of your pathetic team and take back what's ours. Then we'll destroy you all. Just remember, you asked for this."

"Charming," Darby said under her breath, unfazed by the threats. She glanced over at William, who simply sat there confidently, as if he had already won.

"Remember," William said, leaning in closer to Tony, "Seneca also wrote, *Difficulties strengthen the mind, as labor does the body.* We're not afraid of your threats. We've been through worse." He straightened up, his voice hardening. "And we will not back down."

Silence hung heavy in the conversation pit as Tony and Lolita exchanged glances, their confidence perhaps a bit shaken by the unwavering determination of their adversaries.

"Consider this" Darby said, her voice soft but filled with steel, "a turning point" She locked eyes with Tony, noting the flicker of uncertainty that crossed his face before his arrogance returned.

"Fine," Tony said, "You've had your say" He gestured dismissively towards the door, "Now get out."

"In a moment. There's one last thing—a missing piece, if you will—we'd like to mention before leaving."

Just as the tension in the room reached a boiling point, the side door creaked open. Chase Harrison—exuding an air of nonchalance that was almost palpably at odds with the situation; his dark hair and designer suit gave him an air of sophistication, and his eyes sparkled with mischief—stepped into the conversation pit, his eyes scanning the tense faces around him. Justine followed closely behind, her flaming red hair like a beacon amidst the shadows. Her gaze was steady, but there was an unmistakable hint of trepidation in her eyes.

"Sorry we're late," Chase said with a simple grin, breaking the silence.

"Ah, here's our missing piece now," William said under his breath, a wry smile playing on his lips.

"Sorry to interrupt this delightful exchange," Chase said, surveying the sunken seating area with a raised eyebrow. "But I think it's time we skedaddle, don't you?"

Daddy-O

Chase Harrison, CEO of Harrison Capital, reclined in his high-backed leather chair as he surveyed the San Francisco skyline from his office window. The city looked like a sprawling circuit board, pulsing with the energy of a thousand tech startups. And Chase had his fingers on every diode and transistor. He'd built his venture capital empire by taking risks that made other investors quake in their loafers. But today, revenge coursed through his veins like liquid fire.

"Did you get her message, sir?" asked Jenkins, his ever-loyal assistant. Jenkins was a thin man with wiry glasses, always dressed impeccably in designer suits that hid the cold-blooded efficiency of a python.

"Indeed I did." Chase's eyes narrowed at the memory of the video message. Justine had sent him a video two days ago, after three years of silence. That shock of flaming red hair, disheveled but defiant, still haunted him. "I never thought I'd hear from her again."

"Her choice of career was . . . unexpected," Jenkins remarked. Whether they viewed it as the elephant in the room or 800-pound gorilla, the sayings emphasized her choice of professions as a large and powerful presence that is impossible to ignore. He knew better than to bring up Justine's foray into the porn industry directly. It tended to set off Chase's volcanic temper.

"Unexpected? You could say that," Chase said, frustration simmering beneath his carefully composed façade. At 18 years old, his daughter left home with a gleam in her eye, chasing her dream of becoming an actress. Instead, she'd found herself entangled in the seedy underworld of adult entertainment, tumbling down a rabbit hole of exploitation and abuse.

For the first decade plus, they stayed connected. While awkward, their love for each other allowed them to look past things both didn't like about the situation. But three years ago, all of that changed. It was like she was just . . . well, gone.

The video showed a nearly middle-aged woman—her daughter—who appeared to be in trouble. She said she was fine, but she communicated using the nonverbal conversation patterns the two of them always used during her youth. He didn't know the extent of her troubles, but he knew something was off.

"Sir, if I may," said Jenkins cautiously, "what do you intend to do about it?"

"About what, Jenkins?" Chase shot back, irritation creeping into his voice. "About my daughter's misguided career choices or about the vermin who prey on vulnerable young women like her, or the trouble she's in?"

"Yes, I picked up on that, too. I suppose all of it, we—or you—should address all of it, I suppose." Jenkins was unfazed by his employer's sudden mood swing.

Chase clenched his jaw. "I'm going to find out what's going on. Then we can bring down that godforsaken industry and everyone in it. Then, maybe, just maybe, my daughter will see that she deserves better than what she's been through."

"An admirable goal, sir," Jenkins acknowledged, a hint of admiration in his voice. "But you'll need help. I'd suggest we call Chuck."

• • • ● • ● • • •

"Talking to yourself now, Mr. Harrison?" said Charles, Chase's longtime friend and fixer, as he strolled into the office. Known as Chuck to his closest associates and infamous in certain circles for running the West Coast's largest underground gambling empire, he'd been Chase's confidant for decades. His eyes flicked to the closed laptop.

"Chuck," Chase acknowledged with a tight nod. "I'm trying to figure out how to pull Justine out of this mess."

"Not only has an industry that sees her as nothing more than a piece of meat has used and abused her, they held her captive at CAYA for three years . . . she couldn't leave, Chuck!"

They rarely discussed Justine in all those years. Chase would relay occasional updates, and Charles—despite his vast network of connections in the gambling world—saw Justine around town only from time-to-time. But all of that ended. The stories stopped years ago, Charles realized. He never asked about Justine—what did that say about him as a friend, he wondered—as he continued to golf and boat and work with Chase.

Chase relayed the story—as best he knew it—of the past three years. Charles was shocked and his body visibly tensed up the deeper they got.

"Three years?!" Charles' eyebrows shot up in genuine surprise. "How the hell did that happen? And why didn't you loop me in? I could have helped!"

"I wish I had told you, Chuck. God, how I wish I had," Chase said, his eyes welling with tears. He took a moment to look out his window at the beautiful foggy—not a surprise—mist-filled view of San Francisco. "During those three years, I didn't know where my daughter was or whether she was even alive."

"Jesus, that must've been hell for you."

"Understatement of the century, my friend. But now that she's out, I need to ensure her safety and make sure those bastards pay for what they've done."

They began to plot and plan how they could help her escape. Who they could hire. What equipment they might need. After a week, they had what amounted to a plan, wobbly as it was. But Chase was desperate and wanted it done. Now.

• • • ● • ● • • •

Two nights before their hired guns were going to take over the compound, Chase sat in his lavish home office, the dim light casting shadows on the mahogany walls. He slouched in his leather armchair, nursing a glass of water as he mulled over the plan and the last conversation he had with Chuck. Just as he lost himself in his thoughts, the door creaked open.

"Hey, Daddy-O," Justine said softly, her flaming red hair cascading around her face. She hesitated for a moment before stepping inside.

"Firecracker!" Chase said, setting his glass aside. "How? What? We were just about to—Oh my goodness!"

They embraced for a full five minutes and didn't want to let go even then. She told him about the last three years. About the video. About the ventilation shaft, the fence, the forest, hitchhiking.

"I'm so sorry, Daddy," she said, tears spilling from her eyes as she looked up at him. "I know I've made a mess of things. But I'm here now."

She slept for 15 hours, had a bite to eat, then slept for 12 more. The two got in a habit of walking through Fisherman's Wharf and Pier 39 in the afternoon, sometimes just walking sometimes grabbing a Dungeness crab from one of the food carts or eating at Scoma where they dined on "Lazy Man's" Cioppino and Shellfish Sauté Sec.

Gradually, over two months, she shared larger and larger bits of her story. Chase felt a sense of peace as he allowed Justine to proceed at her own speed.

• • • ● • ● • ● • •

"Just couldn't sleep, you know? Thought I'd see what you were up to." She perched on the edge of the office desk, her legs swinging slightly. Despite her casual demeanor, Chase could see the tension in her eyes.

"Been thinking about our talks?" he asked, searching for a way to breach the topic.

"Kinda hard not to. It's been eating away at me, really," she said, fidgeting with the hem of her shirt. "I guess . . . I guess I'm ready to talk about it."

"About Cum As You Are?"

"God, I hate that name," she said, rolling her eyes. "But yeah. I escaped, but I don't want anyone else to go through what I did."

"Tell me everything, Firecracker," Chase said, his voice steady and determined.

Justine took a deep breath, steeling herself. "The things they made us do, Dad . . . it was beyond degrading. And if we didn't comply, they'd threaten us, or worse, hurt us." She looked away, her jaw clenched. "I wasn't the only one. There are so many girls there who need help."

. • . • ● • ● • • • •

Chase stood staring out the window at the distant skyline. Taking a deep breath, he dialed Charles' number on his phone.

"Chuck . . . look, I need your help. Do you have someone in that Rolodex of yours who can help with the plan I hinted at the other day? A re-do of the plan we put together some time ago?"

"Well . . ." Charles began, surprise clear in his voice. "I do have someone in mind. She has hinted that she's open to all sorts of opportunities."

"She?"

"Exactly," Charles confirmed, an edge of gradually growing excitement in his tone. "And the more I think about it, the more I like it. I've introduced her to countless powerful people around town; she's no shrinking violet. She has a knack for taking down people and, well, stealing things. I think she's just what we need."

"Alright, set up the meeting."

"Chase, I'd suggest you let me handle this. I know this part better than you. I do certain things for other people, too, you know. Let me take care of it."

"Fine, let's just get this done."

. • . • ● • ● • • • •

A few days later, Charles entered the Broken Halo, his eyes scanning the dimly lit room before settling on a statuesque blonde woman chatting with great animation to a male at the table. She was wearing a black shift dress with cap sleeves and a point collar with split neckline and had her long blonde hair parted in the center, a classic look that framed her face and drew attention to her facial features. He found a booth on the other side of the room and saw that her piercing blue eyes found him up like a lioness sizing up its prey.

Charles ordered a margarita mocktail and waited for her to approach. Waiting for people was not uncommon, so this didn't bother him. While waiting, he alternately took a drink and checked messages on his phone.

• • • ● ● • ● ● • • •

"Hello, Chuckles, it's good to see you again."

Charles looked up and smiled at his best enforcer's nickname for him. Though he ran the gambling ring with iron-fisted authority, he'd always had a soft spot for Darby's irreverent attitude.

"You've got guts meeting me here, Charles. This isn't exactly your scene, is it?"

"Desperate times call for desperate measures," Charles said with a wry smile. "Besides, I thought you'd appreciate the ambiance, given some of the places I send you to collect."

"Cut to the chase," Darby said, rolling her eyes at her boss. "What kind of job is it this time?"

"Actually, this isn't about gambling debts. This is . . . personal. I want to bring down a seedy part of the porn industry."

Darby raised an eyebrow, her interest piqued. It was rare for Charles to venture outside their usual territory. "Oh? Since when do you care about the porn industry?"

"Let's just say I'm doing a favor for an old friend, and we can't ignore it any longer," Charles said, his eyes darkening with anger. "We want to expose these studios for what they are and make sure they hurt no one again."

"Sounds like a noble crusade," Darby remarked, her voice dripping with sarcasm. "But why me? You've got plenty of other people on your payroll."

Charles leaned in closer, his voice low and intense. "Because you're the best I've got. And this needs to be handled . . . delicately. Plus, we have resources you could only dream of."

Darby narrowed her eyes, considering her boss's unusual offer. "Alright, Chuckles. You've got my attention. But if we're going to do this, we do it my way."

"Agreed," Charles nodded. "My only request is that you keep certain names out of it. The person I represent is a good man whose daughter ran into some trouble. She got out of it, but, well . . ."

"Your friend wants revenge. I can do anonymity," Darby said, knowing better than to press her boss too hard about his connections.

"But I need to know more before saying yes or no. I need to know who we're hurting, even if I don't know who's behind it all."

"Fair enough," Charles said, a hint of pride in his voice at her caution. "I can give you everything else you need to know."

The two talked for hours. In the end, Darby left with a name and a place. She knew Justine would be at a party next week. Darby would now be there, too.

Interview: Charles

I nspector: *Thank you for agreeing to speak with me, Charles. I understand that you and Chase Harrison are friends and that you do some work for him. Is that correct?*

Charles: *Yes.*

Inspector: *How long have you known him?*

Charles: *Oh . . . 40 years?*

Inspector: *Did you go to school together?*

Charles: *Yes, most of high school, then Stanford for undergrad. He went to the Stanford Graduate School of Business and I went to Stanford Law School.*

Inspector: *Impressive. And you've remained close all this time?*

Charles: *Yes. After some past work in the 'real world,' Mr. Harrison started an investment company and brought me on as General Counsel.*

Inspector: *And that's your role now?*

Charles: *Yes.*

Inspector: *What do you do in this role?*

Charles: *Review contracts. Vet potential employees. Look at investment choices?*

Inspector: *Is that it?*

Charles: *Generally, yes.*

Inspector: *Are you sure?*

Charles: *What are you getting at?*

Inspector: *Are you—as some movies have popularized—a 'fixer?'*

Charles: *When problems come up, Mr. Harrison often asked me about them. I offer suggested courses of action.*

Inspector: *And you do whatever is necessary to make the problems go away. Is that true?*

Charles: *Of course I do. But always within the bounds of the law.*

Inspector: *Sure … so you'd never hire a group of people to destroy and rob a porn agency that held your longtime friend's daughter captive … right?*

Charles: *I'd do—and I did—everything I could to bring Justine back. Yes. But I broke no laws in doing so.*

Inspector: *You didn't pay this group?*

Charles: *Not only did I not pay a group, I know nothing about a group.*

Inspector: *Then how did you try to help?*

Charles: *I contacted the CEO of CAYA—his name is Tony, as I'm sure you know—and tried to negotiate and reason with him.*

Inspector: *Any luck?*

Charles: *Tony had me talk to his number two, Lolita—delightful woman.*

Inspector: *And?*

Charles: *Well, Justine's free, isn't she?*

Inspector: *But no hiring a group who put on an elaborate charade to free her, correct?*

Charles: *Of course not.*

Inspector: *One last thing, if you don't mind. Do you work for other people or companies besides Mr. Harrison?*

Charles: *I do some outside consulting, yes.*

Inspector: *Same type of functions?*

Charles: *In a matter of speaking, yes. But never with companies that compete with Mr. Harrison's.*

Inspector: *Fine. I guess what I'm asking . . . do you run high-stakes poker games for certain clients?*

Charles: *What? Are you serious?*

Inspector: *Quite. We believe you helped arrange underground gambling operations for powerful, well-connected men—and some women. Private games with millions on the table.*

Charles: *I don't know where you got your information, but that is absurd.*

Inspector: *So you're not a glorified bookie for the rich and famous?*

Charles: *Of course not. What a ridiculous accusation. I'm tempted to sue you and the department for libel and defamation if you spout these careless theories to others. I have never. . .*

Inspector: *Save it Charles. We'll do what needs to be done. But for now, we're finished. You can show yourself out.*

Charles: (Red-faced, gets up and storms out.)

Ready to Ride?

"Chase," Darby greeted him, her gaze fixed on Justine. She noted the mixture of relief and determination in Justine's eyes and took it as a sign they were still on track.

"Darby, finally meeting you is a pleasure," Chase said with a sarcastic tone, mockingly bowing to her. "And you must be William. I've read your book. Riveting stuff."

"Thanks Chase," William responded, his gruff exterior not betraying any surprise at their sudden appearance. He stood up, stretching his long runner's legs.

Tony rubbed his temples, feigning nonchalance as he watched Chase stride into the conversation pit with Justine by his side. He couldn't quite quell the unease that gnawed at him; something about this situation reeked of a twist he hadn't seen coming. Lolita had tensed beside him, her jaw clenched tight, and Tony knew she was just as blindsided.

"Chase," Lolita said, her voice ice-cold, "and Justine." She paused, narrowing her eyes. "Care to explain what the hell is going on here?" Her gaze darted between William, Darby, and the newcomers, seeking answers.

Chase laughed, a low chuckle that sent shivers down Tony's spine. "Well, Tony, it's not every day a father gets to help his daughter take down an entire industry." He wrapped an arm around Justine, who beamed up at him with pride. "Surprise."

The room went dead silent, the tension palpable. Tony blinked, trying to comprehend the revelation. Justine's father? How could he have missed this connection?

"Your . . . your father?" Lolita stammered, disbelief etched across her face.

Chase nodded his confirmation, grinning like a man who'd just pulled off the ultimate con. "And it turns out Darby here was the perfect accomplice. You see, I reached out to her shortly before she and Justine met a few months ago,"—he nodded at Darby—"and things just fell into place from there."

Darby smirked, her eyes glittering with mischief. "You really should've kept a closer eye on your star actress, Tony. I mean, it's not like she was trying to hide her disdain for you."

"Or the industry," added Justine, a sly smile playing at her lips.

Tony felt his face flush with anger and humiliation. He'd been played, outsmarted by this motley crew of misfits who had infiltrated his empire. His mind raced, contemplating ways to regain control of the situation. But deep down, he knew the tables had turned and there was no going back.

"Fine," he said, his voice barely concealing his fury. "You've had your fun. But don't think for a second that this is over."

"By the way," Chase said, a sly grin spreading across his face. "The investors I represented to you months ago? They were Darby and her team."

Tony's eyes widened in shock, and Lolita's jaw dropped. This revelation hit them like a tidal wave, leaving them momentarily speechless. The pieces of the puzzle clicked into place, and Tony could see just how masterfully the team toyed with him. And Lolita. And his company.

"Impossible," Lolita said, trying to regain her composure. "You're lying."

"Am I?" Chase smirked, glancing at Darby for confirmation. She nodded, her blue eyes twinkling with satisfaction.

"Truly," she said, her voice dripping with sweet sarcasm.

Lolita clenched her fists, seething with humiliation. She couldn't believe that they had been so blind to the truth. And now, with their world crashing down around them, there was little they could do but watch in powerless fury.

As if on cue, the side door swung open and in sauntered Tommy, his muscular frame filling the doorway. He looked every bit the part of a victorious conqueror, his dark eyes gleaming with triumph.

"Hey, guys," he said, a hint of a Cuban accent thickening as excitement bubbled up inside him. "Just wanted to let you know we packed everything up and it's all snug in the vans outside."

"Tommy," William said, barely able to contain his glee. "Perfect timing, as always."

"Thank you, thank you," Tommy said, executing a mock bow. "I try my best."

"What *things*?" Lolita asked.

"Oh, just the vault you showed me," Chase admitted. "Rebuilding and revamping security really should have been at the top of your list of *to-do's* after your devastating loss. So I told Tommy and his crew about it, how to access it, and when to do it."

"Those gold bricks were heavy, by the way . . . and the diamond barely fits in my pocket," said Tommy. "But I left the tv for you."

"Alright, everyone," Darby said, her voice firm but tinged with satisfaction.

As they filed out of the conversation pit, leaving Tony and Lolita to contemplate their new reality, Darby allowed herself a small, victorious smile. They had won this battle, but they knew they had one more task ahead of them.

"Game on," she said, the words carried away on the cool afternoon breeze.

· · · · ● · ● · · ·

Tommy led them out of the building, his stride brimming with confidence as the cool night air enveloped them. In the shadows, a group of his friends emerged, dressed in black and wearing smirks that mirrored their own satisfaction. Darby couldn't help but appreciate the dark allure woven into the scene.

"Ah, my trusty crew," Tommy said, clapping one of them on the back. "Ready to ride?"

"Always," said Sabrina, with a mischievous glint in her eye.

Darby sank into the plush leather seat, feeling the thrill of their victory electrify her senses.

"Nice ride, huh?" William grinned, settling into the seat next to her. "These babies are like the Batmobiles of getaway cars."

The engines roared to life, and the convoy of Sprinters made their way through the dimly lit streets, their powerful engines purring like a pack of lions on the hunt. Darby couldn't shake the feeling that they were part of something larger than themselves, a force of nature unleashed upon an unsuspecting world.

When they arrived at the Venice house, the doors opened to reveal Josh and Ella waiting inside, their faces alight with anticipation. Well, at least Josh's face was bright with hope; Ella was, well, Ella. The electric atmosphere that had filled the vans now spilled out into the open air, igniting the room with excitement.

"Welcome back!" Josh said, raising a glass of rosemary-and-ginger mule in salute. "I trust the mission was a success?"

"Success doesn't even begin to cover it," Darby said, allowing herself a smug smile as she grabbed a glass of her own. "But we couldn't have done it without you two."

"Really?" Ella asked, feigning innocence as she sipped her drink.

"Never underestimate the power of a brilliant mind," William chimed in, clinking his glass against Ella's. "Especially when it's working in tandem with our collective good looks and charm."

"Truer words have never been spoken," Darby said, raising her own glass. "To us, the unstoppable team that took down an empire."

"Cheers!" they all echoed, their laughter ringing through the air like music.

Interview: Chase

Inspector: *Mr. Harrison, thank you for agreeing to speak with me. I understand that you have a connection to Justine, and I wanted to discuss her involvement in the recent events. Can you shed some light on her actions and motives?*

Chase: *Inspector, I'll be honest with you. I haven't seen or heard from Justine in some time. Our relationship has been strained, to say the least. But I'm willing to provide any information I can.*

Inspector: *Thank you for your cooperation, Mr. Harrison. We believe Justine was involved in a heist targeting the porn industry. Can you think of any reasons she would be drawn to such actions?*

Chase: *I can't believe she'd be involved in something like that, but she's had a tumultuous past. She had dreams of being an actress, but circumstances led her down a different path. Justine felt trapped and exploited in the porn industry, and I saw how it affected her.*

Inspector: *So you believe Justine's experiences in the porn industry could influence her actions?*

Chase: *It's hard to say for certain, but I can imagine how her past might have shaped her decisions. Justine endured a lot of trauma and mistreatment during her time in that industry. But regardless of the dark underbelly of an industry that has caused so much harm, I don't see how she could be involved in something like this.*

Inspector: *Do you have any knowledge of Justine's connections or affiliations that could have facilitated her involvement in this heist?*

Chase: *No. I wish I could provide you with more information, Inspector. As I mentioned earlier, my relationship with Justine has been strained. We lost touch a few years ago, and I'm not aware of her current associations.*

Inspector: *Relationships can be complicated, that's for sure. We're trying to piece together the puzzle here, and any insight you can provide is valuable. This might seem to be a random question, but it's about your general counsel, Charles.*

Chase: *What about him? We've known each other for a long time. Forty years?*

Inspector: *Right. Well, you say you didn't know of Justine's involvement in this, but what about him? Was he involved?*

Chase: *Chuck? Not that I'm aware of. He's a longtime friend and would do anything to help our family, but not that.*

Inspector: *So you didn't task him with breaking Justine out of there?*

Chase: *What? Absolutely not. I'm thrilled Justine is free, and I don't really care how she got out. But no, I didn't have Charles do that. Preposterous.*

Inspector: *Fair enough. If you think of anything else that could help our investigation, please reach out.*

Chase: *Fine. Yes. Of course. I mean, I appreciate your understanding, Inspector. I want to see justice served just as much as anyone. If I come across any relevant information or remember anything that might be of help, I will let you know.*

Inspector: *Oh, one last thing, Mr. Harrison. Is it true that your company invested in CAYA and that you served as a co-CFO?*

Chase: *Well, yes to both. When our company looked at investments, it was impossible to ignore the porn industry. This is a $100 billion dollar company. Their revenue is more than ABC, NBC, and CBS combined. It's also more than the NFL, NBA, and Major League Baseball.*

Inspector: *Yes, obviously this is big business. But following your review of their finances, did anything strike you as odd? Did anything jump out at you?*

Chase: *Let me think . . .*

Inspector: *Take your time.*

Chase: *The only thing that really comes to mind is a couple of secret accounts. There were monies being placed in those accounts, and I couldn't determine why or where that revenue came from. When I asked Tony or even Lolita, I they either ignored me or quickly changed the subject.*

Inspector: *Where do you think that money came from?*

Chase: *Well—and this is only speculation based on some observations and rumors—I think the studios were dabbling in some illegal activities.*

Inspector: *Can you be more specific?*

Chase: *Not with any certainty, no.*

Inspector: *What did you hear?*

Chase: *I know there was a top floor of the production building that was being constructed for a new project. It may already be done; I was never told. But the rumor is that it was for underage pornography. Now I never saw that, and I saw no kids onsite, mind you. And I pray that wasn't true. But that was the rumor.*

Inspector: *We have heard similar rumors and I know others are looking into this.*

Chase: *I hope I'm wrong.*

Inspector: *What do you think happened to all the money?*

Chase: *Not sure . . .*

Inspector: *A guess then?*

Chase: *Well, to be honest, I can't believe Tony and Lolita would allow something like this to happen. Lolita is too smart for that.*

Inspector: *Not Tony?*

Chase: *Perhaps, but Lolita is the real brains behind everything. Again, just guessing here, but it wouldn't surprise me to learn that she orchestrated this somehow.*

Inspector: *And why would she do that? Would she steal it?*

Chase: *She would never do that to Tony. She was—and likely still is—undyingly loyal to him.*

Inspector: *Then why would she do it?*

Chase: *Because she could? While true, I doubt that's the reason. If I had to guess, they stashed away all the stolen money and they're most likely going to file an insurance claim. Again—just guesses here—but it jives with what I've seen.*

Inspector: *Makes sense to me, too. Anyway, thank you for your cooperation, Mr. Harrison. We will continue our investigation, considering all possibilities. If there's anything else you think of, please contact us.*

Interview: Lolita

Inspector: *Good day, Lolita. Thank you for agreeing to meet with me. I would like to discuss recent events and your involvement in the operations at CAYA.*

Lolita: *Good day, Inspector. I am here to cooperate with your investigation, but I categorically deny any involvement in illegal activities or holding porn actors captive. My role as Tony's assistant—I mean COO—is to ensure the smooth operation of the company and protect our interests. I am committed to upholding the law and have always acted within its boundaries.*

Inspector: *We have received reports and testimonies that suggest otherwise, Lolita. Witnesses have offered accounts of your involvement in the coercion and mistreatment of performers, as well as your role in the operations of the company. Can you provide any insight into these allegations?*

Lolita: *I understand the gravity of the situation, but I can assure you that these allegations are baseless and unfounded. I have always acted under the guidance and direction of Tony, who places a strong emphasis on creating a safe and consensual working environment. Any claims of coercion or mistreatment are simply untrue.*

Inspector: *Tell me about the dorm.*

Lolita: *What about it? We built onsite housing for our performers to help ensure their safety.*

Inspector: *Did you hold actors against their will?*

Lolita: *No.*

Inspector: *Really?*

Lolita: *I said, 'no.'*

Inspector: *Did you employ what were, in effect, guards on each floor?*

Lolita: *No. We placed certain people on each floor to serve as a cross between a concierge and a mentor. They helped the actors access what they needed in the community and offered advice as needed.*

Inspector: *So those people—like Lilly—did not force the actors to stay?*

Lolita: *No.*

Inspector: *And you didn't force them to stay?*

Lolita: *Again, no. Of course not.*

Inspector: *No threats if they wanted to leave?*

Lolita: *I would never do that.*

Inspector: *Our investigation has also uncovered evidence that points to your direct involvement in the illegal use of underage actors to be filmed by CAYA.*

Lolita: *This is ridiculous. Absolutely not. That is illegal and we wouldn't do that.*

Inspector: *So you didn't have children work here?*

Lolita: *Well, we had some now and then. But they were for our modeling venture. Always clothed, never in movies.*

Inspector: *I see. Do you have some of these photos?*

Lolita: *Unfortunately, they were destroyed during the break-in.*

Inspector: *And do you have parental consents signed by parents or guardians for each of the children?*

Lolita: *Again . . . destroyed.*

Inspector: *And no videos?*

Lolita: *No! I categorically deny this. We did not shoot movies of any kind with the children who came here.*

Inspector: *Did they stay onsite?*

Lolita: *Occasionally, yes. But only because some of them traveled very long distances to get here. We thought it would be easier.*

Inspector: *And you did not hold them against their will?*

Lolita: *No.*

Inspector: *So if we had statements from some of these children claiming otherwise . . .*

Lolita: *Lies. They'd all be lies.*

Inspector: *I don't go on the dark web often, but this case forced me to. Do you publish movies there under the brand 'Smells Like Teenage?'*

Lolita: *That is not one of our companies.*

Inspector: *The owners registered the company in the Cayman Islands, so we will have difficulty finding its owners.*

Lolita: (Silent, trying to suppress a grin.)

Inspector: *Just a couple more things, Lolita. We found a mostly empty room in the data center. Can you tell me what that was?*

Lolita: *We had a storage room. Is that what you're referring to?*

Inspector: *Perhaps. This room had a tv and a chair. In addition, there were shelves that were mostly empty.*

Lolita: *Then yes, that was a storage room.*

Inspector: *What was in there?*

Lolita: *Supplies for the data center. The tv was for our security team to monitor things in the center.*

Inspector: *So no money? Artwork? Gold?*

Lolita: *What? No, I never saw—*

Inspector: *Tucked behind that tv was an envelope. In that envelope was a photo with a timestamp dated the day of your robbery.*

Lolita: (Silent, staring straight ahead.)

Inspector: *The photo clearly shows what appears to be millions of dollars of gold, art, and bills. Where was that from? Was it accounted for? Where did it go?*

Lolita: *Those are things we collected over the years. And yes, it was all previously cataloged, but as with everything else, those records were lost (thankfully!).*

Inspector: *So you obtained all those things legally?*

Lolita: *Of course.*

Inspector: *And you properly paid any taxes and fees?*

Lolita: *Yes.*

Inspector: *Is there anything else you'd like to add before we close our discussion?*

Lolita: *Yes, I'd just like to say that these claims of theft and insurance fraud are false. My focus has always been on protecting the company's interests and supporting Tony in his role as CEO. While my demeanor and physical presence may intimidate some, it does not equate to illegal activities or mistreatment. I stand by my actions and maintain that I have acted within the boundaries of the law.*

Inspector: *Our investigation will continue, and we will scrutinize all the evidence and testimonies to uncover the truth.*

Lolita: *I am fully committed to cooperating with your investigation, Inspector. We were robbed and we deserve to have our money and data returned. I have nothing to hide, and I am confident that a thorough examination of the facts will vindicate my position. I appreciate your dedication to seeking the truth, but I maintain my innocence regarding any illegal activities or mistreatment allegations.*

Inspector: *Thank you for your time, Lolita.*

Lolita: *I appreciate your dedication to uncovering the truth, Inspector. I believe that the investigation will confirm my innocence and refute these baseless accusations against our studio, Tony, and me. We never took any money or anything else.*

Inspector: *Hold on a second. I never said you took any money. Did you?*

Lolita: *Well, no, we didn't.*

Inspector: *You and Tony didn't plan this elaborate charade to make it appear that someone broke in and took everything?*

Lolita: *No.*

Inspector: *You didn't move all your data to some unknown location to make it appear as though these same unknown perpetrators destroyed it.*

Lolita: *No.*

Inspector: *Are you sure?*

Lolita: *You see . . . someone broke in . . . and they took . . .*

Inspector: *Where were you when all of this happened?*

Lolita: *Well, we were here, in our offices.*

Inspector: *I'm going to be honest with you, Lolita . . . I think you are involved in all of this. I think you held people onsite against their will. I think you produced illegal pornographic movies for pedophiles.*

Lolita: (Silent, trying to hold in tears.)

Inspector: *I don't have enough to arrest you today, Lolita, but we'll get it. I'm done with this interview, but there will be more. For now, don't leave the area. I want you to meet with my associate in the hall; she will hold your passport for you.*

Floor-to-Ceiling Windows

A month later, the sun crept through the blinds, casting a striped pattern of light and shadow across Tony's desk. He rubbed his chubby hands together with glee as he surveyed the stack of contracts before him. CAYA was rising again, fueled by questionable investments from equally questionable characters. Banks had turned their backs on Tony and Lolita, but the criminal underworld was more than happy to lend a helping hand—for a price.

"Looks like we're back in business," Tony said with a smirk, leaning back in his expensive leather chair. "These guys may be shady, but they've got deep pockets."

Lolita was near the window; she was wearing olive green sculpted boot cut pants with a suit blazer over a white corset tank that—as always—proudly showed off her abs. Her black, strappy heeled sandal loudly clicked and clacked as she paced back and forth. Her gaze remained fixed on the bustling city below, emotionless as ever. "But let's not forget that these alliances come with strings attached."

Tony waved a dismissive hand. "Bah, we can handle them. We've dealt with worse." His eyes twinkled with mischief as he imagined the heights his empire would reach once again.

Just then, a notification chimed on Tony's computer. A news article had just gone viral, accusing Tony and Lolita of using illegal methods to keep actors, and mentioned their deep involvement in sex trafficking. The headline screamed:

Porn Kingpin and Ice Queen Accomplice Exposed: Dark Secrets Unveiled.

"Son of a bitch!" Tony said, his face turning red as he read the damning accusations. He looked up at Lolita, who seemed unfazed by the news.

"Who would have thought our dirty laundry would end up online?" Lolita said, her voice dripping with sarcasm.

"We know who did this," Tony said, his fingers tapping furiously on the desk. He knew the severity of the situation, but he wasn't about to let this news story ruin everything he had built. "We'll make them pay."

As the pair began plotting their next move, the weight of the allegations hung heavy in the air. They knew that even with their newfound financial support, they couldn't escape the scrutiny that would come with such a public scandal.

· · · ● · ● · ● · ● · · ·

A day later, Tony found more. He didn't think it could get worse.

He was wrong.

"Surprise, surprise." Tony stared at the screen with a raised eyebrow as he gazed at the scathing headline as he read with mock astonishment. "Another day, another story."

"Really?" Lolita leaned over his shoulder, her sculpted abs on full display. "No one's ever accused us of being squeaky clean before."

Breaking News: Porn Moguls Accused of Shady Practices!

"Sex trafficking? Now they've added underage actresses?" Lolita snorted derisively. "How original. I've seen better storylines in our films."

"True," Tony admitted, unable to suppress a grin. "But I must admit, they really went for the jugular this time. It's hard to shake off accusations like these."

"Are you worried?" Lolita asked, her tone cool and detached.

"Of course not," Tony said, as he slammed his laptop shut. "We'll weather this storm like we always do. Besides, it's not like we haven't faced worse."

"We can't afford to let this affect the company," Lolita said, her voice low and dangerous, "Our reputation is already hanging by a thread."

"Relax, Lolita. I know what's at stake here." Tony stood up from his chair, his chubby frame casting an imposing shadow over the room. "We've got connections, resources, and allies. We'll squash this little bug just like we have all the others."

"Good." Lolita straightened her back, looking down at him with her usual air of cold detachment. "Because if this gets out of hand, it won't just be our careers on the line, it'll be our heads."

"Ah, always the optimist," Tony said, clapping a hand on her shoulder. "But you're right, as usual. We'll handle this with our usual tact and finesse."

"Let's hope so," Lolita said, the closest she ever came to showing concern. She turned away from him, her pencil-thin figure gliding gracefully across the room. "I'd hate for all our hard work to go to waste over some second-rate tabloid trash."

"Couldn't agree more," Tony said, his eyes narrowing with determination. "It's time to remind everyone just who they're dealing with."

He couldn't help but wonder what his father, Arash, would think if he could see him now. The old man had worked his fingers to the bone running that little Persian bookstore in Westwood, treating every customer like family, building his American dream one volume at a time. Tony had inherited that same drive, that relentless ambition—but somewhere along the way, his path had diverged from his father's modest dreams of honest commerce. Would Arash be proud of his son's empire, built on the darker appetites of human nature? Or would he be ashamed of how far Tony had strayed from the simple values he'd tried to instill?

As they began strategizing their response, both were acutely aware of the potential fallout from the allegations. They knew that a single misstep could bring their entire empire crashing down around them. But neither was willing to let that happen without a fight. And as the saying goes, desperate times call for desperate measures.

• • • • ● • ● • • • •

In a dimly lit bar on the outskirts of town, a small group of former CAYA employees and actors huddled around a booth, their eyes glued to the screens of their smartphones as they read the incendiary news article. The atmosphere was thick with tension, the air crackling with a mixture of disbelief, betrayal, and indignation.

"Can you believe this garbage?" spat Rachel, a former actress freed by Tommy and his crew. She tossed her phone onto the table, causing it to skid precariously close to the edge before it came to rest against a half-empty glass of water. "I mean, I knew Tony was bad news, but sex trafficking? Underage girls?"

"Who would've thought, right?" grumbled Mark, an ex-cameraman who had demanded better working conditions for the crew and got fired unceremoniously. "That son of a bitch is finally getting what he deserves."

"Hey, don't forget Lolita," chimed in Heather, adjusting the glasses perched on her nose. Her tenure as a makeup artist at CAYA had been brief but memorable, ending when she stood up to Lolita's tyrannical demands. "She's just as guilty, if not more so. That woman has ice in her veins."

"Too true," said Rachel, her lips curling into a bitter smile. "But at least we're free of them now, right?"

"Free, sure," Mark said, his voice heavy with sarcasm. "But unemployed and informally barred from working in the industry, thanks to those assholes, our reputations are as tarnished as theirs."

"Maybe not for long," Heather offered, her eyes twinkling with mischief. "Once word gets out about Tony and Lolita, no one will want to work with them. And who knows? Maybe the industry will realize they're better off without them."

"From your lips to God's ears," Rachel said, raising her glass in a half-hearted toast.

"Speaking of which," Mark said, lowering his voice conspiratorially, "I heard that rival porn companies have already started circling like vultures, ready to swoop in and snatch up CAYA's top talent."

"Really? That's good news for us, right?"

"Potentially. But we'll have to be careful. Those other companies might not be trafficking girls or using underage talent, but they're not exactly saints either."

"True," Rachel said, her features clouding with uncertainty. "But at least it's something. A chance to rebuild our lives and careers."

"Exactly," Heather said, a determined glint in her eyes. "We just need to stick together, watch each other's backs, and make sure we don't get screwed over again."

"Agreed," said Mark, clinking his glass against those of the others. "Here's to new beginnings, and the end of Tony and Lolita's reign of terror."

· · · ● · ● · ● · · ·

Beyond the office door, Tony heard his secretary protest, "Miss, you can't just barge in here!"

Vanessa burst into the room, her black hair framing a face flushed with anger as she waved her phone in the air. "Have you seen this?" she asked, her voice trembling with barely contained rage. "They're calling you criminals, sex traffickers!"

Tony rubbed his temples, the vein in his forehead throbbing. "We know, Vanessa," he said in a strained voice. "We're working on it."

Lolita, perched on the edge of Tony's desk, crossed her legs and leaned forward. "This isn't the first time we've faced bad press," she reminded Vanessa, her tone cool and measured. "We've weathered worse storms than this."

Vanessa began to pace, her feet pounding furiously against the floor. "But this is different," she argued, her hands gesticulating wildly. "This isn't just some tabloid gossip. They have evidence, sources. They're calling for an investigation!"

Tony stood abruptly, his chair scraping against the floor. He walked to the window, his hands clasped behind his back. "We have connections, resources," he said, his gaze fixed on the skyline. "We'll deal with this like we always do."

Lolita nodded, a calculating glint in her eye. "Your dad's right," she said, sliding off the desk and moving to stand beside him. "We'll spin this, control the narrative. It's what we do best."

Vanessa stopped pacing, her shoulders sagging in defeat. "I hope you're right," she said, her voice barely above a whisper. "Because if you're not, we're all going down with this ship."

· · ● · ● · ● · · ·

A week had passed since the multiple articles first made headlines, and the once thriving CAYA headquarters now resembled a besieged fortress. The atmosphere within was thick with tension, as employees whispered in hushed tones and shot furtive glances toward Tony's office.

"Damn it," Tony said under his breath, pacing back and forth in his sumptuous office while Lolita stood nearby. "This is more than just a bad PR move; this feels like a war."

Lolita's voice was devoid of emotion. "I know we can navigate our way out of this mess together. We always have."

"Is that so?" A wicked grin spread across Tony's face. "Do you have some grand, elaborate plan in mind, or are you just trying to keep my spirits up?"

"Both," she said simply, cracking a rare, enigmatic smile.

Before either of them could say another word, the shrill ring of the intercom pierced the air. Tony sighed and reached for the button.

"Sir, there's a situation outside," the security guard reported, his voice trembling. "A bunch of FBI cars just rolled up to the front gate, and they're demanding entry."

Tony's heart was pounding in his chest. He looked at Lolita, who seemed unfazed by the news. "What do we do?"

"Let them in," she advised calmly. "If we try to keep them out, it'll only make us look guilty. Besides, we have nothing to hide. They took all our files and inadvertently helped us by destroying everything."

"Right . . . you're right," Tony said, trying to sound more confident than he felt. He pressed the intercom button again. "Let them in but watch them. Closely. I want to know what they're up to every step of the way."

"Understood, sir," the guard said before the line went dead.

As Tony watched the security feed on his computer monitor, he saw the imposing black SUVs roll past the gates and come to a stop in front of the main entrance. A dozen agents poured out, their faces grim and determined.

"Here we go," Tony said, his voice tinged with apprehension. "The wolves are at our door."

"Stay strong, Tony," Lolita said, placing a reassured hand on his shoulder. "We'll get through this."

"You better believe it," Tony said, steeling himself for the battle ahead. "No matter what it takes."

As the FBI agents poured into the compound, Lolita stood by the floor-to-ceiling windows, her body rigid and unmoving. She watched the chaos unfold below, her jaw clenched tight, and her hands clasped behind her back. The muscles in her sculpted abs twitched as she took in the scene, but her face remained an unreadable mask. She didn't flinch when an agent roughly shoved Tony against a wall, nor did she blink when they began hauling away boxes of evidence. Instead, she kept her gaze fixed on the horizon, her eyes hard and distant, as if she were mentally calculating her next move. Even as the world crumbled around her, Lolita remained an immovable force, her icy exterior never once cracking.

The FBI continued their raid, confiscating computers and rifling through files. Tony couldn't shake the nagging feeling that this was only the beginning. The future of CAYA hung in the balance, and with each passing moment, the weight of uncertainty bore down on him like a crushing vice.

Just then, he heard a female agent yell to nobody in particular, "Come see what I found on their servers."

Lolita and Tony just looked at each other. Darby and her crew had erased all of that. They searched for archived and deleted files for days. They hired experts. There was nothing to be found. Darby's group destroyed their firewalls. They erased all the tables and their databases. Cloud storage was empty. It was literally all gone.

Then a moment of recognition simultaneously hit them. More specifically, a name.

Ella.

And at that moment, it was all too clear: the end was here.

Interview: Ella

Inspector: *Good evening, Ella.*

Ella: (Stares without emotion at the Inspector.)

Inspector: *Let's get straight to the point. Can you confirm or deny any involvement in the heist that took place at CAYA?*

Ella: *Heist?*

Inspector: *Yes, a group of people stole both money and other sensitive items from that porn studio. CAYA.*

Ella: *I don't steal.*

Inspector: *So you are denying involvement?*

Ella: *Yes.*

Inspector: *Can you elaborate?*

Ella: *On what? I said I wasn't involved.*

Inspector: *So you didn't hack into their computers?*

Ella: *No.*

Inspector: *You didn't download all their data?*

Ella: *No.*

Inspector: *You didn't destroy all their files?*

Ella: *No.*

Inspector: *Did you hack into their banks?*

Ella: *No.*

Inspector: *And transfer all their money to other accounts?*

Ella: *No. I don't steal.*

Inspector: *That's what you said.*

Ella: (Silent, looking down.)

Inspector: *What do you do for a job?*

Ella: *I help people with computer issues.*

Inspector: *Like computer repair?*

Ella: *Not exactly.*

Inspector: *Then what, exactly?*

Ella: *I debug computers. I remove malware and viruses. I help people regain control of their computers after others have hacked them.*

Inspector: *So you don't hack?*

Ella: *No.*

Inspector: *Does this pay well?*

Ella: *It's ok.*

Inspector: *How much do you charge to remove computer viruses?*

Ella: *$250.*

Inspector: *That's it?*

Ella: *It doesn't take me long, so I don't need to charge more.*

Inspector: *Where do you live, Ella?*

Ella: *Right now? Omaha. Nebraska.*

Inspector: *Do you still live at home?*

Ella: *No.*

Inspector: *You live in a loft in a trendy part of town. Is that correct?*

Ella: *Well, it's called the Old Market . . .*

Inspector: *Do you own it?*

Ella: *Yes.*

Inspector: *How did you afford this?*

Ella: (Silence.)

Inspector: *I guess I'm wondering how you could afford to buy such a place. When you only charge $250 for each person you help.*

Ella: (Silence.)

Inspector: *OK, let's move on. A group of traffickers kidnapped you when you were younger. Is that correct?*

Ella: *Yes.*

Inspector: *I imagine that's not something you want to relive, so we won't dive into that, specifically. Instead, I'd like to know a couple of different things.*

Ella: *What?*

Inspector: *When you were being held captive, did they ever take you to the CAYA studios?*

Ella: *I don't remember where they took me. They shuttled me to a lot of different places.*

Inspector: *Could this studio be one of them?*

Ella: *I don't think so.*

Inspector: *You don't think so? Or "no?"*

Ella: *I don't think so.*

Inspector: *Once you escaped, you returned to Omaha. Is that correct?*

Ella: *Yes.*

Inspector: *And that's when you bought your loft, correct?*

Ella: *Yes.*

Inspector: *Do you know what happened to the group that kidnapped you?*

Ella: (Silence, staring into the inspector's eyes.)

Inspector: *Ella?*

Ella: *I heard their operation was destroyed. Dismantled. Terrorized. No longer in business.*

Inspector: *Sounds justified to me. Did you have anything to do with that?*

Ella: (Long pause.) *No.*

Inspector: *Because I wouldn't blame you if you did . . .*

Ella: *No.*

Inspector: *OK, so just to be clear, if we found evidence that you helped with the CAYA hack, that would be fake data, correct?*

Ella: *I understand why you might be suspicious, but I assure you that my activity is purely coincidental. As someone who works in computers, my digital footprints are often mistaken for others, and I've encountered situations in the past where my name has been falsely associated with cybercrimes. I'm passionate about using my skills to make a difference, but I would never resort to illegal activities.*

Inspector: *Ella, we've received information suggesting that members of the heist team contacted you and had discussions about their plans. Can you clarify the nature of these conversations?*

Ella: *Like who?*

Inspector: *William is the name that keeps coming up.*

Ella: *The only William I know is an older guy I used to know when I was younger. He lived by us.*

Inspector: *Did you meet with him recently?*

Ella: *We had lunch a few months ago when he was in town.*

Inspector: *Did he ask for your help with hacking this group?*

Ella: *We talked about a lot of things. Hacking wasn't one of them.*

Inspector: *Were you contacted by anyone else related to this? Darby? Josh? Tommy? Justine? Chase? Charles?*

Ella: *Look, I have been contacted by various individuals seeking my help in different matters. I never engaged in any discussions about any 'heist' or hack or illegal activity. I'm cautious about who I collaborate with, and I prioritize projects that align with my principles. So again, I have no idea what you're referring to.*

Inspector: *So if we have evidence showing that your expertise was used to bypass security systems during the heist. That would be . . .*

Ella: *A coincidence. My intentions are to protect and secure systems, not to exploit them.*

Inspector: (Sigh.) *Ella, we urge you to be forthcoming with any information that may shed light on the heist. It's crucial for us to uncover the truth and identify all those involved.*

Ella: *I understand.*

Inspector: *We will continue our investigation, and I advise you to reconsider any information you may have that could aid us. It's in your best interest to be forthcoming and transparent.*

Ella: *I understand.*

What Lies Within Us

Sydney McKay lived in Echo Park, a trendy Los Angeles neighborhood in which *Gilligan's Island* may or may not have been filmed. Like most who lived here, she rented her home; it was small, it was expensive, but she loved it. The murals that adorned the buildings. Independent book and record stores (yes, vinyl records). Vintage clothing stores. It was home to her, and she couldn't imagine ever leaving.

Life over the past four weeks had been tough. She was freed from a job she hated—a group of strangers and a former resident risked themselves to get her and dozens of her colleagues out of a dorm guarded by house mothers and security guards. Sure, they were there to keep people out. But they also kept them in. It thrilled her to be out of there and not performing in porn movies, something she'd done for the past six years. It was exciting at first . . . even glamorous. The luster, however, very quickly wore off. Besides the forced imprisonment, they exposed her to drugs and prostitution. She even moonlighted as a phone sex operator for one of CAYA's other ventures when she'd injured her back.

No, she didn't miss that. She missed the money. She had no income. As a 22-year-old dropout who ran away from home during her sophomore year in high school, she had no degree, no GED, no *real* work experience. True, she saved some of her earnings, but that would run out in short order. She couldn't buy a job. She considered returning to porn; her looks remained marketable, and she thought she could suffer through the indignity and harassment.

As she walked home from her morning coffee at Woodcat Coffee on Sunset Boulevard, her mind wandered to her plans for the day. Heading to the gym was next. Maybe return to the Barbara Kingsolver book she grabbed at Stories Books & Cafe—or maybe (finally) finish *Walden* by Henry David Thoreau. Approaching her front porch, she saw a rather large box addressed to her from *The Team*.

She hadn't ordered anything recently and didn't know who *The Team* was. Grabbing the heavy, cumbersome, nondescript brown box, she brought it in and laid it on her small kitchen counter. Using scissors in an unintended way, she sliced through the tape and opened the box. She saw the envelope first. It rested upon a black velvet that covered a box. Or something. All of that was secured with a pale blue ribbon.

Sydney's hands trembled as she opened the envelope, revealing the dark blue card inside.

Sydney:

For all you've been through. You deserve this. Here's to a wonderful life!

~The Team

As she read the message, her vision blurred, and a single tear dropped onto the paper, smudging the ink. Setting the card aside, she carefully pulled the ribbon and opened what turned out to be a bag. Inside the large bag was a second blue notecard and stacks and stacks of money. The card read:

$5,000,000

So you don't need to count it.

~The Team

Her jaw dropped, and she grabbed the original card again.

She blinked rapidly, trying to clear her eyes, but the tears kept coming, a steady stream of relief and gratitude. A laugh bubbled up from her chest, mingling with the sobs that now wracked her body. She clutched the card to her heart, feeling the weight of her past slowly lifting from her shoulders. For the first time in years, she could breathe freely, knowing that her future was her own to shape.

This scene played out 46 other times this morning, mostly in southern California, but as far away as New York City.

Ella used the phones they gave the captive actors to track them down and to learn their new addresses. A fitting conclusion for all they'd been through.

．．．●．●．●．．

William's Salem home was a mix of modern sophistication and timeless charm. True, a few shutters were missing on the outside and the front door needed to be re-painted. But its interior was beautiful. The warm glow of the setting sun filtered through the windows, casting shadows across the mahogany bookshelves lining the walls. The scent of aged leather and paper filled the room, a testament to his literary expertise and penchant for collecting rare editions. A plush, crimson sofa—sitting atop an antique rug from Peter Pap—dominated the center of the space, facing an oversized fireplace where a crackling fire burned. Above the mantel hung a framed print of Emerson's *Self-Reliance*—a constant reminder of William's personal journey.

"So good to see all of you in one place again," Darby began, her gaze sweeping over the group. She leaned back in her chair, her long blonde hair cascading down one shoulder as she crossed her legs.

The team gathered here, a home base of sorts to catch up and to debrief. It had been two months since their business in California concluded. After leaving their Venice camp, they attempted to return to their normal lives. But money has a way of changing people. Most of the team had started new ventures, some returned to previous jobs, others retired from, well, everything.

．．．．●．●．．．

Darby was inspired by the *reputation destruction* she and William waged upon Tony and Lolita. The contents of the stolen data and the associated newspaper articles absolutely destroyed their company. The war they brought to Tony, Lolita, and their company—it really wasn't a war, more of a single, slightly protracted battle—was successful. The inspiration led to Darby founding a PR company, *Strategic Shield Communications*.

"We specialize in crisis management, brand strategy, and media relations. And let me tell you, business is booming."

"Really? What kind of clients have you attracted?" Josh asked.

"Let's just say we're attracting quite a high-profile clientele," Darby said with a coy smile, wearing her hair down with a sheer green scarf in a bow around her head. "From politicians with skeletons in their closets to disgraced CEOs looking to salvage their reputations, we're the go-to for anyone in need of an image overhaul." She paused, eyebrows arching playfully. "And who better to handle such delicate matters than someone who's been on both sides of the law?"

Josh had upgraded his already impressive wardrobe, though his colleagues still knew to expect the telltale rustle of snack packages whenever he entered a meeting room. "Fair point. As for me, I've returned to the bank, but I'm no longer working behind the counter. After pulling off the heist of the century, I figured it was time for an upgrade." He swirled the ice in his glass, a glint of mischief in his eyes. "I'm now the Vice President of Security. Can you believe they entrusted me with that after everything we did?"

"Talk about the fox guarding the henhouse," Darby said, her laughter ringing out like music. "But seriously, congratulations on the promotion. I'm sure you'll do a stellar job of catching any potential thieves—or at least covering our tracks if we ever decide to stage a repeat performance."

"Thanks. I'll be sure to keep that in mind when the bank's vault is mysteriously emptied overnight." Raising an eyebrow, he challenged Darby, "So tell me, how did you manage to establish your PR empire of helping the rich and infamous clean up their acts so quickly? It's been what, two months since the heist?"

Darby smirked, leaning back in her chair. "What can I say? I've got a knack for making even the most hopeless cases look good. It's a gift."

"More like a curse for the rest of us," Tommy chimed in, grinning. "With Darby on their side, those bigwigs will be untouchable."

"When you've lived the life I have, you tend to make friends in high places. And as it turns out, those friends are more than willing to recommend their favorite former outlaw to anyone in need of a PR miracle worker."

As the conversation continued, it became increasingly clear that despite their separate paths, each member of the team had found success in their new endeavors.

As COO of Darby's PR firm, Justine had quickly become an indispensable part of Strategic Shield Communications. Her responsibilities ranged from managing the day-to-day operations to coordinating with clients and overseeing staff. It hadn't been without challenges—adapting to a world vastly different from the adult film industry she'd left behind proved difficult at times, but her quick wit and keen instincts had served her well. In just a short time, she'd helped land several high-profile clients and successfully navigated them through treacherous public relations waters.

"Is there anything you can't do?" Chase asked, grinning as he entered the room. His retirement had brought about significant changes to his lifestyle, trading adrenaline-pumping financial conflict management, accounting forensics, and—yes—stealing money for leisurely strolls and fine-tuning his golf swing. He'd even taken up painting, though he refused to show anyone his work just yet. Despite his newfound hobbies, however, he couldn't quite shake the itch for adventure.

"Apparently, I can't convince you to pick up the phone for a few minutes every week," Justine shot back, rolling her eyes but smirking, nonetheless. "But seriously, Dad, how's retirement treating you?"

"Can't complain," Chase said, shrugging nonchalantly. "Sure, I miss work and the thrill of the heist, but there's something to be said for waking up without a target on your back. Plus, I've been exploring the finer things in life—like wine tasting and art galleries." He paused, his eyes twinkling with mischief. "And let's not forget my newfound expertise on daytime television."

"Ah yes, your vast knowledge of soap operas is truly impressive," Justine said, unable to suppress a laugh. "Just promise me one thing . . . if we ever find ourselves in another high-stakes situation, you won't try to resolve it using plot twists from *The Young and the Restless*."

"Deal," Chase said, raising his coffee mug in a mock toast.

Tommy smiled with the others; his broad shoulders relaxed in a way they hadn't been in years. "Guardian International is thriving. I never thought I'd be running my own security firm, but it turns out I'm pretty darn good at it." Tommy puffed out his chest, a playful smile on his lips. "Someone's gotta keep the streets safe from the likes of us. Might as well be me."

"Just don't forget about us little people when you're rubbing elbows with the elite," Ella said, her eyes uncharacteristically sparkling.

"Can't say I miss the days of risking my neck for other people's money," Tommy admitted, cracking his knuckles. "But then again, there's something thrilling about it all."

He launched into a description of Guardian International's various services, from personal bodyguards to cybersecurity. He recounted the challenges he'd faced when starting the business, such as building trust within the industry and assembling a team of skilled operatives. But despite these hurdles, the company had attracted an impressive roster of clients, including diplomats, celebrities, and Fortune 500 executives.

"Thrilling? Try running 26.2 miles from Newton to Boston," William said, stretching his legs out in front of him. Since their caper, he'd devoted himself to training for the upcoming Boston Marathon. This increased time to train was welcome—it's impossible to cram for a marathon—but it also meant contending with the ghosts of his past.

"Emerson once said, *What lies behind us and what lies before us are tiny matters compared to what lies within us.*"

"Running is my therapy," he said to himself. "It's how I outrun my demons."

He looked away as he said it, knowing full well that his friends would roll their eyes at his penchant for quoting philosophers. But he didn't care. Their shared past had given them all a second chance at life, and he intended to make the most of it . . . one mile at a time.

Ella—wearing jeans with several holes, including one from mid-thigh to just below her knee, and an oversized chocolate brown checked button-up shirt—slumped in a swivel chair, surrounded by the glow of a single computer screen in William's living room. The hum of the computer's fan and the chatter of her team accompanied the rhythmic tapping of her fingers as she hacked her way through a labyrinth of firewalls. She grinned to herself, thinking how much demand there was for her particular set of skills these days.

"Breaking hearts and firewalls since '03," she said under her breath, indulging in a bit of self-deprecating sarcasm. She was only three years old in 2003, after all. With a final triumphant keystroke, she conquered yet another cyber fortress. She had been busy since the heist that changed all their lives; business was booming for Ella.

"Is it bad that I'm enjoying this newfound popularity?" she wondered aloud, smirking at her reflection on the screen.

"From social outcast to digital diva, huh?" William said. Though it would never quite be the same, nor would it be what either wished it could be, the two of them had also come a long way since their friendship rekindled. Ella returned to Omaha following their daring crime and William to his beloved Salem, but they FaceTime'd once a week (every Sunday after dinner) to catch up and move forward.

Ella's business was indeed booming. She continued as a *hacker for hire*. But with a twist. She now only worked for people who were down and out. Those who couldn't afford help or didn't know how to help themselves. Because of the situations that faced most of her clients, she did nearly all of it for free. Her share of the spoils allowed her this freedom, and she took advantage of it. She loved helping people. She found her calling. Her purpose. Her new "service" highlighted her commitment to making a positive difference in the lives of others, through acts of kindness—many anonymous—and support. Support she wished she'd had years ago. Support she didn't receive.

"William, do you mind if I say something?" she asked, straightening up in her chair and clearing her throat dramatically.

William quieted the group and encouraged Ella to say what she needed to say. He knew there was a lot of healing that needed to happen for her. Perhaps this was part of it.

"So . . ." she began, addressing the room with a perpetual embarrassed affect in stark contrast to her childhood personality. She nervously looked from side-to-side, catching the eyes of each in person there. She took a deep breath, her fingers fidgeting with the hem of her shirt as the team sat around her, their faces etched with concern and curiosity.

"So you know I'm not much for talking. I have learned that I communicate best by staring into my computer and typing like there's no tomorrow. That's me. That's who I've become. But over the past few months, I've learned there's more to me than that. You've all shown me what I'm capable of, and how much more there is to life beyond the confines of my digital playground."

She glanced at Darby, who looked on proudly. "I've learned that teamwork isn't just about coordinating our efforts online; it's about supporting each other through thick and thin, both on and off the job.

"Tommy began teaching me self-defense . . . sorry for giving you a black eye." She looked at him with a sheepish, wistful smile. "Justine showed me how to shoot pool—and then hustled me out of twenty bucks. Josh taught me about investments and what I should do with my money."

"Those moments may seem trivial, but they've helped shape who I am today: a stronger, more confident woman," Ella asserted, her eyes glistening with genuine emotion. "I may not be Wonder Woman, but I'm no longer that scared little girl hiding behind a keyboard, either.

"I do have a confession to make to all of you, however. Some of you were surprised at how easily I gained access to CAYA's computers."

Each of the team looked at each other. When Ella arrived late to one of their first meetings, she strode to the computers, and almost immediately hacked their system. There was more than one look of amazement and incredulity between them that day. Her skills genuinely shocked them.

"When I was, well, being sent around the country by those perverted evildoers, one of my stops was at CAYA," Ella caught William's eyes, which were now filling with tears. "They brought me there to be part of some kind of underage porn production. I did what they wanted."

William leaned forward, his brow furrowed. "You never mentioned that before," he said, placing a comforting hand on her shoulder.

Ella shrugged, a humorless smile playing on her lips. "It's not exactly a memory I like to revisit," she admitted, her gaze dropping to the floor.

The room fell silent for a moment, the weight of Ella's revelation hanging heavy in the air. Darby stood and walked to the window, her arms crossed tightly across her chest. Josh shifted uncomfortably in his seat, his eyes filled with sympathy and anger.

She trailed off for a moment, thinking back over her time there. Nobody in the room made a sound. Not only had they never heard Ella speak this much, her story mesmerized them.

Ella took another breath, steeling herself. "They kept me on the upper floor of the studio building," she said, her voice growing stronger. "They moved me in and out at night, when the others were sleeping. I think . . . I think they were trying to keep my role a secret."

Tommy clenched his fists, his jaw tight. "Those bastards," he said, his voice low and dangerous.

Ella looked up, her eyes shining with unshed tears. "When they took me to my room between video shoots, they let me use a computer. This was the first time during my captivity they allowed me access to one. They thought they monitored my activity, so I didn't reach out to my family or friends. While I couldn't do that, I observed some of the staff accessing an internal website. So I set up a watering hole attack. I infected their intranet site with malware. That means when employees visit the CAYA intranet, their computers became compromised. When I walked in here a few months ago, that's the first thing I checked. They never found it. I was in."

Josh asked, "Ella, why didn't you tell us this?"

"Well, I didn't know any of you except William. I didn't know how to talk to any of you and barely knew how to talk to him."

"Were you there when I was there?" Justine wanted to know.

"I don't know. Probably. They kept me to an upper floor of their studio building. But I did stay in the same building we freed everyone from. They moved me in and out late at night when others were sleeping. I suppose they did that to keep my roles private."

"My goodness, Ella. This is all incredible," Darby offered. "You are such a powerful person. I truly admire how you've worked to create a life that, despite the abhorrent treatment you endured, is now filled with good deeds."

"I've realized that my hacking skills don't define me—they're merely tools I wield to forge my own path," she concluded, her voice cracking slightly. "One last thing. If it wasn't for William believing in me, I wouldn't be here. My parents are great, but William's friendship and genuine concern are the reasons I'm here. He could have found anyone to do this job. But I think he asked me, as he sensed I needed it. To find a new way forward. To use those tools to help others.

"So thank you all . . . each of us has found redemption in each other, and each of us continues to chase our dreams on our own terms."

William gave Ella a hug, and the rest joined in. This was the most emotion any of the team had shown each other during their time together. It felt good.

"Alright, enough with the mushy stuff," she said, resuming her tapping on the keyboard. "It's time to get back to work."

As she dove into her next digital conquest, she couldn't help but feel a sense of gratitude for the people who had become her unconventional family. Their influence on her life was undeniable—and together, they would continue to make waves in a world that never saw them coming.

Interview: Sydney

Inspector: *Good evening, Sydney. Let's get straight to it. Can you deny any involvement in the heist that took place at CAYA?*

Sydney: *Inspector, I swear on my life that I had nothing to do with that heist. I was a victim, held against my will by the people at CAYA. I can't believe they're still trying to control and manipulate me even now.*

Inspector: *Sydney, I understand that you've been through a traumatic experience, and I sympathize with your situation. However, we have information that suggests you may have played a role in this heist. It's important that you be honest with me and cooperate with our investigation.*

Sydney: *Inspector, I swear, I had no involvement in that heist. The only thing I wanted was to escape that nightmare and find freedom. I can't explain the rumors or why anyone would think I had a part in it. I just want to put all of this behind me.*

Inspector: *Sydney, we've received reports you were seen with members of the team responsible for the heist. Can you explain your association with them?*

Sydney: *I met them after they rescued me—us—from that hellish place. They saved my life, and I'm forever grateful to them. But I did not know about their plans or what they were involved in. I was just desperate to get away and start a new life.*

Inspector: *We've also received information suggesting that you received a substantial sum of money after the heist. Can you explain the source of these funds?*

Sydney: *I have no clue what money you're talking about. No one gave me any money, and I certainly didn't receive any from the heist. I've been trying to rebuild my life from scratch, and money is important, but I didn't steal anything.*

Inspector: *Sydney, I want to believe you, but I need you to be completely honest with me. The evidence we have shows some level of involvement. I strongly advise you to reconsider your position and cooperate fully with our investigation.*

Sydney: *Inspector, I've been through hell and back, and I've been fighting to reclaim my life ever since. I can't imagine being involved in something like that heist. I just want to be left alone and find some peace.*

Inspector: *What are your plans now?*

Sydney: *I don't know. I have no job, no money . . . I don't know what to do. I can return to porn, I suppose. But I hope not.*

Inspector: *I understand—*

Sydney: *I don't think you do, Inspector. Acting in porn is gross. It's dirty. It's guilt-inducing. It's demoralizing. Every time I think about it and what it means, I cry. It's not who I hoped to be, and it's not what I wanted for my life.*

Inspector: *Well then, I'm glad—*

Sydney: *Are you really 'glad,' Inspector? You'll still watch porn. Look at porn. Consume porn. Your actions will enable the industry to continue. I understand this studio you're asking about might be down, but the others aren't.*

Inspector: (Silence, looking at Sydney.)

Sydney: *But if I need to do it so I can pay the mortgage, then I will. I won't like it, but I'll do it if I need to.*

Inspector: *With all you've been through, you must really hate the porn industry.*

Sydney: *I suppose I do. They hurt me. Bad. But look, people can do what they want. If they want to look at porn, fine, whatever. I just wish those viewing better understood the exploitation involved.*

Inspector: *That makes se—*

Sydney: *And other people are being hurt. Sure, the actors often are. But what about those who are addicted? Who can't escape its grasp?*

Inspector: *Fair enough. Regarding my other questions, Sydney, I hope you're telling me the truth. Remember, the truth has a way of surfacing, and it's in your best interest to be on the right side of it.*

Sydney: *Are we done? Can I leave now?*

Inspector: *Yes Sydney, we're done . . . I believe we have what we need.*

Existential Resilience

The morning sun dipped through the trees lining the Charles River Bike Path, dappling the ground with spots of gold. Ella walked along the path—she was on the Cambridge side—her backpack slung over one shoulder, enjoying the solitude. After the chaos of orientation and meeting her new roommate, the quiet calm of the early morning was a balm.

Up ahead, a runner came into view, moving at an easy pace. Ella paid him little mind, instead gazing out at the river and listening to the laughter of a couple jogging together as they turned off the Harvard Bridge onto the path next to her.

As the runner drew closer, something about his stride and the set of his shoulders tugged at her memory. Her steps slowed and when he passed by, her breath caught in her throat. She'd know that shaved head and gruff profile anywhere.

"William?"

He turned, startled, and when his gaze landed on her, his eyes lit with surprised delight. "Well, I'll be damned. Ella?"

He stopped, clearly waiting for her to catch up. She quickened her pace until she stood before him, suddenly shy. It had been over a year since they'd last met, the culmination of a job that had changed the course of her life.

"What are you doing here, William?"

"Same as you. Enjoying the view." His gaze dipped to her mouth, and she pressed her lips together, annoyance flaring. Did he never stop?

"I meant in Boston."

"Oh, I come down here from Salem every few weeks. I love running near the ocean, but the energy of the Charles River is intoxicating." He tilted his head, gaze sharpening. "You look good," he said, giving her a quick once-over. "Happy. Healthy."

"I am." The words, for once, were the truth. "You look the same as always."

"The benefits of a simple life." He jerked his head at the backpack. "What about you? Decided to take those test scores of yours out for a spin at MIT?"

"Actually, yes." She shrugged, a flush creeping into her cheeks. "I took your advice."

"Did you now?" His lips twitched. "Well, what do you know? Maybe this old dog still has a trick or two left to teach."

"Maybe," she said, a smile teasing at the corner of her mouth.

For a long moment, they simply gazed at each other, a wealth of memories and unspoken thoughts passing between them. Ella's shoulders relaxed, tension she hadn't realized she still carried easing from her bones.

William cleared his throat and looked away first, scanning the horizon as the sun crested over the river. "So. Cambridge, huh? Must be lonely in that big city all by your lonesome."

"I keep busy." But she couldn't hide the wistful note in her voice, and from the sideways glance William gave her, he caught it too.

"Well, it's not like I've got anything better to do most days. Why don't we make a routine of this? Meet up once a month or so . . . hit up some new cupcake shop like we used to. For old time's sake."

Ella blinked, struck by the simple generosity of the offer. "I'd like that."

"Good. It's a plan then." William started jogging in place, the gravel crunching under his sneakers. "Now, if you'll excuse me, I've still got another five miles to go before breakfast. Try not to get into too much trouble."

"I make no promises."

In the fleeting encounter of souls, we touch the infinite, and in saying goodbye, we partake in the eternal dance of the universe.

"You know, William, I love the transcendental quotes and words you throw at me now and then. But I think there's something more to life. Or at least there's more to my life."

"Oh?"

"I admire Thoreau. And Whitman. And Emerson. But I think of my view as more of existential resilience. Each of us has individual freedom and choice in creating meaning in this otherwise indifferent and even absurd universe. When we rode our bikes together, I felt free. Happy. Innocent, I suppose. But that illusion was shattered. I was taken. I felt ruined. I became a vengeful freelancer—a sort of existential response to my life. I pursued vengeance on those who had wronged me. I sought control and meaning in my life. But you . . . reaching out to me, bringing me along on this journey . . . I have been able to embrace my agency, and I have chosen a path that aligns with my values."

William wiped tears from his eyes as he looked away . . . existential indeed.

"I realized I can shape my life while finding meaning in my actions."

He shook his head. "Atta girl."

"I also learned to accept my past, heal from that trauma, and find fulfillment in my own terms. So thank you for being you and for believing in me, William."

"Boy, do I have a lot to learn from you, Ella. It's clear that the change from teacher to student has begun, and I'm pleased to see how much you've grown and how you've bounced back."

She blushed as she looked at her feet.

"Now get to class before you're late."

With a wave, he set off down the path again. Ella watched him go, warmth blossoming in her chest. Maybe this whole normal life thing wouldn't be so hard after all, not if she had someone to share it with.

Squaring her shoulders, she continued her walk to campus. Today was a new beginning in more ways than one.

* * * * * * * * * *

Ella quickened her pace as the MIT campus came into view, a mixture of old stone buildings and modern glass and steel structures nestled along the river. Her first class didn't start for another hour, but she wanted time to find the right building and get her bearings.

As she walked through the main gates, a thrill ran through her. She was here. After everything she'd been through, all the obstacles that had once seemed insurmountable, she was finally walking onto a college campus for the first time in her life.

A bubble of laughter escaped her as she took in the sight of students sprawled out on the grass, tossing Frisbees and textbooks. The laughter caught in her throat, edged with tears, but for once they were tears of joy.

She swiped at her eyes and kept walking, deeply breathing the crisp morning air. She had become just another student. Her past didn't matter. She had a chance to build something new.

When she found the right building, she chose a seat by the window where she could watch people walking by below. The class wouldn't start for a while, but she didn't mind. For the first time she could remember, she felt at peace in the simple act of waiting.

A smile curved her lips as she opened her laptop, fingers flying over the keys to hack into the school's system and erase any records of her name or image. Ella might be embracing a normal life, but she wasn't quite ready to give up her anonymity just yet.

Some habits died hard, but she had a feeling that this one would fade in time. After all, when life gave you a clean slate, the smartest thing to do was write your own story.

She was ready to begin.

Epilogue

S o what happened to all of CAYA's money?

As only he could, William began by quoting Marcus Aurelius. "*What we do now echoes in eternity.*"

The team left California with $4,600,000,000. That's 4.6 billion. "With a 'B,'" as Josh told the Inspector. Here's what they did with that:

They founded a charitable organization to combat sex trafficking, porn addiction, and research into this unique addiction. The American Psychiatric Association's *Diagnostic and Statistical Manual of Mental Disorders* doesn't include porn addiction as an actual addiction. The team hoped to fund research projects to validate the struggles so many have. Their nonprofit foundation began its life with $1,000,000,000.

Knowing their foundation could not *do it all*, they also sent $500,000,000 each to Sex Addicts Anonymous, Porn Addicts Anonymous, and the UN Trust Fund for Victims of Human Trafficking.

As highlighted, the 47 freed actors each receive $5,000,000.

Each member of the team—Darby, Josh, Justine, William, Tommy, Ella, and even Chase—pocketed $200,000,000.

That leaves $465,000,000 from Josh's handiwork. The team placed all that money in accounts in Hong Kong, the Cayman Islands, Bermuda, and yes, even Switzerland. They kept this money as a combination rainy day fund and would serve as an investment in any subsequent heists.

The vault's gold, art, and cash bundles? They sold this off and the proceeds brought the team an additional $6,500,000.

(And, no, none of the paintings from the Isabella Stewart Gardner Museum were included in that haul.)

The team thought there should really be a sort of pension for the *innocent* CAYA employees who lost their jobs because of the team's takedown. So each of 26 identified employees—including Chloe Jane and other support staff—received $250,000.

Josh said, his eyes full of steely determination, "Each of us has found a calling. Whether it's our *real-world* jobs or our pseudo-Robin Hood heists. Let's stay focused and continue our fight."

"Stay focused, sure," Justine said, her voice dripping with sarcasm as she pretended to polish her nails on the ornate chair she sat upon. "But a little fun never hurt anyone, right?"

"Fun?" Darby raised an eyebrow, curiosity piqued despite herself.

"Absolutely," Tommy said, with a mischievous glint in his eye. "After all, we can't spend all our time plotting and scheming, can we?"

"True," Chase conceded, a wry grin spreading across his face. "And I have a feeling this is just the beginning of a wild ride."

Ella sat in her computer chair and allowed the hint of a smile to cross her lips. She knew the perfect next stop on their wild ride.

As the laughter died down, William cleared his throat, a serious expression on his face. "As Thoreau once said, *Wealth is the ability to fully experience life*. And I think we've all earned the right to do just that."

Justine rolled her eyes, a smirk playing on her lips. "Oh, great. Another one of William's philosophical gems. Please enlighten us with more wisdom from the brilliant thinkers of yesteryear."

William shot her a mock glare, but the twinkle in his eye betrayed his amusement. "Laugh all you want, but there's truth in those words. We've fought hard for our freedom, and now it's time to enjoy it."

"Enjoy it? You mean like running off to the woods and living in a tiny cabin, communing with nature?" Justine asked, her voice dripping with sarcasm.

"Don't knock it till you've tried it," William said, a grin spreading across his face. There is value in embracing simplicity and solitude.

"Yeah, yeah," Justine waved her hand dismissively, "just don't forget to invite us over for s'mores and campfire songs when you go all Walden on us."

William remarked, as only he could, "Let's be like Thoreau—without Justine's sugar-filled campsite treats—and go experience life while also doing some good."

The team chuckled, the playful banter a testament to the bond they shared. Wherever life led them, they would hold on to and cherish these memories. Together, they had accomplished the impossible—and there was no telling what they might achieve next.

• • • ● • ● • • •

The End

YOUR FREE BOOK IS WAITING

Download your free copy of *The Perfect Fall* and discover Lolita's journey from star gymnast with an overbearing mom to ruthless COO.

waldengray.com/theperfectfall

Afterword

Dear Reader,

Thank you for joining Darby, William, Ella, Josh, Tommy, Justine, and Chase on their journey in *The Emancipation Job: A Righteous Wrong Heist*. I hope you found their story of redemption, justice, and friendship as captivating and thought-provoking as I did while writing it. I should note that while none of the fictional characters I include are real, people I know or have read about inspired some of their characteristics.

In this novel, we saw a group of individuals from diverse backgrounds come together to right the wrongs of their past and take a stand against the corrupt and exploitative practices of the adult entertainment industry. Through their heist, they not only sought personal revenge but also aimed to expose and fight against an industry that profits from exploitation and human suffering.

As the characters grappled with their own demons and learned to trust and rely on one another, they discovered the true meaning of family and the power of working together towards a common goal. Their journey was not an easy one, filled with challenges, setbacks, and moral dilemmas, but in the end, they emerged stronger, wiser, and more determined than ever.

But their story doesn't end here. In the upcoming books of the *Righteous Wrong* series, we will delve deeper into each character's past and explore how their experiences in *The Emancipation Job* have shaped their futures. From William's battle against hospital corruption in *The Hippocratic Heist* to Ella's war with organized crime in *The Digital Takedown* and Darby's high-stakes gamble in *The Final Bet*, the crew's adventures are far from over. There are even origin stories that reveal the paths that led our characters here, including *The Perfect Fall* and *Brothers in Arms*.

So, keep an eye out for the next installment in the series and prepare yourself for more heart-pounding heists, unexpected twists, and the unbreakable bonds of friendship. The *Righteous Wrong* crew will be back, ready to take on new challenges and fight for justice in their own unique way.

And if you enjoyed this book, please review it on your favorite book review site . . . all the words of encouragement help.

Thank you again for your support, and happy reading!

Walden

Acknowledgements

I am incredibly grateful for the constant and unwavering support of my family throughout my life's many adventures. Whether I was training for marathons, embarking on cross-country moves, or pouring my heart into my writing, my family has always been there, cheering me on and providing a foundation of love and encouragement.

To my wife, my partner in every sense of the word: your love, patience, and belief in me have been instrumental in all my achievements. I am so grateful to have you by my side.

To my wonderful children: your love, laughter, and endless enthusiasm have been a constant source of inspiration and joy. Watching you grow and pursue your own passions has been one of the greatest privileges of my life.

To my mother: your love, guidance, and unwavering support have shaped me into the person I am today. Thank you for always being there, through the good times and the challenging ones.

I want to express my heartfelt love and appreciation for each and every one of you. Your presence in my life has been an immeasurable gift, and I know that none of my accomplishments would have been possible without your support. You are my foundation, my inspiration, and my greatest blessing.

From the bottom of my heart, thank you.

About the Author

Walden Gray has spent years exploring the intersection of justice and redemption, both in literature and in life. Like the transcendentalist thinkers who inspire their work, Gray believes in the power of individual action to effect meaningful change in the world, particularly in confronting those who exploit society's most vulnerable.

When not crafting tales of righteous wrongs and moral complexity, Gray can be found running and wandering the shores of New England's beaches, seeking inspiration in the same region that moved Thoreau and Emerson. Their writing reflects a deep appreciation for both the darkness and light in human nature, and a belief that even the most damaged souls can find their way to redemption—while shining a light on industries and organizations that profit from human suffering.

The *Righteous Wrong* series represents Gray's first venture into fiction, though they have written extensively about other topics. Through these stories, Gray aims to expose those who corrupt legitimate enterprises for personal gain, believing that fiction can be a powerful tool in revealing uncomfortable truths. They divide their time between the North Shore of Boston and various urban centers, finding that the balance between solitude and society fuels their creative process.

Gray maintains a deliberate air of privacy, believing, as Thoreau did, that *the mass of men lead lives of quiet desperation*. Through their writing, they hope to show that there are always alternatives to desperation—even if those alternatives sometimes lie outside society's traditional moral boundaries.

* 9 7 9 8 9 9 2 5 7 0 0 1 4 *